THE LOST GIRL OF SEAHAVEN

PHILLIPA NEFRI CLARK

Storm

This is a work of fiction. Names, characters, businesses, places, events and incidents are either the products of the author's imagination or used in a fictitious manner. Any resemblance to actual persons, living or dead, or actual events is purely coincidental.

Copyright © Phillipa Nefri Clark, 2025

The moral right of the author has been asserted.

All rights reserved. No part of this book may be reproduced or used in any manner without the prior written permission of the copyright owner. This prohibition includes, but is not limited to, any reproduction or use for the purpose of training artificial intelligence technologies or systems.

To request permissions, contact the publisher at rights@stormpublishing.co

Ebook ISBN: 978-1-80508-762-5
Paperback ISBN: 978-1-80508-763-2

Cover design: Miblart
Cover images: Shuterstock and Depositphotos

Published by Storm Publishing.
For further information, visit:
www.stormpublishing.co

ALSO BY PHILLIPA NEFRI CLARK

Temple River
The Cottage at Whisper Lake
The Bookstore at Rivers End
The House at Angel's Beach
The Secrets of Willow Bay

Rivers End Romantic Women's Fiction
The Stationmaster's Cottage
Jasmine Sea
The Secrets of Palmerston House
The Christmas Key
Taming the Wind
Martha

Detective Liz Moorland Series
Lest We Forgive
Lest Bridges Burn
Lest Tides Turn
Lest Nobody Lives
Lest Angels Weep
Last Known Contact

Charlotte Dean Mysteries
Christmas Crime in Kingfisher Falls
Book Club Murder in Kingfisher Falls

Cold Case Murder in Kingfisher Falls
Plans for Murder in Kingfisher Falls
Festive Felony in Kingfisher Falls

Bindarra Creek Rural Fiction

A Perfect Danger
Tangled by Tinsel

Doctor Grok's Peculiar Shop Short Story Collection
Simple Words for Troubled Times

For my beautiful sister. No star shines brighter.

PROLOGUE

14 September 1952

The little girl's squeals of laughter forced the man to stop walking and close his eyes as waves of grief surged up from his gut.

Vernon slumped against the wide trunk of a gum tree, as repelled by the sound as he was drawn. Such a sweet thing, the joy of being so young and finding wonder in every new experience. The world was a glorious adventure.

One which his own daughter would never have.

With a grunt he straightened and blinked away sudden tears. The clearing was only a few yards distance. It was a popular place for picnics and a family was enjoying the warmth of the early spring afternoon. He couldn't afford to waste time and picked up the bag he'd already partly filled with foraged mushrooms – most likely the last of the year. At this rate it would be night before he finished his task and hiked to where his car was parked.

He moved away from the clearing toward one of several creeks which ran through the long range of hills between Rivers

End and his own home. Here he found a motherlode of fungi and went back to work.

'Lou Lou? Dad says we can't go to the creek alone.'

The man stepped out of sight, peering through bushes when he remembered his bag sitting open on the bank. He'd only make himself known if they touched it.

'Dolly's face is dirty!'

This had to be the little girl who'd been laughing. She was maybe three and a half or four, wearing a pretty dress, with blond hair curling past chubby cheeks then falling below her shoulders. Other than the length of her hair, the likeness to his own lost child stabbed at him until he wanted to be sick.

'Give me Dolly and I'll wash her face, then!'

The boy was her brother, for sure. Same blond and curly hair and blue eyes. Older by a few years. He took the doll from his sister and dipped its head into the running water.

'Mattie! Too much. Stop.'

She tried to grab the doll and almost fell in, but the boy managed to steady her. 'Fine, here's Dolly. We have to go now.'

Laura glared at Mattie but followed at a distance. She suddenly ran back to the creek and scooped some water in her hand to clean the doll's arm, setting it on the ground while she scrubbed.

Go to your family, little one. Go now.

He must have moved in the bushes because the child stared in his direction with wide eyes.

'Mattie! Mattie, there's a monster!'

'Oh come on, Laura. Where are you?'

The man rattled the branches and she let out a shriek and ran.

Once the children were out of sight he stepped out and collected his bag of mushrooms. The children were gone. But the doll lay at the side of the creek.

. . .

Bag full enough to make his wife happy, the man pulled the drawstring tight and secured it. The air was cooling as evening approached and if he got a move on, he'd get to the car before it was completely dark. His path took him along the creek and he almost tripped on the doll.

He scooped it up, peering toward the clearing. Surely the family was long gone?

But there were sounds in that direction and his feet moved of their own accord. He would return the doll. See a smile on the little girl's face... Laura. They'd never be able to have another child, his wife and him. Complications after birth. Not that it stopped their daughter thriving and filling their hearts with such love it rivalled that of their love of God.

He slammed the memory down. Loving a human more than the Almighty was the reason she was taken. A lesson which tore at his faith but not that of his wife. She accepted it was God's will but her spirit was broken.

We are both broken.

Stopping, he held up the doll. The child had abandoned it. She didn't deserve it.

The voices were closer. Urgent.

'Laura! Laura, where are you?'

Adults and the boy, all screaming into the air from different parts of the forest.

He hurried away, heart pounding. How had they let such a small child become lost up here? It was dangerous at night... at any time. Plenty of places to fall. Snakes were out of hibernation. Kangaroos and wombats were everywhere and coming across one at the wrong time could end in tragedy, especially for a child.

He forced his way through the undergrowth until the voices were gone and then, panting, he stopped to get his bearings.

There was a whimper nearby and he couldn't believe his eyes when the little girl stumbled toward him. Her hair was clumped on her forehead with a bit of blood and her eyes swollen from crying. Even her dress was torn.

'Laura?'

He could save her. Reunite her with her family who were so frantic.

'You're safe now. Look, I found Dolly.'

Her hands reached for the doll and he lifted her into his arms.

'I'll take you to your family.'

She leaned her head against his shoulder. Just like his daughter used to do.

He had to take her to her family.

They let her wander alone. They don't deserve her.

He tightened his grip and strode in the opposite direction of the clearing.

ONE

Between the end of the night and the beginning of the day was a moment which paused the world. The air would still and all sounds cease, other than the endless washing of waves against the beach. Stars stopped twinkling and time itself rested within this precious cocoon.

When she was a child, Angie Fairlie had been certain this was a long breath of delight the world drew as it prepared for daylight.

As a teen who'd just lost both parents in a car accident, it became a symbolic sigh of sorrow at leaving the protective cover of night behind.

And as a thirty-year-old, it was a moment she occasionally wished to stay within forever.

Now was such a time.

Warm waves whooshed over her feet and retreated with a gentle tug which she resisted by digging her toes into the wet sand. If she stood here long enough the high tide would come and carry her out to the deep blue of the Southern Ocean where she might float endlessly or else drift to some distant island to find the solitude she craved. No more problems to deal with other than food and shelter.

The moment passed and the sky subtly lightened and Angie shook her head at herself.

At least she was home again and able to drink in the beauty of sunrise at Rivers End beach. It was long overdue and Angie waited until the last star faded before stepping out of the sea.

She trudged through the softer sand to where Temple River cut through a natural tunnel beneath the cliff, leaving the magic behind as she emerged a couple of blocks from Rivers End. Turning left, she followed the road which skirted the town. There were no houses on either side, just a park which took up a whole town block, then another road before the shops started.

This was her first day home – at least as a resident again. She was born here and at the age of thirteen came to live with her grandparents. After her marriage seven years ago and move to Perth, all the way across the country, she'd only been back once, and it had been an uncomfortable visit she cut short. Easy enough to blame the vast distance and her new married life but the reality was that Gramps hadn't approved of her choice of husband.

None of the history mattered now though.

Everything had changed and Gramps needed her here. He was moving into the new assisted care community and had only just begun the big job of packing up Seahaven, his family home. Her new job teaching at the local primary school would officially begin a few days before the first term in three weeks and it would take most of that time to help him move and find herself a small place to rent. The husband Gramps had so disliked – for good reason – was the one left behind this time.

Angie stepped onto the bitumen to cross over.

A squeal of brakes and a horn blaring made her jump back to the verge but her toes caught on the gutter and she fell onto her hands and knees on the grass. Her heart pounding from the shock, she dropped her head, willing them to drive on.

How had she missed hearing a car approach? She hadn't looked, her mind elsewhere.

You could have been killed. How could you be so—

'Are you alright? Are you hurt?'

'Just catching my breath. Thanks.'

'Can I help you up?'

The voice was male and deep and concerned. Instead of answering, Angie pushed herself to her feet and brushed herself off before raising her eyes with a quiet, 'I seem to be in one piece, thank you.'

The owner of the voice didn't look convinced. There was a scowl on his face. And it was a very handsome face. In the gloomy light his hair looked dark brown and flopped over his forehead. His jaw was square and his cheekbones defined. Dressed in black suit pants and a white business shirt undone to the third button, he had a James Bond air about him.

All he needed was a half-smile and martini to complete the picture.

'I almost hit you; walking straight out in front of me like that could have been catastrophic.'

'I didn't hear your car.'

'That's why looking first matters. Did nobody teach you how to safely cross a road?'

Angie blinked at the anger in his tone but she knew she was at fault.

'Well, thanks for checking on me. I'll be going.'

'Wait, hang on a second. Can I drive you somewhere? Take you home?'

Yours or mine?

Clearly adrenaline was messing with her head. She didn't need some man taking care of her. Men were great at promising the world and delivering nothing but heartache and debt and humiliation.

'Look, I don't want to just leave you here. You've had a shock.' His voice had softened and he stepped closer.

'Really, I'm fine. Have you been drinking?' She wrinkled her nose at the mix of cigarette smoke and alcohol coming off him.

'Good grief no. Not when I'm driving. I was at an end-of shoot-event.' He lifted the corner of his shirt collar and sniffed. 'Ew. Any tips on removing smells like that?'

'Do I look like your housekeeper?'

He laughed and then gestured to his car, which Angie finally noticed. It was a red and sporty convertible and the headlights were on so, had she checked the road before stepping out, she'd have seen it coming.

'Lift?'

'Again, no. Sorry I gave you a fright.'

'Sure you're okay?'

'Certain.'

Not waiting for him to keep asking questions, Angie checked the road then sprinted across, not looking back until she was halfway across the park.

He was just climbing into the car and she was sure he'd been watching her. Probably making sure she didn't run in front of anyone else. The car drove away, deadly quiet. Electric. In a moment it disappeared from view.

The sun made an appearance at last, casting beams of light onto the road she'd just left. A second later or a driver response slower and she'd have been injured. Angie was used to making monumental mistakes but that one might have been her last.

Happy homecoming, Angela.

. . .

The gracious home which had housed many generations of Fairlies was destined to be sold for the first time. Set in one of the highest streets in Rivers End on just over an acre of sprawling gardens, Seahaven was built from limestone and hardwood with a metal roof and verandah across the front. Inside were five bedrooms and a large study, a formal living room, dining room, and casual living area. The kitchen was a real country-style affair with a double stove and oven, long timber counter, and big walk-in pantry.

The latter was where Angie stood when she returned from her walk, trying to work out what to make for breakfast.

When she'd arrived late yesterday afternoon she'd been exhausted from the final leg of her drive from Perth. More than three thousand kilometres – across the Nullarbor Plain then through South Australia before reaching Victoria – all over the course of a few days. Gramps had helped her unload her suitcases and then pushed a plate of food in front of her, watching to make sure she ate. There'd been few words exchanged and she'd gone to bed before nightfall. She'd cried herself to sleep at how reserved Gramps was, wishing she could bridge the tense gap between them. He'd known she was coming home from their recent phone conversations and had said she was welcome to stay.

She didn't feel welcome though.

There was a loaf of bread in a paper bag with the Rivers End Bakery logo on it. Angie took it from the pantry to the counter and checked the fridge, pulling out a carton of eggs, butter, and cream. The latter didn't pass her sniff test and she poured it down the sink just as Gramps joined her.

'There's nothing wrong with that.' He watched the last of it vanish down the drain helped by a bit of water. 'Can't waste food.'

'And I can't let you or me become ill. It had turned.'

He grunted.

'Eggs on toast okay?'

'Aren't you still tired from the drive?'

After rinsing out the container, Angie tossed it into the recycling bin Gramps kept next to the regular rubbish bin.

'There's not a lot in the pantry, Gramps.'

'Only used to catering for one. Wasn't sure when you'd get here.'

He was right, of course. She'd only given him a few days' vague notice about coming back and he was in the middle of downsizing his life. In her haste to be here for him – and maybe escape her life in Perth – Angie hadn't even considered the impact on her grandfather.

'I can find somewhere else to stay.'

'Don't be daft. This is your home.'

Her stomach churned. It had been her home once, and maybe it was now, but not for much longer.

Think of something to say. Change the subject.

'I went down to the beach earlier. Before daylight.'

His bushy eyebrows rose for a second and he nodded. 'Like you always did. Some things stay the same.'

Angie gazed at her grandfather. There were extra lines in his face and his shoulders were more rounded, making him appear a little smaller than she remembered. Emmett Fairlie was almost eighty-one and there were fewer signs of the strong and resilient man who'd helped raise her, but his fierce spirit still shone in his eyes. He'd told her he wanted to move to the next phase of his life before his mind went but there was no sign of mental weakness. Never had been.

'Staring at me won't get breakfast made.'

Before she could stop herself, Angie threw her arms around Gramps, holding on to him until he patted her back.

'Like to breathe a bit.' His voice was gruff.

'Sorry.' She immediately released him and collected a frying pan, but not before the smallest of smiles on his face lightened her mood. 'Would you make the coffee and I'll whip this up?'

They ate at the counter, perched on stools the way they had so often in the past. Back when Angie had been a teenager, Nan would shoo her and Gramps from her side of the kitchen and they'd sit here and chat as wonderful meals were prepared. She'd been a terrific cook, Nan, a member of the local Country Women's Association for decades who loved preparing meals using ingredients fresh from the garden.

I miss you.

The loss had come only two years after Angie's parents died. Somehow, she and Gramps got through another funeral and the sad process of adjusting to life on their own. He'd been her rock and strength and eventually, she'd become his friend as well as grandchild.

Until she'd married the wrong man.

Angie's eyes were misting over and she gulped down a sudden lump in her throat. The memories were to be expected but she wasn't here to fall apart. This time she had to become the strong one as Gramps had been for her.

Breakfast was quiet but once they'd washed up, Gramps announced he had to show her the garden. It wasn't as though she hadn't seen it a thousand times but if he was making an effort to put things right between them Angie wasn't going to stop him.

They wandered along a winding path between flower beds at the back of the house, each carrying a second cup of coffee. There'd always been a wide selection of varieties which were often very old or had been carefully propagated over the years. Roses, geraniums, carnations, poppies, snapdragons and so many more. It meant there was always choice for floral arrangements inside.

'Look at the lupins. Have you ever seen them so tall?'

'Oh, beautiful. And how do you have peonies still blooming?' Angie leaned down to smell the gorgeous scent and sighed. 'Absolutely wonderful.'

'Yes, the season is normally over for them but this time they lasted right through Christmas and as you can see, there's still a few showing their colours,' Gramps said. 'I've not managed much success with vegetables this summer. Can't work out what went wrong with the tomatoes. Come and give me your opinion.'

Through a wrought-iron gate was a wonderland of vegetable beds and a greenhouse. The beds were mostly raised and there was a fence of chicken wire around the plot to deter rabbits. Tomato plants were growing in a large bed and Gramps was right, none were thriving.

'They look pest free,' Angie said. She put her cup down to use both hands to gently part the growth between two which had plenty of leaves and almost no fruit. 'Hang on, what's this?'

Gramps's face appeared from the other side and he had a trowel in his hand. 'Can't believe I did that.' He dug into the soil around a plant which had leaves not entirely dissimilar to the tomatoes. 'Your Nan would tell me off.' A moment later he lifted a perfectly formed potato. 'Not going to take the plant out because its happy. And I love spuds.'

'Who doesn't? Was this in here last year?'

'Thought I'd dug the entire lot out but potatoes are sneaky; all it takes is a remnant and bang, whole potato plant.' He smoothed the soil and put the potato into a pocket, shaking his head. 'I know better than to plant enemies in the same bed so soon.'

'What if I give the tomatoes a trim and feed and see if we can salvage them.'

'Worth trying and that was a good pick-up, Angie. Eyes aren't what they used to be.'

Before she could respond, Gramps headed out of the plot.

Angie caught up with him almost at the back of the property. It was elevated and looked back to Rivers End across the neighbouring streets as well as a lovely view of the sea over the limestone cliff. This was where Nan had her office.

Gramps stood on its doorstep, palm on the door, his eyes on the ground.

This was her space. Nan was a talented author with several published books and would spend a few hours each day in her little sanctuary. She didn't mind visitors and Angie had often been one, reading while Nan wrote at her desk, or helping with research. There was a wall of bookshelves inside, as well as in the house, and Angie was spoiled for choice with both her grandparents being avid readers.

'Lass? Never been able to pack her things up. I wondered if you would.'

Angie drew in a long breath.

Gramps turned his head. 'She loved you to the moon and back. I don't trust anyone else to go inside.'

Before the tears could come, before she could even think about what it would feel like to be back inside that precious space, Angie put on one of her masks. The one she kept for the most difficult moments in life.

'Of course I will.'

Her grandfather nodded. 'Keep whatever you want from inside and anything not salvageable can be disposed of. She collected old newspapers and books from all over the place when researching and I imagine much of it is of no interest to others.'

The idea of throwing away anything Nan loved was incomprehensible.

'I'll take a look a bit later and see what's what.'

'Good girl. I'm going to get into the living room today. Work on what I want to take with me.' His face gave nothing away but his tone was flat. 'Not much space where I'm moving to so I'm hoping you might keep some of the books and art and I can come and see them from time to time.'

And me, I hope.

She didn't have a chance to say it because he was already retracing their steps to the house.

TWO

Angie unpacked two of her suitcases which was mostly clothes and shoes. The rest of her luggage was for when she found her own place, stuff like books and a few household items. She reflected dismally that those, her laptop, phone, and car, were all she owned.

Being back in her bedroom offered a long-forgotten sense of comfort mixed up with a feeling of displacement. She'd lived here from the age of thirteen to eighteen, then been back for breaks between university semesters. And while she'd been a student teacher, she'd worked close enough to commute and stayed here for almost another year. It was the only home she clearly remembered. Her parents had moved a few times, thanks to her father's job as a miner. Sometimes they'd be in a mining town for a year then cross the country for a different company. Her mother preferred they moved with him rather than having a home in one place and him being away for months at a time as a fly-in, fly-out worker.

She sat on her bed which Gramps had made up with her childhood patchwork quilt made by Nan. Growing up, she'd come for holidays with Mum and Dad and as she got older, sometimes on her own. It was the only reason she was alive, because the car accident that claimed them had happened while Angie was on school holidays in Rivers End and her parents were a thousand kilometres away.

With one phone call her happy life had changed.

Angie jumped up and went to the window. The view was pretty across the manicured lawn surrounded by more flower beds and a couple of weeping cherries. There was a garden bench which Gramps made long ago and Angie could almost see him sitting there chatting to Nan, both with a cool drink, their laughter drifting across on a summer breeze. A stab of pain was so real and raw in her heart that Angie touched her chest.

'This was my home,' she whispered. 'My safe haven.'

And there wasn't a thing she could do to stop it being sold. She certainly couldn't buy it. Two years of court battles to retain her good credit rating and distance herself legally – including going back to her maiden name – from her ex and his crimes had left her close to broke. A credit rating was of little use when she had no deposit to buy a house, let alone this one, which she expected would fetch an amount beyond the means of her teacher's salary. And it had to be sold to cover Gramps's future needs.

In another few years... maybe. Angie knew how to live frugally and if she could find a small place to rent and poured every spare cent into savings, then the time would come she might afford to own a house. But Seahaven would be long gone by then.

'Angie? Would you give me a hand moving something?'

Gramps was attempting to slide a heavy old entertainment unit away from the wall in the living room. His face was alarmingly red.

'Stop for a sec! Why are you moving it?'

He stopped pushing, panting a bit.

'Shall I get some water?'

His head shook but he perched on the arm of the sofa.

'I think this is too big for us alone. Maybe if we take the television off... but do we need to move it right now?' It made no sense to her.

'Something dropped behind it.'

'Oh.' Angie took a look but it was too dark back there so she opened the flashlight on her phone. 'Is that a photo frame?'

'Just leave it. I'll get Jack to help move it.'

'Jack?'

'Renting the house next door. Helpful chap with good manners.'

Hiding a smile at the description, Angie went in search of an extra-long ruler she had in her bedroom cupboard from some school project as a teen. Gramps was trying to reach behind the unit when she returned but there'd hardly been room for Angie's much slimmer arms.

'Let me try this.'

'No, we'll leave it for now.'

Waiting until Gramps moved away from the unit, Angie dived back to her original spot and slid the ruler over the top of the frame, gently guiding it until she could reach it.

'What did I say?' Gramps sounded resigned, rather than mad.

With a triumphant grin, Angie straightened, the frame in her fingers. 'Got it. I'll put it back... oh.' A dull weight dropped into her stomach as she stared at the photograph. It was her parents on their wedding day. Both were so happy. So *alive*.

A firm arm came around her shoulders and for a minute, Gramps squeezed her in silent understanding. This was why he'd said to leave it.

'When did you get this framed?'

'Just the other day, lass. Found it among a box with other photos and it felt wrong not to have the two of them there with all the others.' He took the frame and placed it in between a dozen or so others, including ones of Nan and Angie and himself. 'Now we're all here again, even just in spirit.'

Angie and Gramps worked together in the living room until late in the afternoon, stopping only for sandwiches. She was impressed by his stoic approach to relegating decades of possessions into three groups. Keep. Sell. Throw away.

The 'sell' list was the longest and included anything which could be donated. She couldn't imagine him having much which couldn't be of use to someone else. Both he and Nan were careful with their money, made good choices with purchases, and maintained what they owned. No treating items as disposable. It was refreshing, coming from the past years Angie endured, where money came in and went out even faster. She hated waste and seeing Gramps in action reminded her why she did. Old-fashioned was often a good thing.

With a comprehensive list of the living room contents, they decided to call it a day.

There were two boxes packed and taped with 'Living Room' written in black marker. Several Post-it notes were stuck to other items such as two small framed paintings, a tall lamp, and the record player. These would all go with him.

'How much space *is* there in your new home, Gramps?'

'Tomorrow we can take some of the boxes down and I'll show you. Two bedrooms, bathroom, living room, kitchenette. Anything which doesn't fit I'll reconsider. Now, I need to attend to some Historical Society business, if you'll excuse me.'

Gramps was gone before Angie thought of anything to say. He probably needed a break from the packing and sorting.

And from me.

Angie bit her lip. The negative self-talking had to stop. Shane was no longer her husband and she'd never see him again. He might not have laid a hand on her but his legacy of verbal and emotional abuse remained. Coercive control, she'd been told by a therapist who'd assessed her for the court hearings. She hadn't known a thing about his gambling debts and subsequent illegal attempts to scam others to pay his way out of trouble. Not until the knock on the door late one night from a desperate woman who'd lost everything believing Shane was part of a legitimate investment company.

She closed her eyes and drew in a long, slow breath through her nostrils, holding it for a few seconds before releasing from her mouth. Meditation was something she was learning about and this kind of focused breathing was the quickest way to bring her thoughts and feelings back to the present.

From another part of the house, Gramps was laughing. She followed the sound to his study and peeked through the open door. He was at his desk on his phone, half turned away. There was another burst of laughter before he spoke.

'And then he woke up and had missed the entire party? Oh that is too funny.'

The amusement in his voice made Angie smile. This side of Gramps wasn't seen nearly enough. Even before the loss of her parents and Nan, he'd been a serious man. Reflective. Now and then his sense of humour would emerge and a house filled with laughter was one of her happiest memories.

'Ah, yes. I have confirmed the time.'

Gramps began to turn his chair and Angie stepped out of view. She didn't want to be caught eavesdropping and hurried to the kitchen.

She could prep for dinner. Cut up some vegetables and see what else was in the fridge. Both of them were capable cooks thanks to Nan insisting they do their share when she was busy writing a book, but somewhere along the line, Angie had lost her enjoyment of making a nice meal for someone she loved. Too much criticism from Shane, who never lifted a finger to help.

'You've been in the pantry for two minutes, lass. Are you lost?'

Angie grabbed the nearest item and carried it out. 'Just looking for this.'

He raised both eyebrows. 'For a tin of tomatoes?'

'You're right. I'll need two to make a pasta sauce.'

'Or you could get changed and come out for dinner.'

'Dinner?'

His face dropped. 'I should have asked. Probably too tired.'

'No. No, I'd love that! Give me five minutes and I'll be ready.'

'Funny how you mentioned pasta sauce,' Gramps said. 'My new favourite restaurant happened to have a table available.'

Angie was almost skipping beside him. They'd decided to walk and she couldn't remember the last time they'd gone out together. She'd changed into a summery dress and sandals and tied her unruly hair back in a ponytail. A quick look in the mirror before leaving had her grinning. Thirty she might be but she felt like she'd just turned sixteen with this surprise dinner out.

'Where are we going? The bistro?' she asked.

'Not tonight. There's been a few additions since you were here last. Was that four years ago?'

'Five. And I should have stayed here then.'

'I agree. But you're here now.'

'So what's changed? Oh, there's a bookstore!'

'There is. And we have a florist, the supermarket was extended and updated, the inn is refurbished, and we've some new places to eat.' He gestured down the street lined by shops and businesses, which was the main part of the small town. 'Much is the same but we've been blessed with excellent additions and because Rivers End is growing, all the businesses appear to be going quite well.'

They stopped to cross, Angie checking twice in case another electric car snuck up on her.

With its dreamy driver.

She glanced at Gramps in case she'd said that aloud but his attention was on the street. He hadn't approved of Shane from the beginning and the man with the red sports car would be even further down Gramps's list of suitable men for his grandchild. Not that letting another man into her life was on the cards.

They crossed and stopped outside a restaurant where tables and chairs were under bright umbrellas outside and a colourful sign announced *Rivers End Italian Delights*.

'Ah, now I understand about the pasta sauce,' Angie said. 'This looks inviting.'

The door was open and inside was a mix of round and square tables, each with a red and white checked tablecloth. A smiling gentleman in his early seventies approached, wearing an apron with the logo on the top with a name beneath it. Franco.

'Ah, Emmett. Would you prefer to sit inside or out this evening?'

Gramps looked at Angie. 'Your choice.'

'Oh, outside sounds nice. If you don't mind?'

'Outside it is.'

In a moment they were settled at a small square table and had menus in front of them. Franco poured water from a glass bottle and promised to return shortly to take their drinks order. There were people at all the other outdoor tables and quite a few inside.

'Busy for a weekday.'

'Always like this. Same as the wine bar further along and unless you book, you run the risk of missing out. What would you like to drink, Angie? A glass of wine?'

'Oh… I don't want you to go to any great expense for me. In fact, would you let me pay for this?'

With a frown, Gramps reached for her hand. 'Do you have any idea what your nan would say if I invited you to dinner then let you pay?' He squeezed her fingers. 'This is my treat and I don't have anyone else to spoil. So, enough of that.'

Angie forced a smile as he released her hand. Gramps was being so kind but it wasn't the same as before her marriage. Their easy-going relationship felt strained. Or maybe she was overthinking it all.

'Have a look at the menu, Angie. I think we should start with the bruschetta. Very garlicky.'

'How often do you come here?'

'Every couple of weeks. It's important to support local business.' His eyes twinkled. 'Plus, the desserts are good.'

Night softly fell and the street remained busy, but now there were more pedestrians than cars. People out for dinner or for a walk, some greeting Gramps as they passed. A few glanced at Angie but apart from some polite smiles, there was no hello and it was unsurprising. She hadn't lived here in years.

They enjoyed a coffee after the meal, which was one of the best Angie had ever eaten. Her main was a creamy pumpkin and sage sauce over handmade gnocchi and they'd shared a trio of gelato for dessert, not having room for much else.

'I don't remember Franco,' she said. He'd just checked on them with his friendly smile, a wiry, cheerful man with a full head of white hair and matching moustache. 'You mentioned earlier he opened the restaurant, so he's the owner?'

'Part owner. He and his wife moved here a few years ago and fulfilled their lifelong dream with this lovely place. She was the chef.'

'Was?'

Gramps nodded, his face serious. 'About a year ago she had a stroke. She's slowly recovering but will require care for the rest of her life. For a while it seemed she'd be unable to leave the hospital because of her needs.'

Angie glanced at the restaurant, where Franco was clearing plates from the table. His smile was still wide as he chatted to customers who were leaving. 'What a terrible shock for them both.'

'And financially. Franco took a lot of time off at first to support his wife and then when he did return, he had no head chef of course. Hiring one and managing Cara's special requirements almost ruined him. Then someone stepped in and changed everything for the better.' Gramps finished his coffee and dabbed his lips with a napkin. 'His godson bought a part share in the restaurant. It was a generous cash injection and has given Franco the freedom to work when he wants thanks to more staffing and Cara is now a resident at the assisted living facility. There's all levels of care and hers is on the high side.'

'What a wonderful thing to do. Does the godson work here as well?'

'Goodness, no. Silent partner. Let me go and pay and we'll waddle home with our full bellies.'

While he was inside, a car slowed and then parked close by. A red, quiet car. Its driver climbed out and began wandering in Angie's direction.

Flustered, she stood and busied herself looking inside her handbag. Of all the luck.

'Good evening.'

Bother, bother, bother.

Meeting his eyes, Angie clutched her handbag against herself. 'Good evening.'

'No ill effects? From this morning?'

There was a slight smile on his full lips. Maybe she was staring too intently. Angie lifted her chin. 'None at all.'

'Excellent. Did you enjoy your meal?' He glanced at the table where there was only the coffee cups.

'I did.'

Now I sound like I'm stuck up. Why are you making me so nervous?

He didn't seem interested in moving on and the longer he stood there, the harder Angie searched for a way to say goodnight. Gramps would be back in a second and then he'd want to know who she was talking to and probably remind her about previous poor choices in men.

'You should go,' she blurted the words and immediately felt heat rise in her face.

For a moment he gazed at her with an expression of curiosity. Then his hand reached into a pocket and he removed a phone which was quietly ringing. Before he answered, his smile broadened, directed completely at Angie, and then he walked away.

The strangest sensation of light-headedness was simply being tired. Or from the wine. It certainly wasn't a visceral response from a brief exchange with a self-assured if not cocky man who probably had too much money and time on his hands.

As she and Gramps wandered in the opposite direction, Angie snuck a look over her shoulder. He'd gone into the restaurant and was at a window table and Franco sat opposite him. Was he the generous godson? If so, then he couldn't be all bad. Could he?

THREE

Angie was outside the door to Nan's office, keys in one hand and a laptop bag slung over a shoulder. She'd been here for a few minutes, pacing back and forth and even walking away at one point as she mustered the courage to enter.

Almost the minute they finished breakfast Gramps had pushed the keys into her hand and asked again for her help. It had to be playing on his mind for him to insist. He was working on his bedroom this morning and the minute she said she was going, he took his Post-it notes and some boxes and closed himself in. Angie understood. He'd not found the heart to pack up Nan's things in all these years and didn't want to be around to see it done.

In the months after she'd died – a sudden, unforeseen heart attack – Angie came here often. At first it was to weep until there were no tears left. Better here than around Gramps, who was lost without his soulmate. As the grief eased to a dull pain, Angie would talk to her grandmother, imagining her sitting behind her desk, pen in hand, nodding at her grandchild's words. A year after Nan died, Gramps suddenly locked the door and he wouldn't discuss why. Angie had wondered if he was trying – in his own way – to help her move on by closing that chapter of their lives... at least the physical connection.

Now she had the keys but no idea where to start.

'And it's completely up to me,' she whispered. Unlocking the door, she pushed it open and forced herself to step inside.

If not for the heavy layer of dust, cobwebs, and the musty smell of stale air, Nan might have been here minutes ago, instead of years.

Angie took a moment to gaze around, trying to plan her course of action. The office was a timber building which Gramps had constructed when Angie's dad was a teenager. Gramps was a builder by trade and noticed how his wife was struggling to write in their shared study. Instead of working on a book she'd be up and down to cater for the needs of the family and too accepting of interruptions. Out here she could close the door and create work hours. The office space was large enough for a small timber desk, two bookcases, and a couple of comfy chairs for reading or visitors. Gramps had gone to the trouble of adding a small bathroom and between the two was a little counter with a sink, bar fridge, and cupboards with some plates and glasses and the like.

The tiny fridge was turned off, as was the power. Angie made a note on her phone to get it put back on. Gramps must have cleaned the fridge as it was empty. It used to keep sodas cold for Angie's visits and milk for the cups of tea Nan would make during her work day.

Going back to the door, Angie opened it wide and did the same with the two windows. It desperately needed airing. And dusting. She ducked to avoid an old cobweb which began to disintegrate with the fresh air and slowly dropped from the ceiling.

Gramps might have cleaned the fridge but he seemed to have left everything else as it was the last time Nan was here.

Even her writing pad.

Nan did all her writing by hand, right up until finishing a second draft and then she'd type out the entire manuscript. On the shelves of one bookcase were dozens of filled notebooks and a row of boxes which contained other notes and drafts. As an historical fiction author, Nan was meticulous with her research. She loved the local region and used factual accounts from the past to inspire and authenticate her work.

Just like Gramps. Always caring for our history.

His association with the local Historical Society dated back decades. It had briefly disbanded and then reformed to embrace more than Rivers End and he'd been president many times and loved his volunteer work with a passion. Perhaps it was what kept him going after Nan passed away.

Reluctant to touch the writing pad, Angie took her bag to the kitchen counter and opened the laptop computer. It was one of the few things she'd kept private and away from Shane, who used to take her phone when she was asleep and review every call and message. If she locked it, he'd stop talking to her, sometimes for days on end. All the time they'd been married, she'd only worked part-time as a teacher. He wouldn't tolerate her continuing her career and insisted she take short-term assignments. The laptop had been her one rebellion. She'd always kept it with her, or else hidden next to the spare tyre in her car, and looking back, Angie cringed at her compliance with his demands when she'd known they weren't right.

The laptop booted up and Angie quickly created a spreadsheet. She'd make a list of everything in here and use Gramps's formula of 'keep', 'sell', 'throw away'.

But exactly where should she begin? She settled on the idea of working on the larger items first. The desk was old but in great condition and Angie didn't want to let it go. Hopefully she'd have a rental before the school term started and Gramps wouldn't mind her keeping it as a reminder of her beautiful grandmother. He had said she could keep what she wanted.

The remainder of the furniture as well as kitchen items could be donated. All were in good enough condition but not worth the time and effort to sell.

Angie completed that part of the spreadsheet and sighed because now she had to move on to the rest of the office. The heart of it. She stood in front of one of the bookcases, hands in the pockets of her shorts. On the shelves were all manner of wonderful books. Classic and modern novels... at least, modern for when Nan was alive. Craft books about writing as well as several dictionaries and a thesaurus. And so many historical non-fiction books across several eras, with a heavy leaning toward Australian titles. One shelf had a glass front and contained multiple copies of Nan's published works in pristine condition. Surely Gramps would want at least one of each of her five books, and she did as well. But what of the rest? Would Gramps know anyone Nan would have liked to have them? Angie made more notes about that, including the word 'bookstore??'.

'Lass? I brought up a couple of boxes but once they're packed don't lift them. Wait for me.'

'Do you want to come in?' Angie went outside.

He shook his head and handed her the boxes. 'Have to keep going in my bedroom.'

'I'm making lists like you do. Would you mind me keeping the desk?'

Gramps headed down the path. 'Anything you want, you keep.'

Angie sighed as she watched his retreating back. Last night he'd been warm and cheerful but now the tension seemed to be back between them. This was too hard on him. Selling his home. Downsizing his life. And more than anything, dealing with Nan's things. Life wasn't fair.

. . .

The boxes were useful for packing the kitchen stuff into. Angie began a pile in a corner of things to throw, such as the ancient kettle, and some mugs too old and stained to keep. When there was nothing more to do in the other parts of the building, Angie turned to the first bookcase, first closing the door and windows to keep the rising heat out.

You're doing this to help Gramps. Get on with it.

Deciding to start with the hardest part, Angie picked up one of the boxes from the bottom shelf and sat in the comfy chair which was her favourite. These boxes were like an oversized shoebox, able to hold a completed, printed manuscript with room to spare. She slid off the lid, sneezing as dust rose.

Inside was a collection of notepads. Each was A5 sized and had a pretty cover, some spiral and others bound. Opening one, Angie smiled at her grandmother's sprawling writing. Nan always encouraged her to write neatly yet her own penmanship was the opposite, although readable for the most part. Each notepad began with a date and a short description on the first page. Some were research based while others were early thoughts. And all in this box pertained to one published novel.

Unable to contemplate this wonderful insight into a creative and talented mind being lost forever, Angie replaced the lid and placed the box on the desk. Somehow she'd find a way to keep these. Or find a home for them worthy of her grandmother's legacy.

The next four boxes were similar and joined the first. One for each of her published titles.

There was a deeper box, bound with heavy string. Angie couldn't slide it off, it was tied so tightly, so she searched for a pair of scissors in the desk drawers. Opening the first she almost wept on the spot to see an envelope addressed to Nan in Angie's childhood handwriting. The postdate was twenty-two years ago.

You kept this?

She snatched the scissors from the drawer and closed it.

It took a moment back on the chair to stop her hands trembling. No matter how she approached this task it was going to hurt. Angie wasn't good at compartmentalising things. She led with her heart. Living with Shane had shocked her into keeping her mouth closed as much as she could but that never meant the emotions weren't there. If anything, they were stronger because she'd kept them private.

Action was the best way to manage the rising tide of feelings so she snipped the string and removed the lid.

The contents were different from the previous boxes.

In here were newspaper clippings, lots of them, held together with a bull clip. Two large envelopes, one which jangled when lifted. Beneath those was a book titled *The Loneliest Girl by the Sea*. It was small – pocket sized and quite thin – and the author was... anonymous.

Angie knew of books which were anonymous and had read a few, such as *The Arabian Nights* and *Beowulf* but had never heard of this title. There was a publisher's information she didn't recognise, not that it meant much. The year of publication 1973. Not really old enough for Nan's books if this was for research purposes.

Delicately, she opened the cover and turned to the first page. There was a dedication. *To Mattie. The only one I never forgot.*

The only what? Friend? Relative? Lover? Something about it felt sad and Angie closed the book and put it back in the box. One of the envelopes contained some letters written in beautiful cursive which all began with 'Dearest Opal' – which was Nan – and signed 'M.W.'

'Who is M.W.?' Angie whispered. It might be as simple as a pen pal or old school friend of Nan's, but why keep them out here?

In the other envelope were two items. An old hymn book

and a set of keys. Well this was interesting. There were three keys on a plain ring. One looked like a house key, another was smaller, perhaps for a letterbox, and the remaining one was quite little. For a padlock?

Putting everything back in the box and closing the lid, Angie returned it to the bookcase. This was a mystery she'd need to ask Gramps about. Nan must have been researching a different kind of book, either set in more recent history or even someone's memoir. She'd always said she'd like to write someone's life story. But the keys. That was kind of strange.

'Ready for lunch?'

'Is it that time?'

'After one.'

Suddenly realising how hungry she was, Angie left the office, blinking in the bright sunlight. It was hot now and she pulled the door closed. There was no sign of Gramps so perhaps she'd imagined their brief conversation, but she made her way to the house, happy to step into the relative cool.

He was in the kitchen pouring iced tea from a jug. It was Nan's recipe, with lemon slices and mint floating and not for the first time Angie wished with all her heart her grandmother would walk through the door with her beautiful smile and warm hugs.

Gramps was even quieter than usual over lunch. He grunted rather than spoke and barely looked at Angie. Her heart went out to him but what could she do or say to make him happier? She collected their empty plates and washed up.

'You helping me, Angie? It takes some of the pressure off.'

She hadn't heard him come into the kitchen and turned with a smile. 'I'm happy to do whatever you need. You and Nan did so much for me. Letting me live here with you and giving me everything I needed to grow up and have a career I love. I can't wait to start teaching again and couldn't have done it without you.'

'You're family. Nan loved you deeply.'

And so do you, or you did.

Pushing away a surge of panic that her marriage had destroyed more than her own life by also taking away the one thing she'd always relied on – Gramps's love, Angie switched subjects without thinking.

'Was Nan working on someone's life story? I found a box with newspaper clippings and handwritten letters and—'

'*If* I wasn't completely clear earlier then listen carefully, Angela.' The palm of Gramps hand was facing her in a 'stop' position and his face had darkened. 'That office was your grandmother's work space. Not mine and not yours. Whatever is in those boxes was her business, not ours or anyone else's. Her plans went to the grave with her.'

'I didn't mean to upset you.'

'Tell me now if I've asked too much. I can hire someone to empty the office.'

'Gramps, no. Of course I will. I said I'd do so and you told me I can keep anything I want.' Angie gripped the tea towel she'd been using. 'Please don't be angry with me.'

His eyes held such pain that she wanted to hug him. And she wanted him to hug her back, tell her he didn't mean his hurtful words and curt tone. He dropped his hand. 'Not angry. The past needs leaving alone.'

She nodded and put the tea towel where it belonged. 'I'll get back to it then.'

'We'll go to my new residence at three. Take some boxes there. Show you the place.'

'I'll set myself an alarm for five to.'

Back in the office, Angie fought against the seemingly never-ending urge to cry. Gramps was right that Nan took her plans to the grave but one thing her grandmother made clear to

Angie was how welcome she was, not only to visit the office but to read anything within its walls. Gramps said the past needed leaving alone yet he and Nan shared such a love of local history that it made no sense.

What if she'd intended for the Historical Society to have what she was working on?

Drawn to the box with the letters in, Angie opened the lid and gazed inside. Gramps was mistaken. Nan wouldn't have minded Angie reading any of this and even letting her help with research. She'd done so in the past. Pushing aside a little voice which insisted that Nan would have asked for help with this if she'd wanted her involved, Angie picked up the small book.

Remembering to set the alarm on her phone, Angie sank onto her chair and opened the book, rereading the dedication before going to chapter one. It began with a short paragraph in italics.

The child was old enough to understand a terrible event had befallen but too young to know what or how or why. Her stomach ached with hunger and her throat was parched. Her tears had long since dried. The pretty dress she wore was muddy and torn. Her head hurt and there was blood when she touched it. She'd stumbled about in the forest, alone for a long time until a man appeared through the trees and lifted her into his arms. He told her she was safe now and he'd find her family. Find her parents and brother. It was the first lie of many.

FOUR

May 1960

The air is bitterly cold, more so on the hill above the rocks where waves crash and the wind cuts through my cardigan and skirt. I should have worn my coat but that's meant to be for Sundays only and if Mama notices I've been wearing it I'll be in trouble.

She's at a meeting of the church committee and I'm supposed to be mending the hem of my school skirt but right now, sitting on the grass gazing down at the water is a better choice.

This is the first day of school holidays and I need fresh air and freedom.

Way out at sea is a yacht with its spinnaker full, racing ahead of rain clouds. They'll be here soon enough so I'm watching closely to avoid being drenched.

The ocean is grey-green with white, foamy peaks as far as I can see. Overhead, there's a bit of blue sky but the sun – when it appears – offers no warmth despite winter still being some weeks away. Even so, I love this time of year. Maybe even more than summer when it can be so hot that I have to find a tree to sit beneath or even climb down the hill to where there are caves to hide inside. The hill is steep. Not really a cliff but a grassy incline which should have steps or at least a real path but has nothing. I guess being away from the main beaches like Driftwood Cove it doesn't matter because not many people venture here. There isn't a beach, just lots of rocks which are usually safe enough to walk on when the tide is out. My father used to fish from them and when I was younger I'd sometimes follow him around and splash in the pools of water finding all manner of interesting seaweed and shells. One day he went fishing and never came back.

My mother said he'd been swept out to sea.

There was a funeral but he wasn't inside the coffin. Mama said it was God's will he be lost at sea and we read about Jonah and the whale and when I asked why the whale didn't come and save my father, she slammed the Bible shut.

'Vernon disobeyed God, that's why. But unlike Jonah, your father never repented his sins and there were many.'

I still remember the chilling look she gave me. 'Never, ever disobey God, or anyone who represents him. Do you understand?'

At the time all I could do was nod vigorously because I was terrified but as I got older, I began to question why the same Christian god that we worshipped each Sunday, who was merciful and kind, wouldn't save my father. In what way had he disobeyed God? I mustered up the courage to ask her.

She refused to answer and I got so angry that I yelled at her and then she made me go out and cut a switch and used it to punish me, after reading a scripture aloud about sparing the rod and spoiling the child.

I never asked her anything important again.

And I never went onto the rocks either.

A sprinkle of rain catches me by surprise and I jump to my

feet. Thinking about that stuff always upsets me. My mind comes up with so many questions about life that I feel it will explode but there's nobody to ask. Girls are meant to be quiet and learn how to cook and sew and help other people. I'm almost a teenager, not a girl for much longer and I know how to do that stuff already. There's a yearning inside to discover the secrets of the world.

By the time I reach the house the wind is even stronger and I'm lucky to get inside just as the rain really starts. My hair is damp but my clothes are dry enough. The living room looks out to the sea and I stand there, peering through the streaks of rain.

'I know this isn't something we normally do, but there's a new couple who recently moved to town and joined our church.'

Mama had come back from her meeting in a happy mood. She'd inspected the skirt I'd quickly hemmed and said it was good enough then walked into the dining room. It was rare for her to go there. We always eat at the table in the kitchen.

'The committee thought it would be charitable to invite them to meet other members of the congregation and it's been a long time since we had guests... but I did invite them for dinner next Sunday.'

I'm surprised and a bit excited. Some of my school mates talk about their parents hosting dinner parties and having family over for meals each week. We don't have any family. Mama says she lost touch with hers many years ago and that Father didn't have anyone. And we don't ever have friends over. Not even from the church.

'We might need to dust in here and find the nice plates and cutlery. Would you like to help me, Mary?'

'Yes, please. What will I do first?'

She smiles and I stare at her. How pretty she is with her

eyes gentle and lips lifted on the corners. Mama rarely smiles so her face looks cross or sad most of the time.

'Shall we plan the meal first? Then we can do a spring clean of the house even if it is a freezing autumn day.'

We check the pantry and cold safe and while Mama tells me what's in there, I write a long list, doing my best to be neat and sorting items by type.

'I like what you've done, Mary. Having all the baking items together and all the dairy and so on really makes it easy to see what we have.' She frowns. 'If we're going to cook a delicious meal for strangers though, we might need to buy a few ingredients. Can you think of anything we can make with what we have?'

I feel so grown up. 'Let's see... you make such nice pastry so what about a pie?'

'A pie seems a bit plain for visitors.'

'The fish pie you make is nice. What about with piped mashed potatoes on top instead of a lid? And there's plenty of cabbage growing in the garden we could do as a side dish?'

All of a sudden, Mama hurries to a cupboard and leans inside, looking for something. She pulls out an old recipe book I'd never seen. Really old, with the pages falling out and it is in another language.

'This belonged to my grandmother and I had a sudden memory of a cabbage recipe.' She lays it on the bench and carefully turns the pages.

'What language is it?'

'German.'

'Can you read it?'

For an instant I wonder if my mother is quite well because she bursts into laughter. Smiling and now laughing. Was this all because we were having guests over?

Is she as lonely as me?

'Oh, Mary. My mother was German and my father was

Dutch and we lived in Holland until we came to Australia when I was little. A baby, really. And my mother taught me to cook the same way her mother did. But I grew up here and became accustomed to different foods and your father loved his plainer-tasting dinners. Ah, here it is.'

The page is faded but has a drawing of a meal with a long list beside it and what is probably instructions beneath.

'Is it cabbage?'

'Yes. Basically you take a whole cabbage and cut out the centre. It is cooked in a big pot with milk inside until slightly soft then you add a mix of stuffing. Minced meat and onion and carrots with plenty of herbs. In the oven until all is cooked.'

I must have screwed up my face because she laughed again.

'Promise it tastes nice. We can make a gravy and serve with potatoes and bread rolls. And we have some preserved fruit left from summer?'

'Yes, plums.'

'Then we make a plum pie for dessert.'

I'm not convinced it will taste good but nothing can make me spoil today. 'Shall I start cleaning the dining room?'

After church on Sunday we hurry home to prepare dinner. Our house is over two miles from Driftwood Cove where the church is, and normally we'd walk. But the rain is still here and Mama reluctantly drives our old car. We've only ever had this car and it needs new tyres and something called a tune-up but we can't waste money on it when there's so little coming in. Since Father died, we've lived off Mama's sewing which she does for a lot of people and she sometimes cleans houses for money.

The car makes some weird noises as it goes up the last bit of the hill to our house. I jump out to open the gate then race ahead to pull the doors of the big shed across. Mama drives in and before she turns off the engine, there's black smoke puffing out of the pipe at the back.

She helps me close the big shed. 'God will look out for us, Mary. The car will be fine.'

I'm not so sure but she's an adult and must know.

By the time the guests arrive the dining room looks nice with our best plates and glasses and a water pitcher. We moved the oil lamps from our bedrooms in there as well as a spare to give the most light possible. I'd met Mr and Mrs Godfrey at church so am not too nervous about them being here. Mama asks Mr Godfrey to say grace.

The cabbage meal is delicious and Mrs Godfrey asks for the recipe. She talks a lot and Mama becomes very quiet. She folds and refolds her napkin until there is a break in the conversation.

'I'll check on our pie.'

She starts collecting plates and I help her, following her to the kitchen.

'Mary, go and talk to our visitors and I'll be just a moment.'

Her face is a bit strained but I do as she asks.

'How old are you, dear?' Mrs Godfrey beams at me.

'Almost twelve.'

'You are?' She looks surprised. 'I would have guessed a little younger.'

'Dear—'

'Sorry.' She leans close to her husband and whispers loudly enough for me to hear. 'She just shows no signs of... well, development.'

I don't know what to make of it but feel uncomfortable. What does she mean by development?

Mr Godfrey gives her a funny look then smiles at me. 'So if you're twelve, are you at high school?'

'No, final year of primary school. I'm looking forward to attending high school but the closest one is in Green Bay and that means a bus ride each way.' Still, it is exciting to know I'll be learning a lot more than at the little school in Driftwood Cove. If I can get a good education then I'll find a job which pays enough money to properly help Mama. Even buy her a new car one day.

Mama must have overheard because she has a look I've seen a few times when the subject of high school arises. I know she'll worry about me travelling so far each day but I'll be fine.

'Mary love, would you fetch the cream?' She puts down the lovely pie she's cooked and steam rises and, along with it, delicious plum and spice smells.

I hurry because I can't wait to try it.

As I get close to the dining room I stop because Mrs Godfrey is talking about me again.

'Does she take after your husband?'

'Why do you ask?'

'Well, you have such a pretty heart-shaped face but Mary is quite different, don't you think? Her face is narrow and long. Not at all like you.'

With my spare hand I touch my cheeks. They seem okay to me. So does my chin.

'Mary? Where's the cream?'

I wait a second or two then take it to her.

Mama's face is bright red and she doesn't even look at me as she accepts the bowl.

After the Godfreys have gone, and I've closed the gate, I help Mama clean up. She doesn't say much. I tell her how yummy all the food was. Before I go to bed, she suddenly hugs me and tells me I am her precious girl. Her perfect little Mary.

The wind has picked up and I can't sleep so I sneak to the kitchen to get a glass of water. On the way back to bed I pass Mama's bedroom. She is crying.

FIVE

Now

'When did this get built, Gramps?' Following his directions Angie drove into a driveway which opened to a large carpark. They'd gone past a sign saying *Rivers End Assisted Living Community* at the front of a series of new buildings.

'Been a work in progress for a couple of years and opened a few months back. There was a waiting list from the day the first clod was dug.'

'It's much larger than I envisaged.'

The sprawling centre had once been paddocks, a few blocks from the town centre and not far from the school where Angie had been a student and was soon to become a teacher. If the school wasn't doing so already, perhaps she could start excursions to visit here. Children benefited from interactions with seniors and the reverse was true. Too many people in retirement villages or assisted care struggled with loneliness and being away from their loved ones.

After parking, Angie glanced at her grandfather. Since they'd got in the car, his mood had improved and he'd not continued his earlier sharpness with her. He was smiling as he gazed around.

Have you been lonely at the house?

She'd never considered he might be searching for friendship and company beyond his volunteer work. Even though she was back for good this time, he'd be happier with people of his own age and interests, along with not having a big house and garden to look after.

They'd brought a collapsible trolley and piled it with boxes. It wasn't heavy so Gramps gave in and let Angie manage it while he led the way.

'This big building up ahead is the reception area. Inside is also the dining room for residents and the main kitchen. At the furthest end is a wing for those residents requiring more specialist care. People such as Franco's wife, Cara.'

From the carpark it was an easy walk along a wide concrete path to the building. Gramps went through a sliding double door and helped Angie push the trolley around a corner. The reception area was large and airy with a water feature and plants. Soft music danced in the air around them. Laughter came from a group of seniors seated around a coffee table. Near the water feature a young woman gently lowered a baby into the arms of a frail woman in a wheelchair, whose eyes shone with tears of joy. In a corner was a small café.

'They've thought of everything, Angie. The café is open during the day for residents to take their visitors. I've heard it's possible to book it at night for a private event.'

The reception desk was made of two long, curved counters forming an oval with each end open. A woman looked up as they approached, her smile widening when she saw Gramps.

'Mr Fairlie, hello! More boxes?'

'Yes, and plenty more to follow. Paula, this is my granddaughter, Angela Fairlie. She's moved back to Rivers End and is taking up a teaching position at the school up the road.'

Paula was a bit older than Angie with lots of red hair pulled back in a bun and a ton of freckles. She extended her hand over the counter. 'So nice to meet you, Angela.'

'Oh, just call me Angie and it's nice to meet you, too.'

'I'll get your key, Mr Fairlie.'

As Paula disappeared into a small office, Gramps grinned at Angie. 'They're all like this, lass. Friendly and helpful and they know their stuff. Do you know there's even a physiotherapist here most days and a heated swimming pool?'

For the first time in ages, Angie was happy. Gramps actually wanted to be here and she'd do everything in her power to help him make the transition smooth.

Once Gramps had collected his keys they pushed the trolley past the reception desk to another set of doors. These opened to a covered walkway between a lawn and garden beds and trees. About ten metres along was another building, long and single floor like the main one.

'Inside are studio-style rooms which are ideal for those who want their independence but still need a bit of help now and then. We're going this way.'

They followed a footpath around the side of the building to a street. It was wide enough for one car and a dozen or so cottages lined each side. Each had a small front garden and a path leading to the door. Gramp turned into the fourth on the left.

'This is mine, Angie.'

He unlocked the door and pushed it open, then helped with the trolley, wheeling it into the living room. There were already several piles of boxes stacked along a wall. The carpet was new and the room had the smell of fresh paint but there was no furniture.

Together they made a new pile of boxes which were marked up as 'living room' before taking the half-empty trolley across the hall to the bedroom.

'This is a nice size, Gramps. And a walk-in robe!'

'Never had one of those. I've ordered a new bed and a bedside table and lamp plus some furniture for the other rooms. Might need your help picking out some sheets and cushions and so on. You've always had a good eye for colour combinations.'

'Happy to help.'

Trolley unpacked, Gramps showed Angie around.

'The bathroom is already set up for old people. Rails everywhere and room in the shower for a seat. And we'll need to look at towels.'

Angie took out her phone with a grin. 'I will begin to take notes. Bedding, cushions, and bathroom stuff so far.'

Next was a small kitchen. Gramps called it a kitchenette and as it was only a quarter of the size of the one in his house, Angie understood. But it was modern and cleverly designed to fit a half-sized oven, microwave, small fridge, cooktop, and plenty of cupboards.

'The dining room in the main building serves three proper meals a day plus afternoon tea so I only need to keep stock of what I fancy making rather than always going over there. I'm going to build a couple of horizontal vegetable gardens and some planter boxes for fresh herbs. Come and see the back garden.'

The way out was through a laundry complete with new washing machine and dryer opposite a wall of narrow open shelving.

Gramps walked to the end of the garden and turned around. 'Not exactly the same as having a coffee on the bench at home in the morning.'

The back area was only a few metres squared, with lush grass, and surrounded by a post and rail fence about a metre and a half tall. The back fence had a small gate which opened to a large parklike area. Either side was the gardens of the neighbours and apart from a small fruit tree, there was little else.

Angie kept her tone upbeat. 'Once you build your vertical gardens the area will begin to shine, Gramps. Are there any restrictions on what you can do?'

'Can't add a tennis court.' He chuckled. He'd never played tennis. 'There are guidelines and any structures have to be approved. I own the cottage but it is subject to a few conditions. From what I understand I can grow plants which don't encroach on the neighbours and create a comfortable outdoor living space.'

'In that case, how about we bring your bench down?'

'I never thought about that.'

'Under the fruit tree would be nice.' Angie crossed the grass to where Gramps stood. 'You'll make this your home. I know it's smaller but the important things aren't big, are they? Mostly they live in our hearts.'

For a moment, Angie feared Gramps would cry. His eyes welled up and his hands shook as he took hers. But then he smiled and nodded. 'I've always loved that about you. Compassion and empathy. What would I ever do without you, lass?'

She squeezed his hands. 'I'm never leaving the area again. Rivers End is my home and you are the most important reason I feel this way. Maybe I should see if one of these cottages is for rent because it is about the perfect size for me.'

Gramps gave her an odd look. Was it because she'd said that about him? But the moment passed and he offered to show her the rest of the community grounds.

On the way home they stopped at the supermarket and stocked up for the rest of the week. Gramps was tiring by the time Angie helped carry the last of the shopping inside and she poured him some iced water and encouraged him to relax for a while.

She unpacked and scribbled down a few ideas for dinners.

Gramps was housing her so it was the least she could do. For a minute she stopped and closed her eyes. He couldn't house her for much longer. Angie had to start searching for her own home and pray something was available in her budget.

Hearing the tapping of Gramps's keyboard, she left him to do his Historical Society work and wandered back to Nan's office in search of a distraction. The first chapter of the little book played on her mind and raised questions. Was it simply fiction or an autobiography? At this point she knew the name Mary and the couple who'd come for dinner. The Godfreys. Oh, and Vernon, the father.

It was getting too late in the day to read another chapter so Angie opened the first of the letters. The return address was a post office box in Melbourne and the letter was dated 16 May 2010.

Dear Opal,

Your letter found its way to me via the publisher of The Loneliest Girl by the Sea *and I have to tell you how surprised I was to receive it. Only fifty copies were printed because I realised my folly of writing the book almost the moment it was released and made a financial arrangement with the publisher to cease distribution. Of those fifty, I managed to track down forty and destroy them and have often wondered where the remaining nine went. I kept one copy myself, and it is locked away until after my death.*

I am familiar with your own wonderful books and quite touched you have an interest in the life of Mary. The book is not penned with the same talent as yours but came from a deep need to tell her story. Seeking publication was foolish and acceptance by the first publisher I approached was a surprise.

Your questions about Mary are ones I am reluctant to answer at this stage. There seems to be little point in discussing matters from so long ago. They are hardly relevant to my life and I have accepted there is no chance of discovering the truth. The past is best left alone.

*Sincerely yours,
M.W.*

Deep in thought, Angie folded the letter and returned it to the envelope. The last paragraph supported her feeling that the book was a memoir of some kind. The writer had accepted there was no chance of discovering the truth... about what?

Angie checked the date on the envelope. It was the same year Nan died. Whatever this all was – this collection of seemingly random items – had mattered to Nan. She'd gone to a lot of trouble to track down the anonymous author and write to them. It had to be important. Gramps was wrong about any plans going to the grave with Nan because she'd always believed in finishing what she started. And she'd encouraged Angie to be the same.

Maybe... could I finish this? In her honour?

There'd be a lot more reading to do first. The rest of the book. The newspaper clippings. The remaining letters. Nan had obviously been so intrigued by the book that she'd poured hours of research into it. And where had she found the book if only nine copies were in circulation? So many questions and Angie was itching to get started.

'Care for a glass of wine, lass?'

She stuck her head out. 'Oh, it has cooled down a lot.'

'I'm going to go sit on the bench for a bit and thought a glass of red might be a nice addition.'

'Oh, yes please. I'll lock up and meet you there.'

Angie put the lid on the box. The last line in the letter had reminded her of Gramps's words earlier today. *The past is best left alone.*

'Or maybe it needs to be set free,' she murmured, and wondered where the thought had come from.

The sky was hazy after the long, hot day. Angie enjoyed the slow change from light to dark every bit as the opposite. If she was down on the beach the colours reflecting on the sea always amazed her at dusk.

No wonder I love it here.

Gramps sat on the bench holding two glasses of ruby red wine. When Angie joined him he handed her one then gently clicked his against hers. 'To the memory bench.'

Almost choking up as the image of him and Nan sitting here reappeared, Angie nodded and managed to say 'Cheers'.

The wine was welcome after the mixed day. Dealing with Nan's office and Gramps's earlier bad mood and even visiting his new home was a lot to deal with. She'd been walking on eggshells with Shane for so many years that her first response to any negative situation was a wall of protection and that had to change.

'I like the idea of taking this with me.' Gramps patted the timber. 'I'll make a garden bed around it.'

'Your new cottage is really lovely and I'm so impressed by the facilities. All you need is a lawn bowls club to be perfect. Actually, you can probably walk to yours from there.'

'Nothing is too far in Rivers End. Did you want to buy the house?'

Angie almost spat out the wine she'd just sipped. That was the last question she'd ever expected from her grandfather. He'd made it clear during their phone conversations before she'd left Perth that he had to spend the equivalent of a new house to finance his new cottage and ongoing lifestyle at the community. She managed to swallow without dribbling any out.

'I'm just going to find a cheap rental, Gramps. Something small.'

'Because you want a small place?' His eyes were unwavering. 'Tell the truth, Angie.'

'No, not because I want a small place. But after what happened in Perth… well, there's no money left. I'm effectively starting over financially as well as with a new life.' She pushed down a sudden lump in her throat. She'd ruined her life and now it was obvious to Gramps. 'If things were different then I'd do everything in my power to buy the house. This is my home and I love it with all my heart.'

Gramps opened his mouth to speak.

'Good evening, neighbours.'

The cheery voice from the other side of the fence behind them was familiar. Too familiar. Glancing around to confirm her worst fears, Angie looked straight into the amused brown eyes of the man who'd almost run her over.

SIX

How could this happen? Of all the people to rent the place next door, why did it have to be this man?

'Ah, Jackson, good to see you.' Gramps got to his feet and wandered the couple of metres to the fence, extending his hand to shake. 'Lovely evening.'

'Much nicer here than the city. I'm enjoying that breeze which comes in as it gets dark and brings the scent of the ocean.' His eyes moved from Gramps's face to Angie's and his expression subtly changed. Was he waiting for her to tell him to go away again?

'Angie, come and meet Jackson.'

Please don't tell him we've met already.

'Jack, please. Jackson sounds so formal. Hello, Angie.'

His handshake was firm and his fingers warm. And those eyes twinkled as if they were sharing a secret, which they were.

'How goes the packing, Emmett?'

'We took another load of boxes to my cottage earlier. Much quicker with Angie helping but I may need to call on you again at some point to move a couple of larger items. If you are around, of course.'

'Anytime. I've no plans to go too far for a while. I actually wondered if you'd both like to come over for dinner tomorrow? My sister and her family are visiting Rivers End and I know they'd like to meet you.' Jack grinned at Gramps. 'As long as you don't mind two very busy children under the age of eight.'

'I don't mind children one bit. And that's most kind of you but surely you'd prefer to spend time with your family alone?'

'They're in town for a week, staying at Palmerston House, so I'm seeing plenty of them. Any allergies? Dislikes? I haven't planned a menu yet.'

Dinner? What if he accidentally mentioned their first encounter? She'd be mortified if people knew she'd been so careless as to step out in front of a car.

What if the school finds out, or a parent? I'm meant to be sensible and a good example.

'Do you like Mexican food?'

'Doesn't everyone? Not that I cook it often these days but when Angie was a teen we'd make tortillas from scratch and filled them with local fish and lettuce and tomatoes from our garden.'

'You remember that?' Those meals were special memories. Both of them busy in the kitchen and laughing as they ate and bits would fall out of the overstuffed tacos. 'I hadn't thought about that in ages but it was such fun, Gramps.'

'It was, lass.'

'What is this magic talk of making tortillas?' Jack asked. 'I was going to buy some of those kits from the supermarket.'

'Good grief. Are you willing to get your hands dirty, young man?' Gramps sounded outraged at the idea of premade food. 'I guarantee that once you learn how to do them, you'll never buy another kit.'

'Always up for a challenge.'

Jack leaned his arms on the top railing and for the first time Angie paid attention to what he was wearing. No smelly formal wear but a white T-shirt and cotton knee-length shorts. His arms and chest were muscular. He looked after himself. What had he said the other morning? He'd been to an end-of-shoot party? Was he an actor?

He was openly grinning at her. She hadn't meant to stare.

'What do you think, Angie?'

She looked at Gramps, not understanding the question.

'We can teach Jack how to make them.'

What had she missed while she was checking out the subject of the conversation?

'I'm happy to write out the instructions,' she offered.

'I think we can do better than that for our neighbour. How about you join us in half an hour, Jack?'

'As long as you don't mind, Emmett? I'd be most grateful.'

Wait. What?

'See you then. Come on, grandchild, we have some prep to do.'

'Why, Gramps?'

'Why what?'

'Invite a total stranger over for cooking lessons!'

They were in the kitchen doing a rapid tidy to make space on the counter, rather than sharing it with half-packed boxes. Once the boxes were moved Angie began scrubbing the top, probably using more force than was required.

'Jack's not a total stranger. He's rented next door for a year. Why are you upset?'

'I'm not.'

He chuckled. 'Bet that counter disagrees. It's clean, lass.'

'Well I was going to make us dinner when we'd had our wine.'

'Jack and I only need half the counter so you go ahead and cook. What are we having?'

'I can hardly cook while he's here but not offer to feed him.' Hating how whiny she sounded, Angie tossed the cloth in the sink. 'What if we see how long this takes? I can make a big salad in the meantime and adapt to our needs.'

'You know, salad and some of those crusty rolls we bought is fine by me.' Gramps came around the counter. 'Didn't mean to upset you by inviting Jack. I'm just so accustomed to making decisions for me, not for two.'

'No, I'm just out of sorts. And this is still your home. I'd better find some flour.'

The doorbell rang.

'I'll get the ingredients while you let Jack in.'

He was in the pantry before Angie could protest so she rolled her eyes, stalked to the door and did as he said.

'Oh, hi again. Please come in.'

She held the door open, standing as far back as possible to give him space. But Jack didn't move. He carried a six-pack of beer in one hand and a bottle of white wine in the other and stayed where he was, feet planted apart on the welcome mat.

'It's okay. If you happen to be a vampire you *can* come in when invited,' Angie said.

His lips quivered.

'Wait... did I forget the red carpet? I'll go find it.'

'I can't work you out,' Jack said. 'Do you like me or loathe me?'

Whatever had got into Angie wasn't letting go.

'Let me think about it. Do I have to make a choice?'

'Could be both.'

'Choice of what, Angie?' Gramps appeared from behind her. 'Beer or wine? Both welcome and so are you, son.' He turned back toward the kitchen. 'You can decide later, Angie.'

Jack stepped inside, pausing near Angie to whisper, 'Yes, you *can* decide later.'

She closed the door as he followed Gramps but the scent of

him lingered and for a second or two she closed her eyes. It would be dangerous to let this stranger get past her barriers. Oh, but he smelled good.

With a mental shake she joined the men in the kitchen. Jack was opening the beers and handed one to Gramps.

'Would you like one, Angie?' he asked. 'Or a glass of wine?'

Or both.

'Wine thanks. Would you like to stay for some salad and crusty rolls? Do you eat carbs?'

'Good grief, lass. Of course he does. So do I but these days they tend to go to my stomach rather than my muscles.' Gramps patted his belly, which was only the slightest bit rounded. 'Must take up running again.'

'Me too,' Jack said, solemnly.

'And me.'

Then with a burst of laughter, they lifted their drinks with a mutual 'Cheers'.

Gramps was a patient and thorough tutor. He didn't touch any of the ingredients but encouraged Jack to experiment with different mixes until it made sense. Not too much water, but enough. A little less salt. Once Jack had got the consistency close to the one Gramps liked, the pan was heated in order to cook the tortillas.

Angie was happy making a salad and half-watching the cooking class. Cutting and creating a pretty plate was calming and she'd spent a few minutes in the veggie garden choosing some lettuce and onions. If she could stay here she'd replant the beds, giving some a much needed rest and bringing the area to its full potential. Nan was more of a gardener than Gramps but he did a good job, mistake with the tomatoes notwithstanding. He'd be able to start over at his cottage and enjoy his fresh herbs and produce without as much labour.

The plate was looking good. Two varieties of lettuce and some English spinach leaves as a base. Then cherry tomatoes she'd bought today along with cucumber, shredded carrot, radishes she'd found in the garden and thinly sliced onion, bright yellow capsicum, bean sprouts, walnuts, apple, and blueberries.

'Feta or a mature cheddar cheese?'

Both men looked up.

'Feta,' said Jack.

'Cheddar.'

'Cool. I'll use neither.'

Angie diced some Red Leicester cheese she'd added to the trolley earlier, loving the orange colour and nutty flavour. The salad complete, she took some photos, impressed by the end result.

'Those are good ones, Jack,' Gramps said. 'See how pliable they are yet not tearing?'

'How easy is this? I'll never buy tortillas again, that's for sure.'

Angie went over to inspect them.

'What do you think?' Jack sounded like he wanted to be praised.

'Hmm. I'll hold my judgement until tomorrow night.'

'Tough crowd.'

'As a primary school teacher I'm preparing you for the judgement that children bring, especially to food. Open, honest, and unfiltered.'

'I see. So you are actually helping me.'

'I actually am.' Angie almost smiled. The banter was fun.

Gramps began cleaning up. 'If you two are done squabbling then we'll eat. Angie, there's an airtight container in the cupboard to put the tacos in for Jack.'

'Thanks, Emmett. I'd never have tried this on my own. I enjoy entertaining but cooking is a bit of a mystery.'

About to say something smart about him having a live-in chef or else using Uber Eats nightly, Angie bit her lip. Jack had a part-share in the Italian restaurant in Rivers End and whether it was because he was helping his family or it was a good investment, the result was a better life for his godparents. Her mouth had got her in trouble too often and while Gramps knew and liked Jack, he was still a stranger to Angie and she needed to tone things down.

'Always happy to show you some of the cooking tricks my Opal taught me. And Angie. She's a fine cook.'

Her skin heated at the compliment and she piled the tortillas into the container she'd found. After clicking the lid closed she pushed it in Jack's general direction. 'They'll keep in there for a day or two and they can be reheated in the oven for a couple of minutes if you like. Or you can freeze them.'

'Appreciate it. Don't suppose you'd like to come over early and guide me through best practices for the fillings?'

'I can't.' That sounded abrupt and rude and if she'd have spoken to Shane in that tone... 'Sorry. It's just that I'm super busy helping Gramps with packing but I do have an idea. I'll be right back.'

Angie escaped the kitchen before the shaking in her hands was obvious. She hurried to the living room hoping that the bookcase was still full. There was a Post-it note on its top – 'Angie, please take what you want to keep, I've got my favourites'. She ran a finger over a long row of recipes books which Nan had collected over the years, and some that Angie had gifted Gramps for birthdays and Christmas.

'There you are.'

She pulled one book out and hurried back. Gramps had put plates and cutlery out and Jack was topping up her glass of wine.

'Here, this is a terrific book and I'm sure Gramps doesn't mind me loaning it to you.' She glanced at her grandfather, who nodded. 'It's all modern Mexican recipes as well as history of the cuisine. It might surprise you how different the food is from the kits and so forth. But anyway, take that home and have a read. Be inspired.'

Jack's look was searching. Had he seen the trembling of her hands? But then he smiled that heart-stopping smile of his. 'I will. Be inspired.'

For a moment Angie wanted to believe there was another meaning there. He was getting under her skin and that was a terrible idea.

Angie spent most of the shared meal fretting. Her gazed moved from Gramps to Jack to the salad and back again. Over and over. She jumped up twice to add more options of dressings and now there were too many choices on the table.

'Should I make a vinaigrette?'

Gramps stared at her as he chomped on a mouthful of salad, expression questioning her and, to be fair, why wouldn't he wonder about this sudden need to make everyone happy?

It was sudden to him but Angie knew it came from the experience of years spent trying to please Shane. As soon as she recognised the source of her agitation she drew on the mental exercises from her therapy sessions. But even though she managed to stop the urge to keep checking everyone was happy with the meal, it was hard going to make herself eat.

'There's peaches and apricots galore at the back of my house,' Jack said. 'Can I pick some to say thanks for the cooking lesson and delicious dinner?'

'Most kind of you and yes please.' Gramps nodded. 'We'd like that, wouldn't we, Angie?'

'Huh? Oh, yes. I think they're the only ones we don't have growing here. We have lots of plums if you'd like some in return, Jack. I could make some pies from the fruit if you like pies?

Some plum pies and peach pies and even apricot pies. Or jam. Do you like jam?'

The words tumbled over each other and she had the attention of both men. She was talking too much and saying the wrong things but all she could hear in the back of her mind was Shane telling her how bad a cook she was. How she didn't love him because she made no effort to cater to his needs. That she never did enough.

Gramps's hand covered one of hers. 'Deep breath. You know you're safe here.'

Angie gulped, eyes on his face. It was kind and concerned all at once and she drew in a long and slow breath. What on earth would their guest be thinking? Had she embarrassed Gramps?

'I'd love a pie and jam and to be honest, Angie, anything you care to feed me. This salad is delicious.'

She forced herself to meet Jack's eyes, half-expecting disdain.

His forehead was furrowed a little but his eyes were warm and genuine.

They don't hate me. They're worried. Pull it together.

Although her body felt frozen, Angie managed a small smile and lifted the fork to her mouth with a quick, 'thank you'.

The men began a conversation about sport and Angie tuned out. She was suddenly hungry and finished everything on her plate. Nothing was wrong. Gramps and Jack weren't Shane. He was gone from her life forever and there was more than three thousand kilometres and a prison wall between them. It was time to leave the past behind and face her new life, here in the home she loved.

SEVEN

Up before dawn again, Angie had wandered along Rivers End beach for half an hour, inhaling the salty air and allowing the crunch of sand beneath her bare feet and endless motion of the waves to refill her emotional well. The walk home was without incident this time and she bypassed the house to go directly to Nan's office.

She'd woken during the night in a cold sweat thinking she was in her bedroom in Perth. After getting up to check the house was locked and Shane wasn't here, Angie had struggled to get back to sleep. Only letting her mind puzzle over the box in the office helped her drift off again.

The main room was dark. She'd forgotten to ask Gramps about the power but it had to be a matter of flicking a switch somewhere. Angie walked around the small building, finding a power box against the side wall which opened readily and let her put the power back on. Much better. Beneath the reading lamp, she opened the box containing the book and took out the envelope with the letters.

The first letter had told Angie how Nan got in touch with

the author of the little book. An author who was reluctant to discuss Mary further and wanted to leave the past alone.

'So, it has to be a real account or at least a fictional take on someone's experiences,' Angie said. 'Mary who? And now I'm talking aloud.'

There were two more letters and she unfolded the first of them.

21 June 2010

Dear Opal,

How kind of you to assure me that you will keep your copy of The Loneliest Girl by the Sea *locked away rather than share it with others. I am deeply relieved to know Mary's story is safe with you.*

It surprises me that you have such interest in Mary and what became of her… and more importantly, from where she really came. There's been nobody other than the publisher who has given the story credibility. In my twenties I did hear of a girl who disappeared in the hills around Rivers End in the 1960s but she was located within hours.

I've lived in a bubble of secrecy for so long and although I wish to keep my anonymity, writing to you feels as though I have a friend who understands. Your suggestions are all good and I can assure you they've been considered in the last few years. DNA testing may provide some answers but unless someone still searches for Mary, how would there be a connection to find? More than sixty years have passed.

The reality, dear Opal, is that Mary's real family are likely long gone from this world, given the length of time which has passed.

More than that, Mary's memories of her early years consist of little more than fleeting faces and voices and moments which are too vague to use as a starting point. Only Mattie remains as clear as the last time they were together. My understanding is she came from somewhere far away from Driftwood Cove and the idea of searching across a whole continent overwhelms me. Perhaps if we had connected when I was much younger...

I hope you are busy writing a new historical tale to share with your loyal readers. There's no bookshop in the towns around me so I make a special trip once a month to borrow as many books as I can from the library further up the coast. I've read each of yours several times and wait impatiently between releases.

Thank you again for caring about Mary.

With affection,
M.W.

Angie reread the letter, pausing to write some notes on her phone.

- M.W. lives/lived somewhere without bookshops, along a coast.
- Driftwood Cove mentioned again, as it was in the book.
- M.W. refers to Mary as if another person. But is that the case? Is she Mary?
- Believes Mary came from a long way away as a very young child. Kidnapped?

That last word made her heartsick. At the end of the chapter Angie read yesterday, there'd been a conversation overheard by Mary about how different she looked from her mother.

And then her mother had been crying late that night. Surely no person would raise a child as their own after stealing them from their parents? There'd had to be hundreds of other explanations.

Nan had struck a chord with M.W. and by the dates, it was only a few months before the heart attack took her from them all. If she hadn't died, would she have written a book based loosely on the life of this unknown author? Her novels were all inspired by real events, ones from the eighteen-hundreds. This felt different because Mary could not have been much older than Nan. She'd once said she loved that earlier era and the fact that nobody living could be affected by drawing on public domain events. Perhaps this story was so compelling that Nan decided to go outside her comfort zone.

Angie reached for the last letter but didn't pick it up. She had a lot on her to-do list today and Gramps had to come first. And she needed to visit the real estate agencies to begin her search for a rental. The fact was that her bank account had less than a thousand dollars in it. Even paying a bond might be beyond her.

She put the box away.

Now was not the time to get swept up in someone else's secrets.

By mid-afternoon Angie and Gramps had completed their work in the dining room and were partway through the bigger job of packing up his study. They had enough to take to the cottage, using his larger car this time, and on the way back, Angie asked to be dropped in town to visit the real estate agencies.

'I'll walk back.'

'We need to have a proper talk about the house,' Gramps said. 'Why not wait until then?'

Unless you intend to give me the house then I can't waste another day.

'I'm only giving them my name and number for any potential places. I'll walk back and won't be long.'

'Dinner's at six next door.'

'And its only four now. See you soon.'

She was out of the car before he could say anything else. Angie should never have agreed to go. What if she got weird again and wanted to over-please but this time with a whole house full of strangers?

I have so much work to do on myself.

Once she started earning again and knew her budget, she'd find a local therapist and get on top of the residual effects of living with Shane. She'd come so far already – literally as well as emotionally and mentally – and wanted to keep going forward. To heal.

Outside the first real estate agents, one which used to be where the bookshop now resided, Angie checked the listings in the window. All were for sale and so much more expensive than she expected. Rivers End was a small town, hours from Melbourne. Yet from the little she'd seen since coming home, there'd been a lot of growth. It was inevitable that people would discover the magic of this beautiful place.

She left her name and number with the receptionist, who was apologetic about having only several huge houses up in Rivers End Heights to rent which were priced so high it almost made Angie's eyes water.

Hoping this wouldn't be the end of her dream to live here again, she headed for the other agency, stopping outside the bookshop on her way. This was simply gorgeous. Most of the windows had clever and interesting displays, a mix of new releases, bestsellers, and local reads. Through the glass it looked like the bookshelves were full and there were a few spots to sit and read or talk. Once she got Gramps settled, and herself, she'd be in here to take a proper browse.

A young woman, perhaps twenty, was in one of the windows fixing a display. She grinned at Angie and gestured for her to come in. Angie mouthed that she couldn't and the woman hurried out.

'Hi. I'm Olive and of course you can come in!'

'I wish I could. I'm a bit time-poor today.'

'Well that's a shame.'

'It is. I love books.'

'Me too. I guess I have to, right?' Olive laughed at herself.

'The bookshop looks amazing.'

'I'll tell Mum. I mean, Harriet. But do come back?'

'Promise. Bye, Olive.'

With another big smile the young woman went back inside. What a sweetheart Olive was. And Harriet, her mother, was the owner? How long was this even here? Angie had been gone for about seven years and in her entire life there'd never been a bookshop.

Nor in Green Bay or Driftwood Cove. Did M.W. come from this area?

Pushing the thought aside for now, Angie crossed the road diagonally to the other real estate agents. This one was owned by John and Daphne Jones who were lovely people. They'd been friends with Nan as well as Gramps. But when she pushed the door open, neither of them appeared. She stood at the reception desk for a few minutes, unsure whether to hit the bell or just be patient.

A voice in the distance became louder, someone arguing on the phone. Angie moved from her spot to pretend to look at a display of houses for sale.

The owner of the voice was a man in his thirties who didn't notice her as he pulled out a chair and dropped into it, soundly telling someone off. It was impossible not to overhear him tell what must have been a tenant that he had no intention of fixing the gutters yet again and if they weren't happy, then they could break their lease.

Angie tried to leave before he noticed but the minute her hand was on the door handle, he did.

'Excuse me? I'll be right with you.'

She froze as he cut short his call and then his tone changed to one of welcome.

'Good afternoon. I'm Xavier Bolan. How may I assist? Looking to purchase?'

'Actually, no. Not yet, anyway. I'm interested in renting a property. Anywhere within about twenty minutes of the town.'

Cold eyes looked her up and down. 'I see. Just for you?'

'Yes.'

'We require a bond of three months' rent on any property.'

'Three months?'

'Too many people default or damage their rentals.'

'I don't damage property. And I'm here to teach at the primary school, so defaulting on rent isn't something I'd do.'

His face said otherwise. He put a clipboard on the counter. 'Put your name and number on here. Not much around to rent though.'

'I'm only after something small. Even a grannie flat.'

'Cheap, in other words.'

Angie quickly wrote down her details. 'Do John and Daphne still own this agency?'

'Yes. Not for long though. I've been running things while they are off caravanning around the state and I'll buy John out pretty soon.'

And destroy the good name they built over decades.

She couldn't get out of there fast enough. What a dreadful man and the idea of him managing a property she rented was unthinkable. But what was she to do? Two real estate agents in town who had nothing available. Maybe she should try Driftwood Cove and even Green Bay instead. Or ask on local social media. There had to be a solution. For now she'd even rent a room in someone's house. She'd been on the booking website for Palmerston House already but the prices, even for a long-term stay, were out of her reach.

Her route home was quickest on foot if she cut through the back streets and this part of town hadn't changed. Older homes with big gardens. A few cul-de-sacs with laneways between properties leading to other streets.

An SUV was backing the cutest caravan into a driveway directed by a woman with bright purple streaks in her hair and oversized glasses. Daphne Jones.

Angie hesitated. What if she spoke to Daphne and John privately about a rental? The SUV was packed to the brim. They were just getting home and this wasn't the time to reintroduce herself. If that creep at the agency was about to buy them out, perhaps they weren't in the loop anymore. Xavier had said they were off caravanning all the time so perhaps they were more interested in retirement than what was happening here.

Before her spirits could fall any further, Angie rounded a corner and started to jog. There was just time to take another look inside the box in Nan's office again before getting ready for tonight.

Angie decided to shower and dress for dinner first then told Gramps she'd be back in the house in half an hour. As she reached the door to Nan's office the sound of children laughing from over the fence made her smile. The one shining light with her divorce was the chance to return to teaching full-time.

She closed herself in and as before, set an alarm on her phone. Another chapter wouldn't take long and then she could mull it over tonight to stave off the nightmares.

The man was kind. He promised to take her to her family as soon as she'd had some food and had her cuts checked and cleaned. Too tired to complain, she'd let him set her in the front seat of a car. She'd clutched Dolly tightly, eyes closing as darkness fell. When she woke, the car was still and there were voices. A woman and the man, arguing. She didn't like arguments.

After a while the man opened her door and lifted her out. He carried her and Dolly inside a house where it was warm and something was cooking which smelled nice. The woman was there and her face was wet with tears but then her arms opened and she took the child into them.

'You're safe, Mary. Safe.'

EIGHT

17 December 1960

In a bit more than a week it is Christmas Day and I can barely wait. Not just for the day but all the good things Mama and I will do together between now and then. The church committee puts together boxes of food and gifts for the less fortunate and we help by making lots of festive fare and sewing soft toys for children. Some families struggle to even put food on their tables with employment hard to come by. People move to the city hoping for a better future and Mama says that makes it even harder for locals to survive because there's fewer customers in shops and less need for labourers. She also says there are people too lazy to work but we help out just the same.

Some of the women gather at the hall, which is on the church grounds, and work together but Mama prefers to be here, at home. Sometimes I think she'd be happier if she made real friends with the others on the committee, instead of keeping to herself so much and seeing everything else as just a duty.

There are some kids my age I like from school and now that

it's the long summer holidays we can spend time on the beach at Driftwood Cove. Mainly Diane and Debbie who are twins and were in my class. They don't attend our church so Mama had a long talk with me about the dangers of outsiders but after I promised to never let them lead me into wrongdoing, she agreed I could meet up with them once a week.

Today is the second time since the end of school and I run along the beach to meet them right at the far end. They're with about a dozen others, girls and boys, some a bit older. I stop and almost turn and leave because the arrangement with Mama is about Diane and Debbie, not strangers.

Debbie sees me and comes over. 'Why are you standing here? Someone brought soft drinks and there's one for you.'

Soft drinks? Mama refuses to buy them. Ever. A waste of money when water or milk is perfectly fine for a growing girl. I don't think I've ever tasted cola or anything like that. It wouldn't be so bad to have one? Just this once?

I walk with Debbie to where the others are sitting and standing around and then they all look at me. Diane smiles. 'Hey everyone, this is Mary.'

There's a chorus of hellos and I reply feeling a bit embarrassed at the attention. Debbie hands me a cola and I sip the icy cold, bubbly liquid, almost spurting it out as it fizzes in my throat. Nobody seems to notice and I find a spot and sit.

'*What* is she wearing?'

One of the girls whispers loudly and once again, there's lots of eyes on me. Everyone else is in swimsuits and I'm in a dress Mama helped me make. It's too big now but I'm still growing and she wants it to last until winter. The dress stops at my knees and has short sleeves and is a kind of green-brown colour.

Diane shushes the girl.

I don't have a swimsuit. I can't even swim so only ever paddle in the waves. After what happened to my father I have no interest in going in further than my knees and that's only on a calm day. My heart is going fast and I'm not sure I belong here after all.

'Swim time!' one of the girls yells and races toward the sea.

Several follow, all trying to outrun her and one of the boys does just that. He ploughs through the waves and dives in.

'Come on, Mary. Just come and splash around a bit.' Debbie wants to go, I can see it in her face.

'You'll have to hold the skirt up. Wouldn't want to get that expensive fabric getting wet.'

It is the girl who'd whispered. She is smirking at me.

I jump to my feet and race back along the sand the way I came. Debbie calls after me and I can hear laughing. I don't stop running until I am at the path leading up the big hill on the other side of the bay. The bottle is still in my hand and I finish up all the remaining black drink even though it is even bubblier from me running. When I find a bin I throw it away and keep my head down until I reach our gate.

And there, I burst into tears.

'It was a big lesson, Mary. I am sorry you had to find out about outsiders this way.' Mama has her arms around me and has given me a hankie. 'Some of them are decent enough people and I sew for several outsider families who are good people despite not believing. But we have to protect ourselves.'

'I thought I was just going to be with Debbie and Diane, not all the others.'

'When we leave our home we are at the mercy of outsiders. Satan finds ways to entice us from the true path. He used two young people you have come to trust from school to bring others into your life. They won't even have known what control was being wielded, Mary. But ask yourself this. If they were easily fooled, are they good influences? Is your soul in jeopardy when you spend time with them?'

My tears have dried and I sit up, letting Mama settle back in her chair. We are in the kitchen where I'd found her baking bread. There's still flour on her hands.

'What will happen when I go to high school, Mama? Do you think anyone from our church attends Green Bay High School?'

Mama takes a minute to answer and her eyes are looking away when she finally speaks. 'Maybe. I will ask the committee. But Mary, all I can do is worry.'

'Why, Mama?'

Now she looks at me, so seriously. 'High schools are not the same as when I attended. There are drugs being sold to children.'

'Drugs?'

She nods. 'Illegal drugs. And cigarettes and even alcohol! Sometimes the teachers are involved. And some teachers become involved with their students.'

I don't understand what she means but I'm scared to ask.

'How else will I get an education, Mama? I want to become a nurse or a teacher myself. I could be a teacher who does good and brings the Word to the students.'

Mama smiles and touches my face. 'Oh, I left some flour. What a kind and faithful girl you are, Mary. You truly live up to your name. *Beloved.* I once hoped to become a teacher, did you know that?'

'You did?'

'I even had finished a year of education in the city.'

'What happened?'

Her smile is gone and her floured hands grip each other. 'Mary happened. An unexpected, unplanned, but wonderful gift from God.'

But I'm Mary.

She stands and goes to the sink. 'There's flour on your face, child. Go and wash up and come back and help.'

'But, Mama, I—'

'Hurry up. We have much to do.'

Our decorations at home are modest. We don't have a tree but Mama allowed me to plait some strips of left-over fabric and wrap them around a little bush outside the door. It looks pretty with red and green and yellow and I cut out a star from the cardboard on the back of an exercise book from school and colour it with old crayons.

We've made a dozen or so stuffed toys, each in the shape of a koala. They're cute and have brown eyes sewn with wool instead of glass eyes. Mama says that is safer for small children. She did all the sewing and I helped cut the material. There are lots of festive biscuits baked with gingerbread which Mama loves because it reminds her of Christmas as a child.

As we pack all the goodies into a couple of baskets to take, I pick up the last of the koalas and hold it against my chest. A feeling grows inside me and I can't explain but all of a sudden I'm smiling. Just like with Dolly.

I haven't thought about Dolly for so long and while Mama packs one last lot of biscuits I run to my bedroom. *Where is she?*

There isn't much in my bedroom. A bed. A chest of drawers. A narrow cupboard where I hang my best clothes. I check everywhere including under the bed but Dolly isn't in here. *When did I see her last?* I close my eyes and try to remember but nothing is clear.

'Mary, hurry up please. We need to go.'

I know that tone of her voice and waste no time getting to the kitchen but all I can think about is Dolly. I want to ask Mama but she hands me a basket and tells me to take it to the car. She's right behind me and we pack everything in and I run down to open the gate, then shut it once the car is through.

'We'll stay for a little while to help,' Mama says. She's

leaning forward, her chest almost against the steering wheel and she's perched on a cushion. I'm already almost as tall as Mama so won't need a cushion once I'm old enough to drive.

'Did you hear me, Mary?'

'Yes, sorry. Are we going to take some of the charity boxes to people ourselves?'

'We were given the task of sewing and baking. All of the congregation who are able to assist have a different role and for half a dozen of the more senior couples, theirs will be to deliver the boxes. I did help once, though. When your father was still with us.'

'You did? Were the people happy?'

Mama gives a surprised glance. 'Happy?'

'To get such a helpful and kind Christmas gift.'

'Some, I suppose. They all said thank you but only one seemed truly grateful. She cried and I remember wondering how it could be that a family depended on the generosity of the church to get by.' Mama's voice got harder. 'There's always a way to make ends meet without resorting to handouts.'

'Like you are, Mama. The sewing you do for other people and the food we grow keeps us from needing handouts.'

Her hand slips off the steering wheel and pats my leg and there's a funny look on her face. I think it might be pride.

The hall at the church is used for Sunday School and church events and now it is filled with women and girls who are bustling around trestle tables. There's chatter and some laughter and it feels so friendly and warm.

We join a table and unpack our baskets. One of the ladies picks up a koala and coos at it like it's a baby.

'Look at this, everyone! Aren't these adorable?'

All of sudden we are surrounded by people, all admiring the toys and someone asked Mama if she makes them to sell. At first she is quiet and mumbles but then she nods.

'I can make more of these. They'd be a few shillings each.'

'Goodness me, Gertie, you should ask for more than that. Do you have time to make two before Christmas Eve for me? I will pay you a pound for them.'

Mama kind of gasps and her eyes widen. The woman who asked is Mrs Kane who lives in Rivers End in a big house. I think she is very beautiful with glossy brown hair touching her shoulders in waves and a sweet smile. She is on the committee and her husband is an important business man.

'I'll have them tomorrow. Shall I bring them to you?'

'Oh that is so far for you. I'll be here tomorrow as well if you want to bring them sometime? I'll fetch my purse and give you the payment now so I don't forget.'

She hurries off and Mama still looks a bit shocked. A whole pound for two toys!

After she pays, Mrs Kane tells Mama she should think about making more Australian animals and selling them. She's going to show her husband and he knows people who might help get them into shops.

When we are going home, Mama can't stop talking.

'I need to make the koalas tonight, Mary.'

'Then I will cook dinner and you'll only need to stop long enough to eat.'

'Oh, Mary. A whole pound means I can buy some extras for Christmas. Would you do something for me? Tomorrow would you take the koalas to the hall and give them to Mrs Kane? I would like to visit the shops.'

I can't remember seeing Mama so happy. 'Of course I will.'

Mama drops me not far from the church and I walk the rest of the way. She's going to the shops and I'll meet her at home in a bit. Even though she worked late last night to finish the koalas, she was up early and cooked breakfast of toast with fresh eggs from our hens.

Mrs Kane is happy with the toys and asks me to tell Mama that she did speak to her husband and he'd like to have a meeting in the new year about making patterns for other animals. I carefully remember her words and say thank you to her.

'You are a sweet child, Mary. And you remind me of someone who goes to high school with my son. Do you have family in Rivers End?'

'There's only me and Mama.' I'm curious. 'I've never met any girls who look like me.'

'Oh, this is a boy. Not that you look like a boy but he has the same curly golden hair and bright blue eyes.'

She *does* think I look like a boy. First Mrs Godfrey said I don't look like Mama and now this. Why is everyone judging me by my face? I'm beginning to understand why my mother keeps to herself and the minute Mrs Kane turns to speak to someone, I dash away.

On the walk home I wonder if I'll meet this boy when I start high school in the new year. We might say hello and laugh at how Mrs Kane thinks we look alike and thought we might be related.

NINE

Now

It was only the insistent beeping of the phone alarm which forced Angie to close the book. She longed to read on. This story – whether Mary's, or M.W.'s – had a grip on her. What began as a tale of a girl who was at the cusp of being a teen was becoming a mystery. One which had drawn Nan in enough to gather newspaper clippings and write to the author.

Gramps was in the kitchen drinking a tall glass of water. He'd changed into slacks and a checked short-sleeved shirt.

'You look nice. Am I underdressed?' The worry was already swirling.

'Let me look at you. Rose-coloured dress which is pretty and looks nice and cool. Sandals which show off your rose-coloured toenails. Long, wavy hair mostly contained behind a rose-coloured hairband.' Gramps smiled. 'I judge you as dressed for the occasion.' He picked his house keys off the counter. 'I water-loaded because one thing I know about young Jack is he has a fine collection of craft beer.'

'Ah. So that's why we're going?'

'I do enjoy a nice beer and he always has something new to offer me.'

At the end of their driveway they wandered along the grass verge.

'When did the Bensons sell the house?' Angie asked. Their old neighbours were a quiet, friendly couple who would swap produce over the fence. Much as Jack suggested he do with Gramps.

'Still own it. They moved to Adelaide to be close to their daughter and her growing family and they rent it out through John and Daphne's agency.'

'Ew.'

She hadn't meant to say it aloud and Gramps shot a look her way.

'I was in there today and the man who wants to buy it was less than nice. He was actually telling a tenant off for needing help with their gutters.'

'Oh, him. He's not made himself popular in our town with his heavy-handed manner and he's pushy.'

'Pushy, how?'

Gramps grunted. 'Been up at the house a few times trying to get me to list with him.'

They turned into the next driveway.

'I guess there's not a lot of choice here for agents.'

'Always liked John and Daph and I feel they don't know what their manager is doing to their business.'

'On the way home I saw them backing an adorable caravan into their driveway.'

'That'd be Bluebell. Last couple of years they've spent more time on the road than in Rivers End. Did you know Daphne is now a wedding celebrant?'

'I'm not surprised. She is such a people person.'

They reached the front of the house where an SUV was parked and plugged into an electric point. The family must prefer them and Angie had nothing against electric cars herself, other than the risk of being run over by one if you weren't looking.

'Think they'll be round the back,' Gramps said.

There was a swimming pool and nice covered outdoor area with a barbecue and furniture. This garden wasn't as big as Gramps's but still made for a great place for kids to play which was what two were doing. Both had water pistols and were chasing Jack around some trees. Suddenly, Jack turned on them, firing water from his own pistols – one in each hand. With shrieks, the children hurtled back toward the pool and ducking around the fence and through an open gate, they dive-bombed in. Water splashed high and a woman called from a sunchair.

'Not funny, Jack.'

'Seeing water cascade down on you is always funny, Ruth.'

Unnoticed, Angie couldn't help grinning. She'd always wanted a sibling and enjoyed the teasing between the two, because Ruth had to be Jack's sister. She was a few years older but had the same dark brown hair and was every bit as attractive as he was. Jack leaned over the pool fence and squirted water directly onto his sister. She squealed and was on her feet in a second. He took off around the outside of the fencing, skidding to a halt a few feet from Gramps and Angie.

'Oh. Hi.'

He probably meant both of them but looked directly at Angie with a wide smile.

'Sorry to interrupt your game,' Gramps said. He didn't look the least bit sorry.

'You saved me from a terrible fate.'

'You will keep for later, Jackson.' After wrapping a sarong around herself, the woman came to meet them. 'How on earth do you cope with him living next door? I'm Ruth.' She held out her hand to Gramps and then Angie.

'Emmett and Angela,' Gramps said.

'Angie, please.'

Two sopping wet children ran over and threw themselves against Ruth.

'If I wasn't wet before, I am now! This is Holly and Josh.'

'I'm five.'

'Holly, you don't have to tell everyone.' This was Josh who only looked about eight and was completely serious. 'Come on, let's find Dad.'

They were gone as fast as they'd arrived.

'Come and sit. I have a new beer to get your opinion on, Emmett.'

'I was hoping you would. Where is this one from?'

The men wandered off in discussion, leaving Angie with Ruth.

'Is it true my dreadful little brother almost ran you down?'

Oh no, this was bad. Why had he told her that?

'Um...'

Ruth began to walk toward the house. 'I'm going to quickly dry off and change then let's get a drink and you can tell me what you think of him. And I won't breathe a word to anyone.'

'What I think of Jack?'

'Absolutely. How about we open a bottle of bubbles? Best way to break the ice and then I want *all* the gossip.'

Angie decided she liked Ruth a lot. They sat with a glass of sparkling wine each at a small round table not far from the pool, in the shade of an old oak. The children were back in the water, now with their father, who'd introduced himself as Ivan. Gramps and Jack were talking beers in the covered area.

'So after I met Ivan I spent a year determined not to get close to him. No more men for me after too many duds yet there he was, far too good-looking and charming in a quiet, brooding way. I even took a job overseas to put distance between us but alas, it turned out to be true love and all it took was one long phone call late one night and I threw in the towel.'

Romance readers would love a story like this.

'We married a month later and Jack walked me down the aisle. Parents were long gone, and Franco and Cara were visiting their family in Italy and although Jack was only about twenty-two or three, he was still the obvious choice. We've always been close.' Ruth was gazing at her brother with a small smile and he waved with a broad grin, raising the water pistol with his other hand. 'But he has his moments.'

Jack returned to his conversation with Gramps. Angie was struck by the friendship between the two.

'I will say that Jack appreciates the kindness of your grandfather.'

'Kindness?'

Eyes back on Ruth, Angie took a sip of the bubbly wine.

'I heard you've been living away for a few years until recently?'

Angie nodded, unsure where this was leading.

'You probably don't know Jack was injured in the line of duty a while ago.'

Line of duty? Was he in the armed forces or something?

'His story to tell but I thought I'd lost my little brother for a while. Over time he recovered but his career was finished and he needed a place to continue his rehabilitation and find a new direction. He couldn't stomach being in the city and when Cara was so ill he came to visit. Our family has always had money so it wasn't a hardship to help with the restaurant but when he saw the difference it made for Franco… well, it was like he was finding himself again. Going back to Emmett… let's just say Jack needed a friendly face and no sooner had he unpacked than your grandfather visited with a warm handshake and a box of homegrown produce.' Ruth's eyes glistened. 'I'm grateful to Emmett.'

All this new information did was raise questions. Angie's first opinion of Jack was of a rich playboy. He drove an expensive car, wore a designer suit, and arrived home at dawn from what he called an 'after-shoot party'. She had been under the impression that he was an actor. A rich one, who'd been generous in helping his godfather's business but still liked himself a bit too much for her taste.

And what are your tastes, Angela? Gamblers who swindle people and have a side serving of spousal emotional abuse?

'I'm sorry.'

Angie blinked. Ruth gazed at her over the rim of her glass.

'I don't understand.'

'Once you get to know me you'll see I like to offer far more information than is asked for. And you just had an expression of such worry. More than that, I sensed some distress and didn't mean to cause it.'

'You didn't distress me. It was great that Gramps was able to make Jack welcome. I guess sometimes people just get on well from the start.'

'They do, Angie. I feel that you and I have hit it off.'

'Likewise.'

'Well, before this turns into a love-fest, I've prattled on too much and want to hear your story. If you care to share, of course.'

Angie didn't. Talking about the last few years wasn't easy and she'd barely told Gramps the worst of it, let alone a complete stranger. Well, a bit less of a stranger and a woman she felt she could trust.

'I love the sea.'

'Me too. Is that it?' Ruth's smile was warm.

'At dawn. And dusk.'

'Rules me out. I'm definitely a daytime beachcomber. Sun and sand and sea. I'll leave the romantic sunsets to Jack.'

As if he knew he was being talked about, Jack looked over at them. Angie half-smiled and he winked.

There it is. He loves himself.

'You said earlier you hadn't wanted another man in your life… I'm the same,' Angie said. She picked up her glass, holding it without drinking. 'I made a mistake and married someone who wasn't the person I thought. In my future I see a little cottage overlooking the ocean, solitary sunrises, and probably cats and dogs my only companions.'

Ruth looked ready to say something but Jack stood and Gramps with him.

'Half an hour until the best Mexican dinner you've ever had!'

'Not if he's cooking,' Ruth muttered. 'Store-bought everything.'

Amused by the whole sibling thing going on, Angie was a bit surprised at how much she wanted Jack to succeed at his newfound skills.

'Uncle Jack, may I have another?' Holly had left her seat and stood beside Jack, holding her plate out.

Looking pleased with himself, Jack wasted no time preparing one for his niece. 'Want to try some tomato this time?'

'Yuk. No 'mato.'

'Right. No 'mato for you.'

'Can I have her tomato added to another tortilla for me? Please?' Josh had joined his sister.

'You certainly can, young man.'

Last night's efforts had paid off. Jack had prepared a

wonderful meal with plenty of tortillas he'd cooked during the afternoon, and enough fillings to feed an army.

Gramps watched the exchange between Jack and the children but he wasn't smiling like everyone else. Instead, a profound sorrow sharpened his features. How often he'd looked this way after her parents died and then Nan. But what was it about two little kids which would make him so sad? His focus suddenly moved to Angie and he blinked rapidly, then returned to his plate of food.

Her eyes met Jack's. His forehead was creased and he did a little gesture with his head in Gramps's direction and mouthed 'All okay?'

She kind of shrugged and hoped her face explained she was just as puzzled. He nodded and for a second there was a sense of connection between them. Then his attention was taken by more requests for extra tortillas.

By the time everyone said goodnight – complete with hugs from the children – Gramps was his usual self. They wandered home, arm in arm.

'Nice people, Angie.'

'Very nice.'

'They liked you. Jack likes you.'

Goes both ways.

Unsure if now was the time to explain how they'd met and her fear of mentioning him in case Gramps disliked Jack, she pushed the story away. Something had upset her grandfather tonight and bringing up her poor choice of husband might add to whatever it was.

'Might head straight to bed. If we can finish the study tomorrow, would you like to get fish and chips for dinner and we'll eat on the jetty? Think it shouldn't be too hot to sit there early evening.'

'I'd like that a lot.'

Inside, Gramps kissed Angie's forehead. 'I'm glad you're here, lass.'

She hadn't expected those words and couldn't respond because her throat tightened. Once his bedroom door was shut she turned the light off. But she wasn't ready to sleep and after making a cup of tea, decided to go to Nan's office for a while. She wanted to feel close to her grandmother tonight.

TEN

For a long time Angie sat in darkness, even after the tea was finished. She'd left the door open and a soft breeze carried the faintest scent from the ocean and if she listened hard enough, the waves were just audible.

I wish I was on the beach. Sitting on the sand. Tasting the sea salt on my lips.

When she was younger she'd have followed her desires and done that but now... it was one thing to be on the beach around dawn and another entirely at close to midnight. Caution came first. At least, when she wasn't miles away and stepped in front of a car. That wasn't normal behaviour at all. She'd learned to evaluate risk and avoid putting herself in a position of danger. It was better this way, even if she missed out on things she longed to do.

Angie would never have gone next door for dinner but it wasn't really her choice and besides, Gramps was there and out of every person on the planet, he was the one she trusted. But as it was, meeting Ruth was the first nice thing to happen in ages. They'd even arranged to have a coffee before the family went home in a few days. The children were adorable. Angie had enjoyed a conversation with Josh about his school and sports and it was obvious he loved little Holly, even if she was a typical five-year-old with few filters. But she'd caught Gramps staring at her while she and Josh talked and he'd had that same sadness in his eyes.

Was this about his son? Her father?

Even though he'd died so long ago, the pain was within easy reach. Her dad was such a good human. Smart and funny and thoughtful. So good at his job.

Before her emotions could rise any more Angie got up and put the teacup on the counter. She turned on the lamp over Nan's desk and sat behind it. At some point she'd have to go through the desk drawers but tonight was not the time. Instead, she reached across to the bookcase and lifted the box over. The one which had her interest.

Rather than keep reading the little book, Angie took out the folder holding the newspaper clippings.

She started with the top one which was a full front page from the *Warrnambool & Region News*. Directly under the masthead was a large photograph of a clearing surrounded by bushland and with a fallen tree in the background. The headline was alarming.

DESPERATE SEARCH FOR MISSING CHILD.

In breaking news, a young girl is understood to have disappeared from a family picnic late yesterday afternoon. Believed to be around four years old, the girl wandered away as the picnic was being packed up. Frantic searching by the family was fruitless. Police and volunteers were only able to search until darkness fell due to the risks posed by difficult terrain. More to come in the evening edition.

Angie reread the brief piece but there was no mention of the name of the child or the family. The date of the paper was 15 September 1952. More than seventy years ago.

Nan had been corresponding with the author of the little book around fifteen years ago. She turned to the next clipping which was another front page. Clearly this story was newsworthy and in small-town Victoria in the fifties would have been shocking to the community.

This edition had a photograph of a group of people huddled around a map somewhere in bushland. There was a smaller image below, to the side of the text. A map with a circle drawn around it.

Where is Laura? The search continues.

More than one hundred police, emergency service workers, and local volunteers spent the day combing the bushland just west of Rivers End in a desperate attempt to locate a three-and-a-half-year-old child. The young girl, known as Laura, was enjoying a picnic at a popular clearing in the hills surrounding the town during a family holiday from Melbourne. She was last seen by her older brother only a few yards from the clearing. Laura was wearing a light green dress, buckled shoes, and may have been carrying a doll. Police ask that anyone with any information contact their local police station.

Angie sat back in her chair. Her heart hurt for the little girl who'd now been missing for two full nights. How terrified the child must have been, not knowing where her family was and hungry and cold. It was early spring then so the weather might have been warm enough or else freezing, so variable were Victorian seasons.

She took a closer look at the circled part of the map which

was a couple of square kilometres in size. A huge area to cover by foot. It was familiar territory to Angie, who'd spent many hours bushwalking as a teen and young adult and had a firm idea where the clearing was. Who knew what it was like seventy years ago but last time she was there, it was almost park-like with a rotunda, a toilet block, and several tables with benches. Not at all like the photo on the newspaper clipping.

'But surrounded by dense bushland. Oh, the poor little girl.'

Her voice sounded tired and a yawn came from nowhere. She'd look at one more then settle down for the night.

There was a gap of two days before the next article, which was on the third page.

SEARCH SCALED DOWN FOR MISSING CHILD.

Following the fourth full day of combing the difficult terrain around the site that Laura was last seen, a police spokesman has announced that there is little chance the child has survived without human intervention. Concerns for the safety of volunteers during the past twenty-four hours of heavy rain led to a recall from the area apart from trained officials. Search and rescue personnel and dogs have failed to find any evidence of where Laura is, or even where she was.

There will be ongoing patrols through the area over the next week but tragically, the expectation is that it will be to bring her body home. Her family have made arrangements to stay in the area until this occurs and have requested anonymity at this time to grieve privately.

Angie wiped a tear from her cheek. How devastating for the family. Coming to Rivers End for a holiday and potentially going home without their dear little girl. With the search hampered by bad weather they were powerless to do more than they would have already. She yawned again. It was late and if she didn't stop now, she would end up seeing in the dawn.

Sorting and packing up the rest of Gramps's study took almost the entire day and it was with sighs of relief and much rubbing of sore shoulders that they stepped back from placing the last of the boxes for the cottage in the hallway.

'Tomorrow we might take this lot down.'

'Is all your new furniture arriving in the morning?'

'Living room and study. The rest isn't far away.'

They wandered back to a room which was bare other than for the massive old bookcase and equally large desk and a few smaller pieces.

'Seems strange, Angie. A lot of work done in here. First with my building business before we could afford a proper office. Then with the society and your nan with her writing.' He sighed again but this time it was from the weight of his memories. 'Always enjoyed her being in here, writing by hand or tapping away on her typewriter and staring out of the window while she sorted her thoughts. But my constant phone calls were a nuisance and that father of yours would poke his head in here asking if his mum knew where his shoes were or was there anything to eat.'

'I can't imagine it.'

Gramps chuckled. 'Hair sticking up everywhere. Looked like he'd not eaten in a week. Speaking of food, I promised you fish and chips.'

'You're not too tired?'

'To sit on the jetty surrounded by squawking seagulls? Never. Meet at the car in ten minutes?'

He was in good spirits despite today's difficult task. Angie admired him for being so strong. She knew all too well how hard it was to reduce your belongings to the ones which would squeeze into a few suitcases. In his instance, it was a new home which would fit four times over into this one. Gramps's resilience, his fortitude in the face of everything life threw his way, inspired her.

If only I could be even a little bit like you.

With a quick reminder to hurry up rather than get into a mood, Angie collected a sunhat and her handbag and at the last moment, a picnic blanket from the linen cupboard. This would be one of her jobs tomorrow, going through all the shelves.

Gramps was in the car when she locked the front door and she threw everything on the back seat and climbed in with a wide smile. 'I cannot wait to eat.'

This was what life should always be like. A delicious simple meal – or was that a simply delicious one? The creaking of old timber boards. Waves sloshing against pylons below. And seagulls cawing and carrying on about wanting a chip.

There were no chips yet though because Gramps had sent Angie to find a spot for them to sit while he collected their dinner. When she arrived there'd been people at the end of the jetty so she'd paddled for a while, letting the low tide gently take away the stress in her body. The ocean did that better than anything else she'd ever found. The other people left and she took the picnic blanket and made a spot where they could sit with their feet dangling over the edge.

The jetty had changed since she'd left Rivers End. Previously the end had been open and one could dive off any part of it. But the last few metres were made of a different timber now and two sides of the end had railings. The third side was open with a new ladder going down beneath the surface as well as a small area where a boat could safely tie up. There was a plaque on one of the rails and Angie read it aloud.

'Rivers End Jetty was severely damaged during the worst

storm in one hundred years. Many local traders and individuals donated money to rebuild and the work was done at no cost by Dan Harrington and his crew. May the jetty survive at least another hundred years.'

Wow… must have been some storm to destroy part of the jetty. It had originally been built a few years after the town was founded as a place safe for rowboats from ships to bring goods. Rivers End wasn't a good choice for larger vessels but the closest deep harbour was too far on barely usable tracks for the drays. Better to make the poor sailors row in multiple loads of supplies, including furniture and artwork.

Angie leaned back on the railing, facing the beach. The jetty belonged here every bit as much as the town. There were no cargo ships anchored a kilometre from shore, nor sweaty sailors cursing their lives, but over time, this special place had listened in on proposals and break-ups, whispered declarations of love and sad words of goodbye.

Gramps was trudging across the sand and she ran along the timber boards to take the white package of yumminess from him, almost burying her face against the paper to inhale.

He laughed loudly and she lifted her head and joined in. This was like her childhood and teenage years. Although there'd been such grief and sadness somehow her grandfather always found a way to make her laugh… or she'd make him. Moments like these were precious and she wanted to wrap them up as tightly as the paper was around their dinner.

They moved the picnic blanket to the open side of the jetty and accompanied by a few groans, Gramps sat and removed his sandals then dropped his legs over the side. Angie copied, without the sound effects.

'Tide is too low.' She peered at the water about a metre beneath them.

'Better than a shark nibbling your toes.'

'I'm no longer ten, Gramps, and I don't believe you.'

He gave her a look of mock astonishment. 'No sharks?'

'No nibbling. More like an entire foot. Followed by the other.' She kept her expression serious for at least five seconds before giggling as if she was a child again.

'Time to feed you, lass. Lack of nutrition is playing with your mind. Or your sense of humour. Here, you open the food and I'll open the drinks.' He had a carry bag with him and pulled out two icy cold colas in glass bottles.

'Oh. My. Goodness. I haven't had a cola in years.'

Angie unwrapped the fish and chips. Inside was a container of tartare sauce and she opened the lid for them to dip the crispy battered whiting fillets. The chips were salty and tangy from vinegar.

For a while they ate without speaking, devouring the meal until only a few crusty chip pieces remained. Gramps entertained himself tossing one at a time as high into the air as possible and watching the seagulls hustle to catch them. Angie savoured the cola as if it was the first time she'd ever had one.

Just like Mary.

The imagery invaded her mind. A young girl from a devout Christian family stretching her wings – ever so cautiously. Mocked by others for her attire she'd panicked and fled, taking only the bottle of cola. Her first ever taste of any soft drink. And she'd run until she could run no more.

You poor sweetheart. How cruel were those who hurt you. And how brave you were for trying.

The strongest sense of a connection to young Mary brought tears to Angie's eyes.

She had to find out what happened to the girl and the puzzle her grandmother had felt so passionately about solving. But would Gramps be willing to help? He'd shut her down quickly last time she'd raised what she'd found. He was smiling to himself as he sipped his drink. This evening had reinforced her need to have her grandfather as an active part of her life.

Angie's mistake with Shane and unwillingness to listen to Gramps's warnings had estranged them for a while until she'd seen the truth of his concerns. She wasn't willing to risk his love a second time and he'd made it clear he didn't want to know about Opal's last project. She'd work on the mystery alone.

ELEVEN

The sea air and all the hard work of the day sent Gramps and Angie to bed earlier than usual and even though she expected to stay awake and eventually go up to Nan's office, she fell into a deep sleep.

Just after breakfast Gramps had a phone call from Paula to say the delivery truck was arriving early and would he come down to the residence and get the furniture placed where he wanted it. He and Angie had already packed his car in anticipation and drove down, arriving only a minute after the truck. It took little time with two delivery men doing the heavy work and Gramps already knew where he wanted everything. The truck packed up and left.

'This is perfect, Gramps. Everything fits but more important, it all is so nice!'

Angie gazed around the living room which now had a two-seater sofa and two tub chairs, one large coffee table and a smaller one, a modern, streamlined entertainment unit, and a couple of floor lamps.

'It's looking like a home now and once you put up some art and add the television it will be so comfortable.'

'Come and see the study.'

The cottage came with two bedrooms and he'd immediately decided to use the smaller one as his study. In here was a lovely timber bookcase which took up an entire wall, a timber desk which was a third the size of his one at home, and the biggest office chair Angie had ever seen. It had a high back with a headrest and arms, and reminded her of a racing car seat.

'My little indulgence, Angie.' Gramps grinned and sat on the chair. 'Everything adjusts and look at this...' He pressed something and the back reclined until he was virtually staring at the ceiling. 'I might fall asleep on it.' His fingers tapped away at the same button but nothing happened. 'A little help?'

'Um... how?'

'Maybe a push from behind?'

Angie put both hands beneath the head rest and added some pressure and the seat abruptly returned to its original position.

'That was too much excitement!' Gramps stood. 'Might read the instructions. Apparently this is a chair for people who play computer games.'

'Are you planning on playing them?'

'Already do.'

'Okay. Like?'

The idea of Gramps playing *Grand Theft Auto* was almost too much.

'Solitaire. Quite addictive if you ask me.'

Trying hard not to laugh, Angie gestured to the boxes that the delivery men had helpfully brought in from the car. 'Do you want to unpack these or go home and pack some more?'

'Actually, lass... do you mind if I get started here? But you take the car and I'll walk home a bit later.'

Angie kissed his cheek. 'In that case, I might do a bit of shopping but I'll leave you the car and walk. The weather is perfect.' And then he wouldn't have to walk the couple of kilometres home tired from unpacking. 'The keys are on the coffee table.'

Gramps was already opening boxes when she left. Setting his new home up to his tastes a room at a time was probably the best thing he could do to make the transition easier.

The morning sun was pleasant and Angie enjoyed the walk of a few blocks into town. Before shopping she ordered a coffee and sat outside the corner café. She felt as if she'd barely stopped since arriving home. Not to relax, anyway. And she was a long way from having a real break because there was still so much to do for Gramps, let alone find her own rental and prepare for the upcoming school term.

'He's rather dashing with his tweed jacket and white hair, you have to give him that.'

The words drifted from another table and when Angie snuck a look, the speaker was one of three older ladies sharing a plate of pastries. She'd seen them at the assisted living community in passing and two were familiar – people she had probably crossed paths with when she was much younger.

'Once you get past his gruff personality, you mean.'

'I think he's a big softie, Annette. We've both known Emmett for so many years but not ever had the chance to be more than acquaintances through different committees.'

Emmett! Gramps?

'If not acquaintances then what do you want to be, Bess? Planning to get married at last at your advanced age?'

'Goodness, Marge, that's not very nice.' This was the lady called Annette. 'For that matter, Bess is younger than you.'

'Good thing I'm not looking for a new husband then. The first one was bad enough.'

'How can you say such a thing, Marge? You still treat Tim like he's your best friend, even after the divorce.' This was Bess. She had a sweet face which currently looked affronted.

The one named Marge had a stern expression but her lips were quivering.

Bess wagged a finger at her. 'Not funny to tease me.'

'I can assure you it is very funny.'

All three suddenly burst into peals of laughter.

Hearing the ladies talk about Gramps was a bit uncomfortable but also amusing. He might be in for more than his expectations of new friends and time in the pool if there were women around his age keen to be more than 'acquaintances'. Angie had never thought of him as dashing but it somehow suited him.

For the first time Angie noticed a small dog beneath Marge's seat. A cute cavalier. Well, dogs were great icebreakers.

Angie, stop! Gramps doesn't need matchmaking.

Before she could overhear any further conversations about her grandfather, Angie decided it was time to do her shopping and go home.

With a shopping bag over one shoulder, Angie revisited both real estate agents in the hope of good news. As before, the nice woman at the first one shook her head, promising she would call the minute anything turned up.

Do I even want to step foot in the other one?

Perhaps Daphne or John would be there today.

Angie pushed the door open and her heart sank when Xavier look up from behind the counter. It was obvious he recognised her but all he did was drop his head again. Once she got to the counter she stood waiting. He was making notes in a ledger.

Why was he so rude? Didn't real estate agents make their livelihood from rentals and sales which meant dealing with people of all kinds? And it wasn't as though Angie came in here with an aggressive or demanding demeanour. She thought she presented okay... not that it should matter but he'd been dismissive of her twice now.

'Excuse me? Xavier, isn't it?'

He actually sighed, placed down his pen, and met her eyes. 'Mrs Fairlie.'

'No. Miss Fairlie but Angie is fine, thanks.'

'There isn't anything in your budget to rent. Sorry.'

'You haven't asked for my budget.'

Xavier didn't even blink. He looked bored and that irked Angie.

'I think I should speak with John or Daphne. When will one of them be here? Please?' Angie managed to get the words out, thankful her voice sounded normal even if her stomach was turning.

'I believe I told you they are travelling.'

'You did tell me that.'

'Angie? Angie Fairlie?' With a squeal and a blur of dark hair with bright purple streaks, Daphne Jones threw her arms around Angie, squeezing her so tightly she couldn't breathe. 'Oh my dear Angie, I can't believe that's you.'

Daphne finally released Angie and stepped back to look her up and down. 'Well you are every bit as gorgeous as you ever were! John will be just as happy to see you and I can only imagine the delight of dear Emmett that you are home.'

Angie had forgotten how warm and wonderful Daphne was.

'Now, tell me why are you visiting our little place here?'

What would Daphne think of Angie's recent past? Would it make her think twice about renting her a house?

'Actually, I'm looking for a place to rent for a while. In a few weeks I start teaching at the primary school and with Gramps moving, I need somewhere small to stay. Preferably in the next fortnight.'

Daphne beamed. 'Well you've come to the right place.

There's a nice two bedroom cottage almost ready to rent. The owners are finishing up the painting today, I believe, so we can arrange a viewing once they give the all-clear. Have you already given Xavier your contact details?'

Xavier stood and gravely shook his head. 'Sorry to tell you but that property is all but promised to another client.'

The little ray of hope inside Angie withered. Or was this just him being obnoxious? And if so, why?

'Well, that's interesting but let's not rule Angie out of the equation. Nobody has been able to view the place yet so how certain are you the other client is a firm candidate?' Daphne stared up at Xavier with a friendly smile. 'The final decision always belongs to the owner so have they approved the first person?'

'Not yet. As you mentioned, the cottage isn't ready to occupy but the potential renter has good references and fits the criteria of being a long-term prospect. My understanding is that Miss Fairlie prefers a shorter term rental.'

'Actually, I—'

'And the rent the owner is asking is on the high side for a small home.' Xavier had a glint of triumph in his eyes.

'Angie, dear, let me get some additional details from the owner and I'll get John or Xavier to call you once we have all the information. In the meantime, we'll have a hunt around for anything else on the books and see if we can't get you into your own lovely home. Now, will you please give my very best wishes to your grandfather and tell him we'd love to have you both over for dinner soon.'

'I will. So, you're staying a while?'

'We are. At least a month.'

Daphne had her back to Xavier and didn't see his face wince at her answer.

'I'm sure Gramps will want to chat to John about selling the house.'

'Of course! Although he can speak with Xavier if we're not around. He'll be the owner in the not too distant future after all.'

Sending a big smile in Xavier's direction, Angie couldn't help her words. 'I think it will be John or nobody. After all, there's so much respect and trust between Gramps and the two of you.'

Daphne kissed both of Angie's cheeks. 'You are so sweet. Go on, enjoy this beautiful day we're having.'

Angie had been home for two hours and was almost finished packing another of the bedrooms when her phone rang. She didn't recognise the number and her heart sped up. What if it was Shane? He'd promised to find her. But he was in prison for a long time and she couldn't live her life frightened of every phone call. She touched the accept button.

'Angie speaking.'

'This is Xavier from Rivers End Real Estate.'

She dropped onto the side of the bed.

'Yes?'

'We seem to have got off on the wrong foot. Daphne has asked me to show you the cottage tomorrow. Shall I pick you up at ten?'

Be with you in a car? No thanks.

'I would prefer to meet you there. If you send me the address I'll be there on time.'

The pause was a tell. Angie had learned much during her marriage. Any push back, any sign of being independent resulted in silence or verbal abuse. No wonder her hackles were up with Xavier. He gave off the same vibe as Shane. Presumably though, John and Daphne had vetted the man and were comfortable with him managing their lifelong business and prospective sale of it. Something wasn't adding up.

'Let me pick you up, Angie. The cottage is in a bit of a funny spot and the online maps don't give good directions to it. So, ten tomorrow?'

I do need a rental.

'Sure.'

His tone was warm. 'Excellent. I'll be at the bottom of your driveway at ten.'

She tossed the phone to the other end of the bed once the connection was cut and wrapped her arms around herself. If only Gramps didn't have to sell.

'I wish I could buy Seahaven,' she whispered. 'I love living here.'

But it was a waste of time, let alone hope, to wish for it.

Instead, she'd suck up her fears about Xavier and tolerate him if it meant having the chance to find her next home.

She finished working on the bedroom as quickly as possible, leaving only one box for Gramps to check. After carrying all of the bedding to the laundry, she packed the washing machine and turned it on. Gramps might choose to take spare sheets and the like so she might as well give them a freshen up and he could decide later. Another quick check of the room left her happy with the result. She scooped up her phone and a text message popped up.

> Confirming 10am tomorrow. X.

'Ew. At least write your name in full so it doesn't look like you love someone.'

If Gramps saw that he'd think she had a new man in her life and that wasn't a conversation she wanted to have. She deleted the text, shoved the phone in her pocket, and went to Nan's office.

. . .

The next newspaper clipping was an article published more than two weeks after the last. A quick look through the remaining pages showed that all were in date order, so had Nan been unable to locate any to fill this time frame? Surely there'd been more updates, regardless of the news.

A series of images and maps accompanied the article, including the ones from the previous dates. There was a larger map as well, extending even further from where the child disappeared. And then a heartbreaking photograph of people laying flowers in the clearing. Among the group, a man and woman and a boy stood a little apart but the photograph was taken behind them. Even so, this could have been Laura's family.

Friends and members of the local community gathered today to mourn with the family of little Laura, missing now for more than two weeks. The three-and-a-half-year-old wandered away from a family picnic late in the afternoon of 14 September 1952 and has not been seen since. A large and prolonged search including the use of tracker dogs failed to locate her or any signs of where she might have gone. Police have expanded a door-to-door search to neighbouring towns in the hope that Laura may have been found by someone and taken to their home. Anyone with information about seeing a child sharing Laura's description anywhere out of the ordinary is asked to speak to their local police station. Information can be provided in confidence.

The article continued for a while, going back over the same details as previously covered and then reiterating the request of the family to keep their names out of the paper for reasons of privacy.

Angie understood the desire for privacy during such an awful time. Newspaper reporters back then must have been more community-minded if they were willing to withhold Laura's full name. And the family were visitors to town rather than long-term residents so their names wouldn't have been known locally.

Who would recall what happened these days?

Gramps must have been quite little then, too young to remember the tragedy, and Nan was even younger. The Historical Society surely would have some record of it which meant Gramps might have come across some records but if so then Nan most likely had spoken to him about it already. Angie was unwilling to upset the current good feelings between them and decided to raise it only as a last resort.

She replaced the clippings, wanting to read a chapter before Gramps returned.

The sheets were cold but the woman wrapped the little girl in a dressing gown and sat on the edge of the bed, singing a song over and over in words which made no sense. But the sound of the woman's voice was like her own mother's and she was so, so tired. When she woke it was pitch black and she screamed. Light flooded the room when the man and woman ran in carrying a lantern. Not her daddy and mummy but these strangers. She cried out to go home and the man lifted her onto his lap and rocked her back and forth, telling her this was her home now. Here was where she was wanted and loved and she would be safe here. Mary belonged here.

TWELVE

11 January 1961

The early morning is glorious as the sun rises behind me and turns the ocean into a kaleidoscope of colours and patterns. I'm sitting on the hill above the rocks and got here just before dawn, waiting for the first light to appear.

I've decided to become a writer of children's books. How wonderful to create stories for the youngest minds and hearts. I love children – small ones – not the ones my age who are so unkind. It still hurts a bit thinking about those girls on the beach but Mama was right about keeping to people within the faith. I miss seeing the twins though and being part of a small group of friends.

Out at sea is a boat with a tall sail. I think the sail is white but the sunrise makes it kind of golden. I'd love to paint it. The boat and the sea and the sky. I like drawing things. The house. The chickens. Even Mama although she doesn't know I sketched her pretty face. She doesn't even like looking in the mirror so I don't want to upset her. And it is only for me to see because I don't have even one photograph of her. Nor of Father.

I remember him so perhaps I should sketch him before the memories fade too much.

I could illustrate the books I write!

This idea is the best one ever. High school will have art classes and then even if I still become a teacher first, it could be for art.

Mama doesn't keep many books. Mostly the Bible and some others she calls classics. There's a couple of beautiful-looking books written in German which I'm not allowed to touch because they are so old and precious. None for children though.

And that is strange because I have clear memories of being read stories from books. And even when I was little I knew words. Big words which Mama told me I shouldn't know at my age and mustn't use around other people. They were never *bad* words! Ones like brontosaurus and invincible and outrageous. Sometimes I don't understand my life. I remember playing with a boy who was older than me. Mattie. I told Mama once and she sat on the floor and cried and I was so scared that I never spoke his name again.

But I thought about him.

He was fun to play with. And bossy. If only I could clearly see his face and work out how I know him. Nobody at church is called Mattie. There are boys older than me but none of them are him. And I have the strangest feeling... a small, faint memory of him calling me his little sister.

Impossible.

There's only me, Mary. No other children.

The rooster is crowing his head off and I might as well go collect the eggs before Mama reminds me. Today is the last chance to finish the enrolment into high school so I want to make sure Mama doesn't have anything which might stop her. She's been busy sewing a lot of toys hoping Mr Kane will buy them. I'm proud of her.

. . .

By lunchtime I'm getting nervous about whether there's time for Mama to sign the form and for me to run into Driftwood Cove and post it. The envelope has to be stamped with today's date or I might not be accepted at school.

She comes out of the room where she sews to make a cup of tea and I quickly finish making sandwiches for us both.

'Is the sewing going well?' I ask.

'I'm tired. My fingers need a little break but then I want to do some more so there's enough to be worth Mr Kane's time.'

'I wish I was good enough at sewing to help.'

'You've cleaned up the kitchen. And prepared vegetables for dinner. As well as making lunch. Thank you, Mary.' Her eyes stop on the paperwork which I've placed on the kitchen table. There's a pen and the envelope is ready. 'We need to talk, child.'

Something in her tone makes my heart sink. Why do we need to talk? Have I done something wrong and will be punished? I hate being punished. My fingers curl into the palms of my hands and I summon my courage to accept whatever is coming. Mama is never unfair and I know she only corrects me to teach me important lessons but I have been so good. The tears are prickling at the back of my eyes but I hold my head high.

'Let's sit at the table. This is an important conversation.'

I didn't expect that and almost throw myself on the chair in case she changes her mind.

She takes a seat and pulls the paperwork closer. 'This is the most difficult decision I've made in a long time, Mary, and I want you to understand how much I have prayed and read scripture to come to this conclusion. I've watched you worry about when I will sign the document to enrol you in the high school and my heart is sad because my decision will disappoint you.'

'Mama?'

'Mrs Kane asked me after church recently if you were related to anyone in her town.'

'Oh... the boy her son knows in high school?'

'That one, yes. You didn't tell me she asked you.'

'It was such a silly thing. I'm sorry. I shouldn't say a grown-up is silly but the question was. I told her I only have you. And I forgot about it because it didn't make any sense to me at all.' I lean forward a bit. 'It was a mistake not to tell you.'

Mama pats my hand. 'Yes, but it wasn't to be deceptive. It made me consider if I should pursue making the toys for Mr Kane because on reflection, I believe Mrs Kane is not true to the faith. She allows her son to mix socially with outsiders and wears a lot of makeup and dresses as if she is better than her station.'

This is hard to follow. Mrs Kane is pretty and does dress nicely but I'm not sure why that means she is not faithful. I guess I still have a lot to learn.

'Mr Kane is a businessman but he contributes much to the church, so I decided to keep sewing. If he decides not to purchase the toys then I shall sell them at the markets in town and Green Bay and even up in the mountains, if the car manages the steep hills. But my fear is that Mrs Kane and her son are a bad influence. You've already experienced the nasty behaviour of other children at the beach and I imagine they will also be attending the high school.'

I'm finally understanding. She is afraid I will be led astray.

'Oh, Mama, I would never leave God's path! You've taught me well and I want to be just like you.'

Her face screws up and goes bright red and then big tears begin dripping down her face. She opens her mouth to speak then closes it again and I'm alarmed so jump up and pour her a glass of water. After a minute she drinks some of it and then dabs her eyes with a hanky.

How could I have upset her so? My mind races over the last

few minutes but I can't find what I've said to bring my poor mother to tears. I try to hold her hand but she blows her nose, before sipping water again. Then she bows her head in a prayer, her lips moving silently, and I sit quietly so as not to disturb her. When she looks up again, her face is solemn.

'You are truly one of God's blessings, Mary. But don't strive to be like me in any way other than your guide through the coming years as a teenager. Nothing matters more than your obedience to God and to me on this. For you to become a woman worthy of a good husband and children within a Christian marriage, the outside world must be properly feared for its temptations and pitfalls. Satan is everywhere.'

Being a wife and mother isn't something I've ever thought about, even though I love children. I'm not even a teenager yet and can't imagine being *married*!

Mama lifts the papers and holds them in both hands. 'This high school? None of our faithful attend. I can't include Mrs Kane's son but even if he is true, one person is not enough to hold off the forces of evil. My prayers led me to certain scriptures and then I spoke to another sincere woman who belongs to our congregation. She teaches her children at home and has seven. I only have one.'

'At home? But is that kind of schooling enough to gain entry into further education... like as a teacher? Or artist?'

'Artist? Mary, only certain blessed men are called to become God's artists. This isn't something a school teaches and nor is it a suitable choice for a woman. We are best serving people, not entertaining them.'

Something tells me to stay quiet and not debate this because I really want to tell Mama my intention to write children's books and illustrate them but if do it now it will be terrible.

My hands are clasped under the table and I squeeze my fingers together.

'To answer your question though... home schooling is an

acceptable way to educate and if you truly wish to teach, then all you'll need to do is pass exams to enter higher education. This way is better, Mary. Not being with outsiders for hours a day all week. No exposure to Satan in an environment without a loving guardian to protect you.'

I want to cry. If Mama says she won't sign the school enrolment I will be inconsolable. I want to go to high school. I want to learn and be taught and grow.

Then the truth descends and a deep calm replaces the panic. I'm not a boy. All my life I've understood that men are the head of a house. The leaders. The logical and sensible ones who protect women and children from evil. With Father dead, my mother has had to do her best to fulfil his role although it is neither natural nor comfortable. Her weakness as a female had been strengthened by God's love. Who am I to challenge her?

It would be to challenge God.

'Mary... I won't sign this.' Mama tears the paperwork in half. 'You are too important to put at such risk. I can't permit it. In three weeks we will begin home schooling.'

Her face is set. I see how ready she is for me to argue. Well, I won't. I won't get angry with her and be punished for raising my voice or disrespecting her. My stomach is tied in knots but I nod.

'May I please go for a walk down to the sea, Mama?'

There's relief in her eyes. 'Take your sandwich if you wish. Enjoy the nice weather.'

I wrap my lunch in paper and hurry out of the house.

I run all the way down the hill to the rocks. The tide is coming in and they are already partly covered but I don't care and take off my shoes.

The rocks are warm and slippery where the pools are overflowing from the sudden increase in water and I don't want to be swept out to sea so take care with my footing. Waves are pummelling the edges, sending spray into the air and foamy water rushes ever closer. I stop when I'm just out of reach.

Now I cry. I scream at the sky and the ocean and the rocks. I call for my father, longing for him to be alive and turn around from the edge of the rocks with his smile and tell me he will sign the papers. My body shakes with rage and I am so ashamed of myself being like this. Mama is doing what she thinks is best. I am a child. Powerless. For a moment I want to throw myself onto the rocks and let the waves do with me what they will.

My dress will be ruined. We can't afford to keep making me clothes.

I laugh at my stupid thoughts. Then cry some more but now it is not in anger but heartache. High school was the only thing I've ever looked forward to and now, Mama has taken it from me.

Warm water splashes against my bare feet and I look down. The sea doesn't care about my pain but there's a kind of peacefulness it brings. I stand there until the tide is too high for safety and then climb back up the hill. There I sit, my eyes on the horizon. One day I will move far away. I will find the education and adventures my heart seeks. Until then I'll be a good girl.

A good, lonely girl.

THIRTEEN

Now

Angie choked back a sob as she closed the book. A lonely girl. One whose dreams were cruelly stolen and for no good reason.

The parallels to her own childhood struck a chord. Her happy early life was devastated by the loss of both parents. Angie had never had close friends, thanks initially to the constant moves with Dad's work. When they died and she was living here and settling into school in one place, she'd only just begun to relax and get to know other kids when Nan passed away. She withdrew from anything social, deeply afraid to love anyone other than Gramps.

No wonder I was so willing to believe Shane was my way out.

Not out of the town she loved but an escape from the lingering grief and loneliness.

Unable to be in Nan's office anymore she took herself outside and sat beneath a favourite tree almost at the back corner of the garden and there she gave way to the tears. Back against the trunk and legs drawn up so she could hug them,

Angie let herself cry out the sudden emotions. The lost girl by the sea could be her – every bit as much as Mary. Both such lonely children with sadness in their hearts. Both keenly curious and kind-natured and wanting to become teachers.

And I did, but Shane almost stole it all away.

Whatever did become of little Mary?

It was only as the tears began to dry up that she lifted her head and found a hanky and was suddenly aware of another human in close proximity.

Jack was on his side of the fence, sitting against a similar tree, a book in his hands. But his eyes were trained on her and he looked worried.

'Oh. Oh, I'm sorry. I didn't know you were there.' Had he heard her crying? Angie couldn't bear the embarrassment.

'Don't be sorry. I didn't want to move in case I disturbed you.'

'I'll go.'

'Wait. Would you like some water or something? I'm a good listener.'

Share my deepest fears and memories with a total stranger? No thanks.

'Um. No. I just... I was reading something in Nan's office and it got to me.'

'You must miss her so much. I guess there'd be a lot of memories in there.'

'Yes, but this wasn't anything of hers. Well, I guess it was hers but the words weren't.' That didn't make much sense and Angie had no idea why she'd said anything, but Jack had shuffled himself around to face her and maybe a total stranger was better than a close friend, even if she had one. 'There's a book someone wrote. A memoir, maybe. It meant something to Nan.'

'And it distressed you.'

Why was Jack so nice? His voice was calming in an odd way. He looked genuinely interested. But some men were like that. Until they showed themselves for who they really were. Others were blatant.

'And on top of that I have to get into a car with someone who makes me uncomfortable tomorrow morning. But if I don't then I might miss the chance to rent a little cottage that fits my needs.'

'Hang on… why do you have to get into their car?' Jack leaned forward, his eyes suddenly serious.

'I'm overthinking it. It's a real estate agent and he said the way to get to the place isn't on a map which sounds ridiculous now I say it aloud. But I'm just overreacting to my general impression of him which isn't fair.'

'Angie, it is completely fair. Listen to your instincts.'

'They are pretty mixed up these days.' Annoyed with herself for blurting so much to the neighbour, Angie pushed herself to her feet and brushed leaves off her pants. 'I have to go check when Gramps is heading home.'

Jack stood but he put a hand on the tree to support him and slightly winced as he straightened. 'Just a suggestion. Either get Emmett to go with you or tell this man you'll follow in your own car.'

'Thanks. I'll do that. See you.'

She jogged away before she gave away any more of her thoughts. Gramps would be back at the cottage in the morning, most likely, and she wasn't ready to tell him she had a lead on a rental yet. Jack's suggestion of following Xavier in her car was a good one and as awful as she felt about him seeing her crying, he'd done nothing to make her feel uncomfortable about it. He was a good man.

Instincts, Angie? Or are you completely useless at judging other people?

. . .

A phone call to Gramps left Angie at a loose end. He thought he'd be back in a couple of hours and said he wouldn't be up for much other than an early dinner and a board game, if she was keen. She loved their old habit of playing games through an evening and decided to make a grazing platter instead of a regular dinner. But that meant no time to return to Nan's office... not that she was in the right state of mind right now.

She settled on going through the linen closet. She gathered two washing baskets and two boxes and started at the bottom.

It was best she did this because Nan had rarely thrown anything away and Gramps had barely touched it over the years. He'd purchased new bedding after Nan had passed, as if even touching the sheets she'd once lain upon was too painful. Angie lifted a soft pillowcase to her face and inhaled. It was fifteen years since Nan died and this had been washed and packed away ever since, yet if she closed her eyes she was certain she could smell Nan's rose perfume.

Deciding to keep one set of sheets, pillow cases, and blankets which Nan had bought, Angie placed those selected onto her bed. Later on she'd put them away until she moved. In case Gramps did want a set, she repeated her choices and placed them in one of the boxes to show him another day. She did the same with towels, tablecloths, serviettes... all manner of lovely pieces Nan had chosen or made. Angie wasn't big on sewing but had done embroidery at night sometimes. It was too hard to think of simply disposing of such personal items.

She finished the second highest shelf and checked the time. An hour gone.

Perhaps she'd leave the top until tomorrow. She needed a stepladder anyway. One by one Angie moved the washing baskets to the laundry and the boxes to the hallway to go through with Gramps. Probably tomorrow as well.

Turning her attention to dinner, Angie found a lovely timber board which would be perfect for the grazing platter.

This was something she enjoyed making and had done so a lot when first married. Back when Shane was loving and sweet and they'd entertained in their apartment overlooking the Swan River. She'd felt special as the hostess, with a dozen people milling around, drinking and laughing.

Not that they were her friends. Shane seemed to have a never-ending supply of business colleagues and Angie didn't mind. It was enough to do this for him. The cracks began showing when she invited some teachers she worked with over one night. He was pleasant and polite until they left and then he coldly told her never to do it again. *His* apartment. *His* choice of guests. He stalked out before she could speak.

And that was the night I should have left him.

Shocked and hurt, she'd gone straight to bed, feigning sleep when he finally came home. For hours she'd gone over the marriage so far, searching for why her friends and colleagues posed a problem for a social evening and coming up empty. Unable to rest she'd risen and in the kitchen was a huge bunch of flowers. And a note.

I forget how young you are. How inexperienced. Let's put this behind us. I love you, Shane.

Shane was almost fifteen years her senior. He'd been married before and divorced. His life experience was far beyond Angie's and yet he'd chosen her to love. She'd forgiven him but kept the note and years later when she read it again, realised there was no apology there.

Angie looked at her hands, one holding a knife and the other a tomato. The latter was leaking juice, so hard was she squeezing it.

'Get out of my head!' She spoke loudly to reinforce the command.

'Put down the knife and step away slowly, lass.' Gramps chuckled from the doorway. 'Killing an innocent tomato is bad enough.'

She had to grin at his words and laid down the knife. 'I might put this into the compost bin.' Her fingers were covered in juice.

'Nan used to keep a bag for all her peelings and offcuts and the like and freeze them until she had enough to turn into a soup base or stock. Dunno why I remember that now but it saved on wastage and you know Nan. The soup queen.'

'In that case do you mind finding a zip lock bag and we will resume the tradition.'

Within a few minutes Angie had filled one bag. Gramps went to have a shower then opened a bottle of wine, sitting opposite as she chopped an array of vegetables to use to dip into guacamole and tzatziki she'd made from scratch. These would accompany some cheese, slices of a different tomato, and some pickled onions and gherkins. Perfect.

'I like my cottage,' Gramps announced.

'Good.'

'Study feels a bit more homely with my books in their right places and the desk all but set up. The living room needs some finishing touches, so would you come and give me your opinion tomorrow?'

'Oh, I'd love to. And I've almost finished the linen closest, so I'd like to run a couple of things past you in the morning.'

'I'm planning an early start to take another carload of boxes down. My videos and the record player and the artwork mostly. Might leave straight after breakfast then you follow me down when it suits.'

Perfect. I won't even have to mention Xavier.

'Want to tell me what had you squeezing that tomato to death?'

Angie had hoped he wouldn't ask. She shrugged. 'Just thinking about my mistakes. Bad choices.'

He looked at her over his spectacles. 'Shane.'

'Yeah.'

'If I'd known what he was really like when he visited the first time then his head would have been like that tomato.'

'Gramps!'

'He hurt you, lass. Lost everyone else I've loved in my life and he almost took you away as well.' His eyes were glistening and his face reddening even though his voice remained neutral. 'He's lucky he's behind bars.'

In a second Angie was on Gramps's side of the counter and had her arms around him. She rubbed his back, shocked at how fragile he suddenly seemed.

He leaned against her. 'Never want to lose you again. Should have come and checked on you.'

'I had to find out for myself though. I never thought of myself as a lost little girl.'

His body stiffened and he pulled back out of her embrace. 'What did you say?'

'Just that I probably wouldn't have believed you. Not for ages.'

'No, the other part.'

'About not being a lost kid? It was just a manner of speech, nothing more. That I was trying to be independent and grown-up. And I messed up.'

His expression softened and he drew in a long breath. 'We all mess up.'

'Do you want to pick a game? Shall we eat and play?'

He nodded and went in search of a board game. His head was down as he walked and his shoulders were slumped. She'd filled her head with Mary's story so much that she was letting it creep into her life and was seeing things where they didn't exist.

. . .

Two hours of Scrabble was enough for Gramps. He'd been quieter than normal and seemed distracted, although he still beat Angie more than she beat him. She watched him carefully, fretting over his earlier response to what was an innocent remark.

He'd lost his son and daughter-in-law. His wife. The same losses weighed heavily on Angie. But his moods were hard to predict at present and all she could think was that the stress of moving, of leaving his family home, was bringing up old feelings. After all, he was losing Seahaven in a way.

'Might get some sleep, lass. Meal was delicious.'

'Company made it good.'

Gramps began to pack the game away.

'Go on, I'll do this.' Angie took the box from him with a smile. 'Shoo, you look exhausted.'

'I've missed this. Games nights. You will come and visit me?'

'Visit you? Good grief, I'll be annoying and drop in as often as you'll have me but I think once you settle in, you might end up too busy for me!'

Particularly if three certain ladies have their eyes on you.

Once his bedroom door was closed and the board game away and washing up done, Angie poured herself the final half glass of wine. She let herself out of the back door and wandered to the bench in the front garden.

She sat right on one end, next to Nan's usual spot. Gramps would be on the other. Even when it was just her sitting with Nan or later, with Gramps, the places would remain the same. How she wished Nan was here tonight. Angie closed her eyes, letting the pleasantly warm air settle around her. Her grandmother enjoyed summer evenings every bit as much and sometimes they'd stargaze on a crystal-clear night. More than ever she needed Nan's wisdom to help her navigate the next few weeks. And to guide her through the story behind Mary.

'It is all there, child. Finish my work. Reunite them.'

Angie's eyes flew open and she jumped up, almost dropping the glass.

Nobody was there. The bench was empty. So was the garden.

Yet Nan's voice echoed in her mind.

Sitting again, she half-turned to where Nan used to sit. 'I will finish your work. But reunite who?'

The only response was a lifting of the breeze which rustled the leaves of the old tree above.

FOURTEEN

Gramps was gone long before Xavier pulled up across the driveway exactly at ten. Angie was already there. She hated keeping people waiting and as much as her nerves were rattled, was determined to treat this like a business meeting.

At the last minute she'd remembered Jack's suggestion of following Xavier but it was too late to run back and get her car keys now.

She climbed into the front passenger seat of a white sedan, almost jumping back out as cigarette smoke swirled around and her foot crunched something in the footwell.

'Needs a clean. Just ignore the mess.'

I'll need a shower when I get home!

Angie clicked the seat belt on and tried to avoid the pile of empty soda cans and takeaway wrappings around her feet. There was an open ashtray overflowing with butts and the interior was filthy.

Xavier gave her a cursory glance before doing a U-turn. 'Daphne insisted you get the chance to view the cottage.'

'That's kind of her.'

'There's another client who is prepared to pay whatever it takes to get in to it so don't expect too much.'

Yesterday Xavier had said they'd got off the on wrong foot and now he was obviously planning to revert to how he'd been with her from the start. She should have brought her car. Angie kept her eyes forward. This wouldn't take long and would be worth it if the cottage was suitable and the owners willing to rent to her. Daphne might have something to say about a potential renter trying to outbid another.

Xavier drove toward town then turned onto the road leading to the Otway Ranges. They passed the primary school and a church and the last of the residential streets and the car sped up once they were on the open road. He was an impatient driver, tailgating a slow-moving van before overtaking well above the speed limit. Angie's hands gripped each other. Shane was like this. Always thinking about his convenience and needs over the rights and comfort of others.

A few kilometres from Rivers End was a narrow bridge crossing Temple River and just before it, a road forked to the left Xavier barely slowed as he tore around the curve and despite her best intentions, Angie grabbed the handle above the window.

He smirked at her and it was all she could do not to tell him to pull over and let her out. She had once with Shane and he'd just ignored her and driven even faster and she'd never been so afraid in a car. Not until now.

A chance glance in the side mirror brought with it a sudden rush of relief. If she wasn't mistaken, Jack's car was a short distance behind them. She focused on it rather than the man beside her. *Why* Jack was trailing them was a question for later but right now Angie wanted to hug him. Surely Xavier wouldn't do anything else dangerous with another car following.

Without indicating, Xavier abruptly slowed and took a driveway, bumping along what was basically a dirt track full of potholes. Surrounded by dense bushland, a cottage appeared and the car stopped.

'Long way from town. Big drive for you to work. To the shops. Beach. All that stuff.'

Angie pushed the door open and climbed out, peering down the driveway.

No Jack.

Xavier was out of the car and striding toward the cottage. 'Coming? The owners are back soon so let's do this and get back to town.'

I will walk back.

It couldn't have been Jack.

There was no time to analyse what might have been disappointment. Angie hurried after Xavier, traipsing through long grass. Weeds, really. He opened the front door and went straight in.

Angie's phone beeped with a message.

> Parked at the end of the driveway but if you need support (aka, a boyfriend/ best friend/ long lost brother) then text HELP and I'll magically appear.

Almost laughing aloud with relief, Angie replied.

> We will talk about how you got my number. But thanks. Don't leave.

> I'm here for you.

For the first time in forever, Angie's heart lightened.

She followed Xavier inside.

He stood at the end of a narrow hallway, facing her. 'Living room to your left. One bedroom to your right. Second bedroom next door on the right. Dining room next door on the left.'

She peered into each of the rooms. All were small and

devoid of furniture. They were freshly painted but the carpets and curtains were threadbare.

'Down here is the kitchen and bathroom and laundry. Everything a woman needs.' The tone of sarcasm wasn't lost on Angie.

After a quick inspection, she faced him in the hallway. 'What are they asking for rent?'

The figure he quoted was ridiculous. It was higher than a city apartment in Perth and this was in the middle of nowhere and had a bit of a creepy feel about it.

'Now do you see why I discouraged you?' Xavier stepped closer. 'Daphne might think this is a nice option but she's too busy swanning around the countryside to bother herself with a personal visit.'

'Well, thanks for showing me around.'

'I thought you were desperate?'

'I'll see myself out.'

As she walked back along the hallway she quickly texted Jack then slid the phone back into a pocket.

Xavier overtook her, putting a hand against the door to stop her opening it. 'You shouldn't leave so soon, Angie. We should take this chance to get to know each other better.'

'Let me out, thanks.'

Angie was about done with being civil to this man. Until Shane, she'd never have tolerated the rudeness and whatever it was Xavier was doing but life had taught her caution around people – around men – and she would remain calm until she could get out of the cottage. If only her legs didn't feel like jelly.

'Come on. Look around the whole property. There's a cosy shed up the back.'

'Oh, honey! Are you in there?'

Xavier visibly started and flung the door open.

Jack had his hand in the air, ready to knock, with a pleasant smile on his face. But his eyes shot straight to Angie's and narrowed. He changed the trajectory of his hand, stretching it to her. 'There you are. Ready to leave?'

Grabbing his fingers like a lifeline, Angie slipped past Xavier. 'Sure am.'

'Just wait a minute. Who are you and what are you doing here?' Xavier followed her out. 'We're not finished.'

'Angie said she is ready to leave.' Jack went down the steps with her then turned to face Xavier, his eyes boring into the other man's.

She hadn't released his hand and took a tiny step back. 'Thank you, Xavier, for showing me the cottage. As I mentioned it isn't suitable for me but I appreciate the opportunity.' Angie glanced at Jack. 'Shall we?'

Xavier stalked inside and slammed the door.

'You were far too polite with that creep.' Jack tightened his fingers. 'Let's go.'

The inside of Jack's car was the opposite of Xavier's. It was clean and smelled nice. Of Jack. Angie put on her seat belt, trying not to think about him that way. Her fingers still tingled from the warmth of his hand, which had held hers until they'd reached his car.

'How did you get up there so fast after my text?'

'Something felt off so I was lurking around in the trees close by.' He grinned as he started the motor. Not that it made much sound.

'Lurking.'

'Old habits. He didn't do anything inappropriate? Because I'm happy to have more of a chat with him.'

What old habits?

'He didn't touch me.'

Jack turned to give Angie his full attention. 'Touching is hardly the only way of being inappropriate. Men like him get off on intimidating women. Probably other men too. But in this case, you.'

'How do you have my phone number?'

He gazed at her for the longest moment. If a person could see into her soul then Angie thought it might feel like this. Then he faced forward again. 'Emmett gave it me as you being his next of kin a while ago when he had his health scare and I—'

'His *what*?'

Jack's head turned. 'Oops…'

'Tell me.'

Her heart pounded. What on earth had happened to Gramps?

'So that's not why you moved back.' It didn't sound like a question. 'This is a discussion for you and Emmett. He was given the all-clear, Angie. Nothing is wrong with him but he had a bit of a scare in the male health arena and asked if I'd have your number just in case anything happened. But nothing did. Okay? Nothing happened.'

He didn't tell me. He didn't share something so important.

Even as the tears prickled the back of her eyes Angie was forcing them away. Jack was a stranger to her. Gramps might like and trust him but she wasn't gullible. Not now.

Jack just put himself out for you.

'How long ago was it?'

'Almost a year. I'd moved in about a month prior and we just hit it off.'

Angie would have been just divorced and in the middle of the court cases, she had been barely in touch with Gramps while she navigated that awful time. Pulling him into it was the last thing she wanted yet she'd longed for his wisdom and often stared at her phone, trying to find the courage to speak to him. Had he also wanted to call her and say he had his own worries?

'Hey… I'm so sorry to make you sad.' Jack's voice was soft. 'I think I have some tissues somewhere.'

A tear had escaped and she quickly brushed it away. 'Thanks, no, I'm fine. You took me by surprise. He's all I have in the world and means everything to me.'

'He's said the same about you.'

If she didn't get control right now, Angie was going to dissolve into a puddle of tears. She was stronger than that. Or at least, stubborn. Whichever it was, she found her neutral face and plastered it on but wasn't prepared to look directly at Jack. 'I really appreciate you following Xavier and would love a lift home or to wherever it is convenient. Even just to the outskirts of town is fine.'

'Actually, Emmett asked if I'd drop in to the cottage and help him rearrange some furniture, so is that suitable?'

'It's perfect.'

Jack pulled onto the road and went a little further along to turn around. As he did so, another car stopped up near the bottom of the driveway they'd just left, blocking Xavier's car which was driving down. Two men climbed out and headed toward Xavier.

'That's weird.' Angie worried for a moment in case something was wrong but as Jack went past, Xavier was out of his car and all three were shaking hands and smiling.

Jack had slowed and glanced up but then gradually sped up without commenting.

The drive to Rivers End was the polar opposite of the one out. Not only was the car comfortable but Jack drove without bravado and showiness. She had no need to grab at a handle or grip her hands together and by the time he turned into the carpark at the assisted care community, Angie was almost dozing, her mind slowly going over the most recent parts of the book she'd read in Nan's office. She never relaxed in cars. This was a first.

'Now I feel like I've partly made up for nearly running you

over.' Jack undid his seat belt and Angie followed suit. 'What else can I do?'

'Not a thing.'

'There must be something, particularly after helping teach me to make tortillas.'

'It was Gramps who did all the teaching. Anyway, unless you have a keen interest in local history books and love puzzles then I can't think of anything. You're helping Gramps and that means heaps.'

Angie climbed out of the car and slung her handbag over a shoulder.

Jack locked the car but leaned on the roof, gazing at her. 'Do you realise you just described me to a T? Books, researching, uncovering secrets... kind of my thing. I imagine Emmett's told you about my background?'

'Not really. Only that you have been renting next door for a while and are a good person.'

'He said that?' The grin on Jack's face was engaging. 'Nothing from my sister?'

'I like her.'

'As opposed to liking me?'

She couldn't help herself nor keep her face entirely serious. 'Reserving judgement on that.'

Something changed in Jack's eyes. Angie didn't believe she was capable of reading another person anymore but she was convinced he was amused.

'I love a challenge.'

'Your sister only said you'd been injured in the line of duty but I didn't ask what she meant.'

Jack wandered around the car and held out his hand. Slipping hers into it felt like the most natural thing in the world. They headed in the direction of the street of cottages.

'Long story for another day. Preferably over a decent bottle of wine and delicious meal. But briefly, Ruth is right. I was seriously injured at work and it cost my career, but you know what, Angie? It didn't change my fundamental love of solving mysteries and I guess that's why I originally joined the police force. All I wanted was to become a detective.'

'And you did?'

'Yes I did. And now I'm not one, my mind is crying out for a challenge. So how about it, Angie? I'll give Emmett a hand and then you let me give you one.'

FIFTEEN

Gramps was outside his cottage chatting over the front fence to the three women and dog from the other day. The woman holding the little dog's leash stood apart from the small group, gazing in the direction of the nearby hills.

'That didn't take them long,' Angie said, keeping her voice low.

But Jack heard. 'Them? The ladies?'

'I overheard one of them describe him as dashing and there was even talk of marriage.'

Jack chuckled.

As they got closer the woman whose name was Marge – if Angie remembered correctly – turned her attention to them. Suddenly self-conscious, Angie retrieved her hand from Jack's. The woman's stern expression was accentuated by a sharply cut bob but there was curiosity in her eyes and she lifted her chin after scooping up her dog under an arm.

'Bess, Annette, we need to go shopping,' Marge said. 'Come along.'

She didn't wait, turning and striding away at a fair pace.

'I think we're leaving.' This was Bess. 'It was nice to catch up, Emmett, and I'm sure we all look forward to welcoming you to our lovely community once you finish moving in.'

'Later, ladies.' Gramps waved.

Later, ladies? Who are you?

Bess and Annette linked arms and followed at a more sedate speed, the latter using a walking cane. Gramps finally noticed Jack and Angie.

'Just missed some of my new neighbours,' he said. 'Three of the original residents when the place first opened.'

'I'm sure I know two of them. Bess and Annette?' Angie went through the open gate with Jack just behind. 'Were you or Nan friends with them in the past?'

'More like friendly acquaintances. I knew Annette's husband better as my doctor for a long time before he passed away. She and Bess have also been on a couple of the same committees but today is the most we've ever had an informal chat.'

'And Marge? That's the name of the other lady?'

He nodded. 'Yes. First time we've spoken. Unsure if she is naturally standoffish or just shy. Did you both just happen to arrive at the same time?' Gramps headed indoors. 'I just can't manage the big pieces alone and the delivery man had to go.'

Jack leaned close to Angie's ear and whispered. 'Shall we avoid answering his question for now?'

'I think so. Thanks.'

He gave her a funny look. He'd meant about coming to her rescue earlier, surely? Not so much being in the car and then walking around holding hands like teenagers. Angie felt a sudden rush of heat to her face and quickly followed Gramps through the front door.

Shane wasn't an affectionate man, especially not in public. Except there was no affection to show because Jack was virtually a stranger... not her boyfriend.

'Angie, did you happen to bring any boxes with you?'

She followed Gramps's voice to the bedroom. He was somewhere behind a plastic-covered mattress which was propped against a wall and part of the doorway. On the other side a bed was pushed to one side.

'No, but I can run home and get anything you need.'

'Run home? Did you drive down with Jack?'

'Um... yes, I arrived with Jack. In his car. We were going the same way.'

Good grief, Angela. Stop making it worse!

Gramps's face appeared around the side of the mattress. 'Happy the two of you are getting on so well.' He disappeared again.

Angie backed out, straight into Jack. He didn't move for a moment and his hard chest against her shoulders and spine was all-too-nice. She laughed it off with a light 'sorry' and he made room for her to escape. Unlike earlier with Xavier she didn't want to escape and that was a problem she needed even less than dealing with creepy real estate agents.

There was nothing Angie could do to assist so she walked into town in search of lunch for them all. The bakery solved that problem and after buying some bottled water at the supermarket, she cut back between the inn and one of the town's two pubs. To Angie's dismay, Xavier was standing at one of a dozen or so tall outside tables with the men who'd been in the other car at the cottage he'd shown her. They were deep in discussion, heads close together above empty beer glasses.

Turning around would most likely get his attention so she worked her way between people and tables, keeping her head down.

'You sure you've got this one covered, mate?'

'I'm sure. The little princess doesn't like the place after I scared her off, which leaves it all for you. Just the formalities, then it makes it house number five.'

Angie couldn't believe her ears. She kept going, speeding up as she cleared the last of the tables. Overhearing that conversation made her ill and worried for Daphne and John. They clearly had no idea of the kind of person who ran their business... and intended to buy it. What was his game?

At the road she had to stop to let a car past and against her better judgement, glanced back.

Xavier had stepped away from the table and stood, arms crossed, staring at her.

Suppressing a weird urge to wave, Angie instead pretended not to see him and walked over the road once it was safe. She should have avoided going past him but then she'd never have overheard those odd comments. Not only about scaring her off the cottage but saying it was house number five. Five houses for what purpose? Surely those men didn't need to rent five different homes between them... no, something wasn't right.

Angie drove home with Gramps early in the afternoon. Jack had an appointment to attend so left the cottage before they did. He and Gramps had set up the bed and then adjusted some of the living room furniture.

'I put aside a set of sheets from the linen cupboard but you really need nice, new ones,' Angie said. 'When would you like to shop for those kind of things?'

Gramps parked in front of the garage, next to her car. The garage was another place they needed to go through as it had become more of an oversized shed than being used for its real purpose in recent years. There was still so much to do and somewhere in all of it Angie had to find a rental. Even if Gramps let her stay in the house for a bit after he moved out, she couldn't be here for long. School term was looming and having her own place by then mattered because once she began work, her focus would be on the students and learning about her new job. And he'd want it sold quickly to cover his new living costs.

'Later in the week. Early next? I hate shopping.'

Angie had almost forgotten she'd asked Gramps about when they'd go.

'Which is why we'll make a comprehensive list and I will be with you.' She slid her arm through his as they crossed the distance to the front door. 'We can make an early start and plan ahead by looking at each shop's website for ideas.'

'Never bought a thing online.'

'Nor have I, but all we're doing is looking.'

He unlocked the door and pushed it open, stepping back to let her in first. 'Don't all young people buy online?'

'Probably.'

All of Angie's pay had gone into the joint account with Shane and he watched what she spent. It hadn't mattered at first but once the credit cards were being maxed out all the time, Angie began to ask questions.

And be guilted about how I didn't trust my own husband.

'What's wrong, lass?'

Gramps had closed the door and looked worried.

'Do you think I'm a weak person?'

'Now just where did that thought come from? I'll guess. That no-good ex-husband of yours.' Gramps put an arm around her shoulders and directed her toward the kitchen. 'There's not a person on this planet who has met you who would call you weak. None. No, they'd say you are kind and generous and compassionate. You always see the best in folk and perhaps that, in part, explains you marrying the man.'

'Because I was naive?'

They stopped at the kitchen table and Gramps dropped his arm and faced her. His eyebrows almost met, so stern was his expression. She almost squirmed under his scrutiny but his voice was soft.

'Because you are loving and sincere. That man took advantage of your wonderful traits for his own bad intentions and that, my dear, is completely on him. Not you, Angie. Never on you.'

She hugged him tightly. Not ready to completely believe his words, it nevertheless lifted a weight. If he didn't see her as having done anything wrong with her choices then surely she could stop being quite so hard on herself. When she stepped back she was smiling and he nodded.

'Much better. Now I should have asked earlier but are you alright on your own this evening?'

'Sure, but why?'

'Had an invitation to have dinner in the community dining room and then an evening of music and dancing. Sounded fun. And I need to begin to assimilate.'

'Assimilate makes you sound like an alien, Gramps. The rest sounds wonderful.'

'Never thought I'd be so happy about moving but there's a lot for me to look forward to. Might have a shower and get ready.'

If one of those ladies was making him feel positive about the future then that made her happy. And every bit of happiness mattered.

Angie was in Nan's office when Jack arrived. She'd texted him after Gramps left to ask if he still wanted to help her solve the puzzle. His response had been to ask what time, where, and what should he bring.

'I know you said bring nothing but somehow this icy cold bottle of wine found its way into my hand, along with two glasses.' Jack was grinning as he stopped on the doorstep. 'May I come in?'

'You may. There's not a great deal of space though.'

She'd tidied up to make room for him to use one of the comfy chairs and moved a small table between it and hers. The box in question was on the desk, unopened.

'Emmett won't mind me being in here?'

'That I can't answer. He's asked me to sort it all out and said I can keep whatever I want from in here, so I can't imagine he'd be upset at you helping me. Please take a seat.'

He did and poured two glasses of wine, handing one to Angie. 'So where is Emmett? I saw him walking rather jauntily down the street a while ago.'

'Turns out he's been invited to have dinner followed by dancing at the assisted living community. He's walking because he's looking forward to having a couple of beers and I heard him humming earlier.'

Jack grinned. 'Good for him. Shall we toast to Emmett and his future?'

Angie clinked her glass against his. 'To Gramps behaving himself. Or not.'

The wine was cool and delicious and almost immediately took the edge off Angie's nerves about inviting Jack over. It felt a bit weird to be here with the man who'd almost run into her... not his fault but still strange.

'When we first met, where had you been?'

'Me? I thought I mentioned it. An after-shoot party.'

'But what does that mean? Are you an actor?'

Jack threw his head back and laughed.

He was good-looking enough to be one. Had a confidence about him as if used to being on show. And a great body. Angie took another quick sip.

'Not an actor. I consulted on a police film being made at

Dockland Studios in Melbourne. They wanted to make sure they'd kept things as real as possible and I enjoy being able to work on projects like that. I still have the heart of a detective, I guess.'

'Do you still know people? I mean, other detectives or police who can check up on... um, bad guys?'

His eyebrows rose. 'What kind of bad guys are we talking about?'

I'm being silly. This isn't your problem.

But Xavier's comments bothered Angie and another opinion – a professional one – might put her mind at ease. She put down her wine glass.

'When I went to get lunch today I happened to overhear a conversation which sounded a bit off. It was between Xavier and those men from earlier.'

Jack straightened. 'Go on.'

Confident she remembered word for word, Angie repeated the snippet she'd heard. She left out how Xavier had stood to watch her leave. It didn't matter.

'Five houses. Rentals presumably. Could mean anything.'

'You're right, Jack. I'm reading something sinister into nothing.'

'I didn't say it was nothing.' His tone was mild but his face was serious. 'Some of the best tip-offs come from average folk paying attention. And before you say a word I don't think you are average. Not even close.'

Jack's gaze was unwavering and now the room was too warm and there wasn't nearly enough air in here. Angie got up and opened both windows, willing the heat in her face to disappear. He was just being pleasant. That was all.

She collected the box and sat, placing it, unopened, on her lap. It was time to change the subject.

'My grandmother would have liked you, I think,' she said. 'She always stood up for people in a quiet way and wanted justice done for those who were wronged in life. Her fiction books were written in a way which exposed human flaws as well as human kindness and she once told me she hoped they made readers think.'

I can trust you, Jack. I feel it in my bones.

She removed the lid and put it aside. 'At first I thought the contents of the box was research for her next book. But now I believe she stumbled across a mystery and was on her way to solving it when she left us so suddenly.' Angie lifted the book and handed it to Jack. 'This is either a memoir or fiction written as one. There are also some letters between Nan and the author, who she tracked down. As well, she has a bundle of newspaper clippings about a missing child and some other bits.'

Placing his wine glass on the table, Jack opened the book. 'She found the author although they are anonymous? Good for her. Have you read it?'

'Only three chapters so far. I really want to read the fourth but if we are going to talk about this then would you read the first three so we are both in the same place?'

'I'd love to. The chapters are short so I can do so now.'

'Perfect. And I'll set up a spreadsheet on my laptop so we can add our joint thoughts.'

For a while they sat doing their own things with an occasional grunt from Jack, presumably when he reached more difficult parts of Mary's story. When he closed the book, he picked up his glass and took a long sip. His face was sad and that tugged at Angie's heart. Her initial impression of him was wrong and the more she got to know Jack, the more she saw that.

'Why do you think it isn't fiction?' he asked.

'It feels too raw. And then there's the newspaper articles.'

'There was a missing child around that time?'

'A little girl who wandered away from a family picnic up in the hills.'

'Any evidence it is the same child?'

'Not so far,' Angie said.

There was something new about Jack. His eyes were bright with interest. If he'd been a detective, then this was probably right in his wheelhouse.

'Do you want me to read the next chapter aloud? Or you do it?'

Angie settled back in her chair. It had been years since anyone read to her and although the subject matter was emotional and at times disturbing, she was content to hear the words. 'Please go ahead.'

First Jack topped up their glasses, then he opened the book to chapter four.

After a while the dreams changed. Mary was six now yet it didn't seem that long since she was four. At night it was harder to remember what her mother and father looked like. She still could see Mattie's face though. Hear his voice. But her parents lived here, with her. Mary knew this during the day. Mama. Father. Always close by. When she'd close her eyes to sleep there used to be frightening fragments of calling for her mother. Trying to find Mattie. Dolly being beside the river. Lately her dreams were about the child Jesus. He loved and would save her. And her parents were her guides to a godly life.

SIXTEEN

6 June 1962

Today is my fourteenth birthday and I wish it was my twenty-first so I could leave home. I might leave earlier anyway no matter what the law says. Mama is always reminding me that we only obey secular laws which don't conflict with those from God and I can't find anywhere in the Bible which says I need to be twenty-one.

I only asked for one thing for my birthday. I'm allowed to ask for two as long as they both are useful such as clothes or shoes or a new pillow. I thought this was useful because it would allow me to plan ahead as well as keep track of my day-to-day life. And even write my thoughts down.

A diary is all I want.

When Mama asked last week for my choices and I told her, she didn't respond other than to nod. But this morning she gave me two gifts. One was a jumper she knitted for me and I really like it. The other was wrapped in brown paper and obviously a book and I was so excited but inside was a school textbook.

'I had to save up but I know you were using one which was out of date. This is the newest version for arithmetic and although girls aren't good at it, you need to understand as much as possible for your exams.' Mama had smiled. 'You are a diligent student and I am happy with your choice of becoming a primary school teacher one day.'

'Thank you for my gifts. I love the jumper and the book will help me a lot.' I had given her a quick hug and stepped back. 'I really am grateful but I just wondered… I really would like to have my own diary.'

'Diaries are wasteful and offer Satan a way in to the mind of a young girl. You certainly don't sound grateful so put your gifts away and then clean out the chicken coop. I want it spotless.'

She stalked away, her back rigid and I know there's no point apologising or complaining.

So now I am covered in chicken manure and bits of straw but everything is as clean as it can be for a place where birds rummage around all day and perch at night. When I'm done I take the basket of eggs I collected and go straight to the laundry by the side of the house. I strip off the dirty clothes leaving just my underwear on and fill the sink so they can soak. I run back to the house because it is so cold and the air on my skin makes goosebumps. Leaving the eggs in their basket on the table, I hurry to my bedroom and put on long pants and the lovely new jumper. It is soft against my skin. Mama must have spent more money than usual on the wool and I realise I've stopped being cross with her. I might be able to save up to buy my own diary if I can find some work to do outside school term.

I go to find Mama to show her the jumper on me and tell her I've finished the chicken coop. She's in the kitchen, scrubbing the top of the stove as if she is angry at it. There's a nice smell in here and I think there's a cake in the oven.

'Mama? Did you see the lovely eggs?'

'Yes. I've put them away.'

'Thank you. I needed to soak my clothes in the laundry because I got muck all over me but the hens are happy with fresh straw and all nice again.'

'Good.'

Still she scrubs.

'Thank you for my lovely jumper. It is so soft. I really love it.'

Her shoulders drop and she turns around. At first I think she is upset with me. Her face is red and kind of screwed up like when she is about to lecture me or else cry and I don't want her to do either. Not today.

She puts down the scourer and washes her hands, drying them on a tea towel as she looks at me.

'That really should be kept for special occasions, Mary.'

'I won't get it dirty. I promise. I've never had anything so warm and comfortable and I think you are so kind and clever to make it.'

'But am I kind, Mary? It isn't what you asked for. Nor is the textbook. I disappointed you.'

'I'm not disappointed with your gifts, Mama! Or in you. Ever. Not ever.'

'There is only me to raise you, child. Without your father I have to bring in money to pay for our needs and teach you and give you the best chance I can at growing up to be a faithful and humble woman.' She shakes her head. 'You have no idea of what sort of person I truly am. The mistakes I have made... how can I even ask God's forgiveness? I will die without knowing his benevolence and be buried in a grave among the sinners of the world.'

Die? Why are you speaking of this?

I burst into tears and cover my face with my hands.

She is suddenly there and she puts her arms around me, rocking us both back and forth. 'Sorry. So sorry, little lost girl. You never asked for this. What Vernon did was wrong and his burden was too much to bear so he took the coward's way out instead of making it right. I was wrong for letting it happen and I will pay for it through eternity.'

Her words make no sense at all yet her love fills my heart as she comforts me. I don't know why she calls me a little lost girl but then she shrieks. 'I smell burning!'

My birthday cake is only a little singed on the top and once it is cool Mama cuts the bits off and then covers it all with icing.

'This can go into the pantry until later. Would you like mashed potato with some green beans and gravy and chicken for dinner?'

Mashed potato is my favourite. 'Yes please. Can I help?'

Mama smiles. She seems happier now. 'No, you may not help. This afternoon you should do anything that you want. There's no school right now so it is your choice and I'll cook dinner and afterwards we'll have a slice of birthday cake.'

I feel special. And free. Much better than earlier.

First I go for a walk down to the rocks, but only after changing out of the new jumper. There's a chilling wind and the waves are whipped up. I want to talk to my father but the tide is making it impossible to go too close. So I stand on the lowest part of the hill, my hair blowing around my face and my fingers frozen. The sky is as grey as the sea. I kind of like it.

Sometimes when I come here I can feel Father's presence... not that I would dare say so to Mama. She believes he is in Hell for his sins but won't tell me what he did which was so bad. What she said today doesn't make sense about him doing something wrong and taking the coward's way out. I remember him as gentle and funny and hardworking. Not a sinner of the worst type.

Today there's nothing other than the howl of the wind and

I'm sad because my birthday should matter. He is the one thing which would make it complete.

'Happy birthday to you. Happy birthday to you.' Everyone is singing. I'm trying to blow out candles on a cake but I can't and Mattie is laughing at me and I get cross with him. I stamp my foot then run outside into the warm sun and he catches me and swirls me around until I am squealing with delight.

I'm sitting on the grass and don't know how I got there. My legs are weak and shaky and my head is spinning.

'Happy birthday to you.'

'No, stop!'

I cover my ears with my hands and stare at the ocean until the music fades and nobody sings. My teeth begin to chatter and I am crying because it was so real. But my birthday is now, in winter, not a warm summer day. Who is Mattie? Where is Mattie?

On the way home I remember my clothes soaking and go to the laundry. I squeeze the worst of the dirt out and rinse them in clean water. Only a bit because the winter hasn't given us the usual amount of rain and the tank is lower than normal. I leave the clothes in the water. Tomorrow I'll gather all of our laundry and do a proper wash with water boiled on the stove. At least it will be warm in here with the door closed and steamy water.

It isn't until I've taken off my outdoor shoes and closed the back door that I hear voices. Not in my head like at the rocks but a man's voice and my mother's.

We so rarely get visitors that I get nervous in case it is someone we don't know. Mama has cautioned me to never allow a stranger – particularly a man – into the house. I don't know what to do. They are in the kitchen and I have to go through it in order to reach my bedroom. I shouldn't interrupt adults talking so I go to open the back door but the rain we've been wanting decides now is the time to arrive. I'd rather not get soaked.

Between the back door and kitchen is a tiny space where we hang raincoats and stuff and off it is a small storage area with a door which Mama keeps locked. I've been in there often because there are shelves for our preserves and dried food but others with old suitcases and boxes and I'm not allowed to touch those. The door is unlocked and a bit open and I'm so curious to see what might be important enough to keep locked up.

'She is far too young!'

Mama's voice is raised and I jump and move a bit closer. It is wrong to eavesdrop but she sounds upset.

'Fourteen is an acceptable age.'

I know the voice and to confirm it, carefully position myself to see into the kitchen through the slightly opened door. Yes, the priest is sitting at the table. There's a pot of tea in front of him and one of Mama's nicest teacups. She doesn't have anything and is bolt upright in her chair.

He has rarely spoken to me and doesn't like children or teenagers. I feel he only tolerates them in some of his services because parents want them there.

'Today is her fourteenth birthday but Mary is young for her age.'

That shocks me. I think I'm mature and sensible and am intelligent.

'I'm not suggesting they marry immediately, Gertrude. A long engagement makes for a long marriage and as a member of our church and faithful woman I am confident you agree it is a sound path for her to follow.'

'Yes, of course I want her to marry and have children. It is her duty. Not so young though. She is still at school and hopes to become a primary school teacher.'

He scoffs and Mama's face turns red.

'My nephew is a good young man. He is also of means so

Mary has no need to work, other than in charitable volunteering. The good Lord knows we need more charity in this age of poverty where people become thieves just to feed their offspring. It is men who need jobs, not young women. I wish you to think about this. Your daughter lacks your pretty looks. *You* could easily capture the attention of another husband. For her it will be difficult.' He looked around the kitchen. 'She has little to bring to a marriage.'

Mama stood abruptly, her chair scraping the floor.

'She'll be home any minute and I'd rather she doesn't walk in on such a conversation.'

'Quite. Give it serious thought, Gertrude. You do little for God's flock other than sew in exchange for money. It would be a disservice to your faith to keep Mary from contributing. I'll see myself out.'

The priest lumbered from the room and the moment the front door closed, Mama covered her face with her hands.

I can't let her know I heard.

Tiptoeing to the back door, I wait until I hear the car drive away and then I quietly turn the handle. Once the door is open, I close it quite loudly.

'Mama? I'm back.'

When I enter the kitchen she's gone so I go and freshen up, brushing my wayward hair and washing my hands. In my bedroom I carefully fold the new jumper which I'd left on the bed and place it into a drawer.

'Mary?'

I jump. I hadn't heard Mama open my door and can only see part of her the way she's standing. Her eyes look puffy and red and I know it is from the visit with the priest. Is she going to tell me he was here and why?

'You once asked me about a toy you'd lost.'

That wasn't what I expected her to say and I must look confused because she almost smiles.

'It was a long time ago but I remembered where it was. Your father packed it away to keep it safe and I thought today was a good day to find the thing. Although you are far too old for dolls but you really aren't... you aren't so old.' Her voice catches.

She steps into my bedroom and holds out a soft doll with golden hair and big blue eyes. 'Do you remember Dolly?'

SEVENTEEN

Now

Jack slowly closed the book and leaned back in his chair. 'She was a child. Fourteen. Yet the priest wanted her to marry his nephew… how was that acceptable?'

As with every time she delved into Mary's life, Angie was struggling with profound emotions which threatened to overwhelm her. This might not even be a real person yet the injustice and sorrow and loneliness of Mary wound its way into her soul.

She finished the glass of wine to collect herself, aware Jack had his eyes on her.

'It wasn't even legal. The marriage would be illegal even if the priest ordained it.'

'What a strong young woman she is,' Jack said. 'She knows exactly what she wants to do in life even if the path her mother set is different. She's bounced back at every hurdle.' He refilled their glasses after holding up the bottle for Angie's agreement. 'It's her lonely existence which gets to me.'

'Have you picked up the little clues about her age maybe

being wrong? And that she doesn't quite fit into the family with her looks?'

'Ever think about being a detective?'

'Me? Never. But helping Nan with her research was great for learning how to spot anomalies in records and dig a bit deeper. I have a very vague memory of seeing this box when I was a teen but never what was inside, which feels a bit strange as she always said nothing was off limits. Before we go further and this becomes harder to pull together, would you help me with the spreadsheet?'

'As long as I don't have to create it. Numbers are not my thing.'

'Nope, all ready to go and I happen to love numbers. What I need is to start filling in some columns so if you can search back through the book then I'll do the rest.' Angie put the laptop back on her knees. 'I've got half a dozen headings but can easily add more if we come across any other patterns or things of note.'

'I'm impressed. Where shall I start?'

Angie glanced at the headings. 'What about her age?'

For a few minutes Jack scanned his way through the first four chapters, stopping whenever there was something relevant.

'Mrs Godfrey thought she looked eleven when she was twelve. And there's the comment from the same woman mentioning the difference in looks between mother and daughter.'

'Yes, I'll add it now. What pages please? Oh, and what date?'

They worked well together. Jack was meticulous with detail although he kept adding his own thoughts, which slowed the process. At one stage he smiled.

'This is typical of how I used to work a case,' he said. 'Facts might be sparse so in order to get a full picture I needed context and sometimes that required considerable speculation.'

'A bit like how Nan worked. Find whatever was true and build a web or structure around it.'

'Exactly. Some people think police work is all chasing bad guys but there's more desk work than action. Homicide needed hours if not weeks of sifting through information to build a case.'

'But you still loved it?'

A shadow of something like regret appeared in his eyes. 'Almost every part of the job. If I'd been quicker or more aware then I'd still be living that dream.' He shrugged and looked back at the book.

For a while they continued adding to the spreadsheet. At one point Angie watched him. He was so focused on the words in the little book, searching for clues to add to the spreadsheet. It was nice having someone to share this with.

He must have felt her looking at him and glanced up, little wrinkles forming around his eyes as he smiled. She smiled back, her heart doing some weird acrobatics.

It must be the wine. With no food.

'I wonder how Gramps is going.'

'Probably having a great time. You know, when I first moved next door he was very polite and friendly but in a reserved way. There was an air of... I dunno, seriousness about him.'

'He's always been that way. Quiet, reserved in some respects. The happiest I ever saw him was with Nan, out in the garden building something or planting and gardening. There was so much laughter.'

I miss you so much.

'The thing is that once he made the decision to move and especially when he knew you were coming home to stay, he seemed lighter in his spirits.'

'He did? But...'

'But?' Jack closed the book and leaned closer. 'Emmett talked about you so much I felt like I knew you before I met you.' He shook his head. 'Apart from almost running you over but I didn't know that was Angie Fairlie.'

'So if you'd known?'

'Possibly I wouldn't have yelled at you.'

'It was my fault. I must have given you such a scare stepping out in front of you in the near dark.'

There was a shift in the air. Something subtly changed.

'Your face when you saw my car. Good grief, you startled me. My headlights picked you up on the verge but then you were in front of me. Thank goodness for decent brakes.' Jack reached out a hand and gently touched Angie's face. 'What were you saying before? You said *but*.'

Angie had to force her mind back although it was only a moment ago.

'I disappointed Gramps by marrying Shane. He was against him from their first meeting and when I moved to Perth it was like I'd turned my back on him. We didn't speak for such a long time.'

'He never said a word about you turning your back on him. And that's in the past. You're here with him now.'

She wanted to tell Jack everything. Explain what life was like with Shane and how awful the past couple of years were in court and ultimately seeing him jailed. Her fear of never being allowed to teach again if she was found guilty of crimes she hadn't even known were happening. Of being burdened with the debts of a man who had swindled people out of their life savings. She'd gone back to her maiden name the minute she could to disconnect from him on every level.

'Angie?' Jack was on his feet and gently removed the laptop, placing it on the desk before squatting in front of her. He took her hands in his. 'I've stirred up some memories, haven't I?'

His hands were warm.

'A long story for another time. But yes, it is in the past.'

'Have you eaten? I'm starving.'

On cue, her stomach audibly rumbled and they both laughed. Then he pulled her to her feet. 'Your place or mine?'

After deciding to stay at Seahaven and taking a look in the fridge together, Jack offered to poach eggs, announcing it was one of the rare meals he could do well and while he did those, Angie toasted some sourdough bread and sliced an avocado. There was a nice tomato relish in the fridge and between the two of them, they turned the simple ingredients into a fancy meal. It was fun having breakfast for dinner.

'I really should set the dining room table,' Angie said.

'You really shouldn't. I like sitting here in your kitchen and have enjoyed many a good conversation with Emmett while we snacked on cheese and olives over a whisky.'

Angie collected cutlery. 'I had no idea the two of you were so close. In fact...'

'Do you always do that? Trail off in the middle of a line?'

'Probably.' She joined Jack at the counter and gazed at him. Was she about to spoil this newfound friendship? 'I misjudged you at our first meeting. And then the second one reinforced my opinion that you were—'

'Adorable?' Jack looked hopeful.

Ignoring a sudden urge to agree, Angie chose her words carefully. 'Confident. In yourself.'

'Ah. Cocky.'

'I did not say that.' Her lips curled up against her will. 'Self-assured. Actually, I was convinced you were a wealthy actor and was surprised that Gramps approved of you.'

Suddenly aware how that sounded, Angie attended to her plate and loaded her fork with egg and avocado.

The soft chuckle she was getting used to said he knew exactly what she meant.

'Oh, I think he approves of me, Angie. But ultimately, it matters what you think.'

'Well, of course I approve of you, Jack.' Glancing up, she grinned. 'You are a pleasant, mostly quiet neighbour and a good friend for Gramps. He even told me you have nice manners. What's not to approve of?'

Jack made a spluttering sound but was lost for words.

My work here is done.

Gramps arrived home at almost eleven. Angie was dozing on the sofa in the living room and stretched as he tried to tiptoe past.

'And what time do you call this, young man?' She followed him into the hallway, grinning.

'Whatever are you still doing up?'

'I boiled the kettle to make hot chocolate a while ago then got sleepy so lay down for a bit. Would you like one? Or are you heading straight to bed?'

'Hot chocolate sounds good. Let me put my jacket away and I'll join you.'

Angie had them ready on the counter when Gramps came into the kitchen and he sank onto a stool with a small sigh.

'Nice to sit down again.'

'The walk back up the hill is pretty tiring.' Angie sat on the end, where she could face him. 'I'm always puffing by the time I reach the driveway.'

'Sounds to me like you need to get fit, lass. I remember you thinking nothing of running down to the beach, swimming for hours, then running home. Running everywhere or sleeping.'

'I'm sure I did more than those extremes.'

'Not much middle ground. Not as a teen, anyway.' Gramps sipped and nodded. 'Delicious, thank you. But no, it was a few dances too many which has my feet and legs and hips complaining.'

The last time Angie had seen him dance was with Nan and it was in the living room, spontaneous, and with only the music in their own heads. They'd been waltzing around the coffee table and didn't stop even when Angie wandered in.

'Now, why are you smiling? I'm not too old to dance.'

'No, you're not too old. I used to love dancing.'

'I remember taking you to lessons in Green Bay.'

She hadn't thought about that for ages. For a brief time the idea of becoming a professional dancer was appealing but the dedication to training was lacking. But how she loved dancing, whether at a party or later – when away getting her teaching qualifications – in nightclubs or at the occasional formal event.

'You should accompany me next week.'

'To where?'

Gramps gestured in the air. 'Where I was tonight. Once a week they have dancing and everyone is welcome. Not just us oldies. And the music is eclectic enough to suit all tastes. Had to remember how to do the Time Warp.'

Angie almost spat out the mouthful of hot chocolate.

He reached for a napkin from the holder in the middle of the counter and handed it to her.

'Sorry, Gramps. Did you say—'

'It's just a jump to... actually, is it left or right? Anyway, I didn't do any jumping but it was quite invigorating to boogie for a bit.'

Time Warp. Boogie. Next he'd be breakdancing.

'Well, I'm pleased you had a nice time. What was dinner like?'

'Buffet table. Plenty of variety and choice of three desserts. Good thing there was dancing and then the walk home.' He patted his stomach. 'Best thing is the company. Hadn't realised I knew half a dozen of the gentlemen who live there. A couple from the Men's Shed. They say they are happy living there.'

'That's reassuring.'

He finished his drink and then gazed at Angie. 'I admit I was second-guessing my decision to move. I always thought I'd spend the remains of my life here and was resigned to having to get some help later... when I need it. The idea of having strangers in and out of our home if my health deteriorated and I wasn't able-bodied was depressing.'

'But I'm here. I'm back for good.'

'Now why would I expect you to give up your life to look after me?'

'*You* did. For me.' Her throat constricted. 'You and Nan. You... you started over as guardians with a teenager instead of enjoying those years together.' Tears tapped at the back of her eyes. 'I would do anything for you, Gramps.' Her voice dropped to a whisper. 'Anything.'

Gramps took both her hands in his, gripping them tightly, his own eyes glistening. 'Listen to me, Angela. Your nan and I never regretted bringing you home. Never. Not for a second. Not even when you went through the phase of learning to play the drums.'

That made Angie half-hiccup, half-laugh.

'Danged noisy things but your grandmother reminded me how much she'd put up with my hammering and sawing over the years with my projects. Point is, lass, having you in our lives kept us young. You've lost a few years from a bad situation, and thank goodness have emerged in one piece, so this is your time. Do you understand me?'

I have almost nothing.

'Your nan would look you in the eye and tell you that we make our own fortune. Her idea of fortune was happiness for the rest of us, for her, for the readers. Find your fortune and grasp onto it. Eyes on the prize, Angie.'

Once she nodded, he released her and got to his feet.

'Bedtime.'

He picked up both cups and took them to the sink to wash, then added them to the drying rack.

'Two plates?'

Angie jumped up. 'Oh. Um, yes. Jack was here earlier. Had a late dinner.'

A broad smile crossed Gramps's face.

'I hope that was okay? I didn't ask you. It wasn't planned.'

'This is your home too.' He got as far as the doorway and glanced back, still smiling. 'Seems you already have your eyes on the prize.'

EIGHTEEN

The first thought when Angie woke reminded her to speak to Daphne and John Jones today. The second was Gramps's comment last night. He'd made a few which she had mulled over in bed before sleeping but it was his last which occupied her now.

'Seems you already have your eyes on the prize.' He'd said it smiling but the words had unsettled her.

Jack wasn't some prize to chase.

Having another relationship was the last thing Angie wanted. She was still licking her wounds and seeking a better balance in her life. It felt wrong to explore possibilities without her day-to-day world being stable – financially and emotionally. She had so much work to do on herself before inviting another person in.

She didn't even know if she'd end up sleeping in her car at this rate. The time wasn't right.

But is the time ever right?

She groaned and pulled the covers over her head.

How had this even happened? In the space of a few days Jack had gone from being some kind of movie star who loved himself to Gramps's nice neighbour and now her... what? Friend was the only definition she was willing to use.

He was trustworthy. That's what her instincts said – for what they were worth. But Gramps liked and trusted him and if she couldn't rely on her own judgement then she could rely on his. But what did she know about the ex-detective? He'd been injured in the line of duty, badly enough to end his career. He had a lovely sister, brother-in-law, and was a doting uncle. He was part owner of the local Italian restaurant after helping his godfather out financially. And he had rented the house next door for the past year. By comparison there was so much she didn't know. What were his long-term plans? She had no information about what he did for a living now other than consult on a film. And not a hint about past, present, or future romantic relationships.

None of this was helping Angie get him out of her head.

She slid out of bed and a glance at the clock and then out of the window surprised her. It was before dawn. If she got a move on she had time to go to the beach.

The air crackled with humidity as Angie jogged onto the sand. A storm was forecast for late afternoon but she didn't need a weather report to know it was coming in hard and soon. One look at the lightening sky was enough. Heavy clouds loomed over the sea, periodically covering the moon. A hot wind blew Angie's hair back, stinging her eyes.

Despite the uncomfortable conditions the lure of the jetty was too much and she sprinted past the lagoon and onto the timber boards. At the end she stopped, hands on the railing as she sucked in salty air. It was invigorating. Exciting, as a long, low rumble of thunder echoed. Beneath the jetty the sea was high enough to splash up through the cracks in the boards.

Last time she'd been on Rivers End beach at this time of the morning, she'd longed to remain inside the bubble of peace between night and day. It was still tempting yet even after such a short time home, she felt her soul was healing.

When you belong somewhere, it hurts to be away.

Living here again was her future even though she had only a sketchy outline of the details. For the first time in ages, Angie knew everything would work out. Her path had merely deviated for a while with some harsh life lessons.

'And I'm alive.'

The words disappeared into the dawn.

Her future was in her hands, unlike little Mary. Angie stared in the direction of Driftwood Bay. Somewhere there a young girl had lived but did she belong? Was Mary the missing girl from Rivers End and had she lost everything against her will?

As sad as the thought was, it stirred something deep in Angie.

It was impossible not to draw comparisons. Like Mary, she'd experienced an upheaval in her life without having any say in the matter. She'd grown up lonely and feeling out of place. And she'd longed to become a teacher. But unlike Mary, Angie had been raised by people she knew, not grown up wondering if somewhere was a family who loved and missed her. 'I promise you, Mary. I'll discover the truth and wherever you are now, do my best to find you. I think it is what Nan wanted.' Saying it aloud made it real.

With the wind even stronger, Angie put her back to it as she returned to the sand. Above the long, protective limestone cliffs there were no clouds and the stars faded with the coming of morning. At the tunnel she paused to watch the thunderhead race to shore. Huge and filled with lightning.

How thrilling it would be to stay here and watch. Sit beside the river and feel the thunder as much as hear it. But the rain might last for hours and then she'd have to make her way back to the house without as much as a raincoat.

This time she was careful crossing the road.

And just a little disappointed that no red, silent car happened to go by.

The first sprinkle of rain came as she hurried up the driveway. The lights were on inside the house and opening the door, she was welcomed by the aroma of fresh coffee. Home.

'Good thing no more furniture arrived today,' Gramps said. He gazed through the living room windows which were streaked with rain. 'Haven't seen a storm like this in months.'

'Think of it this way. We've finished another two rooms today and you've been able to go through the boxes which I wasn't sure of.' Angie was pleased with the progress they'd made, even during a few hours when the power went out.

'I'll buy new sheets. New towels. Overdue for updating a lot of the things which we'd had for a long time. Other things I could never let go. Those pieces of art I chose and, of course, some of the books. And the record player with all the vinyls. Always resisted the move to get rid of them in favour of the latest trend.'

'The collection is probably worth a mint.'

Gramps turned around. 'I bought a remastered Miles Davis album and had to sit down after seeing the price. Did you find the box with your old records?'

'I did, thank you. Can't believe you kept them for me but they brought back a lot of memories. Once I'm settled and start getting a regular income, I'll buy a little record player. Might even dance around to the music.'

She was smiling but Gramps wasn't. If anything, his expression was severe like it had been the other day.

'Angie, we need to have a proper talk about that.'

'Me dancing?'

'No. Your financial situation. Your housing situation.'

'Nothing to say, Gramps. I'm just starting from scratch but I'm resourceful.'

'There's no need to place yourself under such pressure. Your grandmother and I always intended for the house to be yours one day, but then you married and moved.'

Please stop. I can't bear hearing how I let you down.

Oblivious to her discomfort, Gramps continued. 'There's more as well. When your parents passed away, there was a small inheritance which we gave you at the age of eighteen. It was only a few thousand dollars.'

'I know. I remember. It was how I bought my car.'

From another part of the house, Angie's phone began to ring.

'I need to get that, Gramps.'

'We need to finish this conversation!'

'I'll be a minute.' Relieved to escape, Angie ran to the kitchen where the phone was and answered. 'This is Angie Fairlie.'

'Hello, dear. It's Daphne.'

'Oh, I was going to ring you today sometime.'

'Beat you to it! Is it about the little cottage?'

Angie perched on a stool. 'Sort of.'

'I have to admit neither John or I have been to inspect it since we got back but from the listing details it sounds almost perfect for your needs. Other than being a fair way out of town.'

'It isn't really what I expected, Daphne.'

'Too small? Or isolated?'

'Um... no. It might be worth you having a look though.'

'Oh dear.' Daphne's tone became more serious. 'Xavier mentioned it was just repainted.'

'Yes, I'd agree it was. It's more that the grounds are in poor condition and so is much of the home. To be safe, it probably needs quite a bit of work.'

'Well, isn't that odd. Xavier has been doing such a good job of finding new rentals this year and they rarely even have time to go on the market before he matches them with the perfect tenant.'

Perfect? More like co-conspirators.

'Daphne? My experience with Xavier was unpleasant. I'm truly sorry to have to say this but I can't in all honesty keep it from you.'

There was a long silence. Had Angie said too much? She hadn't thought through how to word it and hated doing this on the phone instead of face to face. But then there was a small sigh on the other end of the line.

'Dear me. Someone else mentioned they'd been disappointed with something he said a while ago and we did talk to Xavier. His explanation was plausible and he promised to be more sensitive to how he spoke to people and nothing more has come up. Until now. Would you be willing to meet with us? John and me of course. Not Xavier if he's made you uncomfortable.'

'I don't want to cause trouble.'

'And I doubt you'd have said a word if it wasn't worse than you've told me, dear. When would suit you?'

They arranged a time the next morning and both hung up. Angie needed to write down everything she'd seen and heard for their meeting so as not to overlook any important details. She straightened and turned. And stopped. Gramps was in the doorway.

'Sit, lass. I want to know what that phone call was all about and then we're finishing the talk we started and no excuses or running off.'

. . .

Angie told Gramps everything about the visit to the cottage. Almost everything. She left out the worst of how Xavier made her feel and also how safe she'd felt with Jack. Neither had any bearing on the facts.

He stopped her a couple of times to clarify where and when this took place then let her continue. She finished with the conversation she'd overheard outside the pub but kept the part about Xavier watching her afterward to herself. Gramps might overreact and decide to get involved.

'So I'll see Daphne and John tomorrow and pretty much tell them the same as I've told you. I can't let this man hurt their business.'

'I'm more concerned about you. I've never heard a good thing about the man and have no idea why the Joneses have let him run things for so long. They love their business, so I have to assume nobody has been straight with them.'

'Until now.'

'Listen to me. Nobody doubts your ability to do anything, Angie. But some men simply can't be trusted and more men – more *good* men – need to let them know there's no place for that behaviour in society. I'll come with you tomorrow to see John and Daphne. Alright?'

Angie nodded. Asking for and accepting help was something she needed to practise.

Gramps tapped the counter with his fingers. 'As to your search for a place to rent? Will you hear me out?'

She had no more fight in her today. If he was going to remind her she'd blown her inheritance on a car which she still owned thanks to her poor choice of husband then she'd sit here and apologise.

'Seahaven has only ever been owned by Fairlies. And I wouldn't leave if it wasn't best for me in the long term. But there's a reason it needs to stay in the family.'

'What reason?'

A strange expression of sorrow disappeared as fast as it came.

'It isn't important. But you seem to have the idea I'll be selling the house?'

'You told me that.'

'I did no such thing. I told you the new cottage was costing me as much as a house and that's because once I move in there's not another cent I have to pay. Not for food or the facilities or rates or anything including any physio or medication. But I paid for it from my superannuation fund.'

'Are you saying you aren't selling?'

'Why would I sell your inheritance? If your dad was still alive then he'd be the one I'd leave it to. And he would have left it to you. So no, Angie. I'm not selling Seahaven. And because I have no need for two homes, my intention has been to sign it over to you as soon as you want it.'

NINETEEN

'But the furniture? The packing up we've done?' How had she got it so wrong?

'I'm quite sure you don't need all of my old collections and outdated stuff. The furniture is yours to keep or change for something more to your taste, other than the few items I'm having. The house needed a decent going over and declutter so you can have a fresh start with it.'

The house is mine?

Gramps got up and collected a box of tissues.

'Why the tears?'

'What tears?' Angie touched her face and laughed shortly. 'Oh, those tears.'

'Take some time to think about what is best for you. Mr Appleby is able to sort out whatever paperwork is required to make it formal, regardless of whether I transfer Seahaven now or you simply become its caretaker until you are ready. And once I'm gone you can sell it if you wish. I'd prefer you don't while I'm kicking around, but I won't try and control what you do.' His smile was forced.

Angie almost threw herself at Gramps, holding onto him as

sobs came from a place of grief. She couldn't imagine a world without him but wasn't living in a fantasy world. The time would come and she would again be alone.

'Shh, don't be so sad. Or happy. I can't tell.'

Gramps patted her back until she finally released him and returned to her stool. After pulling out a handful of tissues, she took a moment to gather herself and dry her face. He was filling the kettle, which seemed like a good idea.

She gazed around the kitchen. This dear place was the heart of the home and might be old and the appliances need updating but it was filled with good memories.

'Already planning how to turn this into a fancy modern kitchen?' Gramps teased.

'Not at all. I love it like this.'

Over their coffee they decided Gramps would retain ownership for at least another year while Angie built up some savings. By not having to pay a landlord her income could go toward the rates and other costs of the property.

'And you can buy yourself another car when you want.'

'I'd rather pay you some rent though. I'd have to otherwise.'

'Rubbish. You'll be maintaining the grounds and covering the day-to-day costs whereas if you were still in Perth, or living anywhere else for that matter, I'd be having to rent Seahaven out.'

The weight of the world lifted from Angie's shoulders. Gramps's generosity meant she truly could have a new start. Unless...

'Do you think Mr Appleby would look at all of my court papers? Including the divorce agreement?'

'I'm sure he would. But why?'

'I have to be certain Shane can't find a way to do anything to try and claim Seahaven as part of the settlement.'

'For your peace of mind, talk to our solicitor. But you've been divorced for what, a year now? Shane is the person the courts found guilty of fraud and all those other financial crimes. Not you. He won't be able to claim anything, lass. Not a thing.'

Gramps was making sense. One day Angie might make decisions without second-guessing herself but for something so important as Seahaven she'd get legal advice.

The storm was gone and the sky clearing when Angie let herself into the office after dinner. Gramps was watching a favourite television show and would then go to bed. She needed to be alone with her thoughts and feelings. And as much as she'd have liked to see if Jack was free to join her, he was part of the reason she wanted to clear her mind.

Stepping inside brought a swell of emotions.

This office could remain as a tribute to Nan's work. A sanctuary where Angie might sit, as she'd so often done, and talk to the woman who'd meant so much. The pressure was gone to sort through everything. Earlier she'd asked Gramps why he wanted the office packed up if he intended to gift her the house.

'Since your last phone call from Perth you'd said you would find a small rental in town. I got the feeling you wanted to find your own home so I couldn't expect you to take on all of Nan's things and my room is so limited.'

They'd both said things in the past which clouded the situation. Too much tiptoeing around and trying not to upset the other. Not anymore. For the first time in years all the barriers were down and they were communicating well. There was little Angie wouldn't discuss now.

Jack was one though. And this research of Nan's was another, because Gramps was so sensitive to anything to do with it.

Angie sat behind the desk.

She still wasn't ready to go through the drawers. The time would come when it felt right. The same for the rest of the books and boxes. For now there was just one box which would keep her busy and even though the time pressure was gone, her own curiosity only grew stronger. And now she'd made a promise to Mary.

Was there really a connection between Mary and Laura, the child missing from Rivers End? Nan had to have considered it, given the newspaper clippings. Angie opened the box and lifted those out.

Jack would find these interesting and might offer some insight into the search for the child from an official perspective. The initial frantic hunt for her, close to the last seen location and expanding out. Increased people-power when she wasn't readily located. Bringing tracker dogs and widening across the region. Dealing with inclement weather. Hope turning to disbelief and then despair.

After the ones she'd already read there was a sudden change in articles. Rather than reporting on Laura, these appeared unconnected. One was a page of classified advertising. Items for sale. Jobs vacant. Houses to rent. None were highlighted. The page was dated 1963.

Another article was about a church in Driftwood Cove. It mentioned a religious sect Angie had never heard of so she did a quick search on her phone. The results were few but it appeared to be deeply conservative and small and no longer existing. Whoever wrote the article was scathing about the abandonment of the church itself by its priest and alleged misappropriation of a large sum of money donated by the congregation. This one was dated 1964.

'Only two years after the priest wanted Mary to marry his nephew… assuming it is the same church,' Angie muttered.

Then was a page which was a mix of birth notices, marriages, and obituaries from 1966. Nobody's name jumped out at Angie.

A mixed page was blurry but Angie made out something

about a spate of thefts reaching from Rivers End to past Driftwood Cove, all being livestock, firewood, and tools of trade. The name Donny Hammond was mentioned as someone recently arrested on suspicion of petty theft along with members of his immediate family.

The final clipping was much more recent. Dated only weeks before Nan passed away there was a full-page article about abandoned houses in the region. Several photos accompanied the article and one stood out. There was a gate and track leading to a house in the distance. Behind the house was a big double-doored shed and possibly a chicken coop.

Angie couldn't believe it. 'Could this be Mary's house?' Her whispered words sounded as hopeful as she suddenly felt. None of the other houses in the article reminded her of the descriptions Mary had included in the book. Nan must have thought so as well. But her heart sank. After so long it might be gone. Demolished in place of a new home or homes. She took a photo with her phone then read the text beneath it.

This property has no owner, according to council records. The building has never been approved and the title of the land is long out of date. Whoever lived here did so without paying for the privilege and did so without electricity or a telephone line.

How peculiar. She'd need to ask Gramps about this. Not the specific property or where the information came from but about how common it was for people to build a house without permits. With his experience running a building company as well as his local knowledge, hopefully he'd have some insight. From the article all she knew was the house in question was on the other side of Driftwood Cove, remote, and overlooking the sea from a hill.

She glanced through the window and sighed. If only it was

an hour earlier she'd go for a drive but twilight was here and there was little point looking in the dark.

Angie's mind kept wandering to the first two letters in the box so she relented and reread them. More than ever she believed the author of the little book, *The Loneliest Girl by the Sea*, was Mary. Even though she'd referred to Mary in the third person in the letters it might be as simple as needing to maintain a distance from a traumatic childhood. Refer to the child as someone else to lessen the burden of pain.

There was one letter unread and with a shock, Angie realised it was dated just one week before Nan died.

For a moment she closed her eyes, forcing down the ever-present tug of loss. What would Nan have wanted her to do? In her heart she knew.

Dearest Opal,

I've thought of little else than our recent telephone conversation.

'You spoke to Nan?'
Angie gulped and kept reading.

Above all, how do I repay you for such thorough and persistent research into Mary's origins? Even my husband, who completely supports my deep-seated need to stay out of any spotlight, has urged me to accept your gracious offer. He only knows a small part of my history and has no idea of my little book because I carry such shame and grief and cannot expose a kind person such as he to this past of mine. As far as he is aware, I am looking for a lost loved one and while this is true, it is not the whole truth.

When you told me you have a theory about Mary's early life I was ready to hang up and cut all ties because, dear Opal, fear overwhelmed me. Fear of discovering the truth, yet it is all I've longed for almost my entire life. Fear of finding Mattie again, only to learn he wants nothing to do with me or, worse, is deceased. And fear of being blamed for what happened. To me and my parents. Or whoever they really were.

Fear has ruled my life. It is time for courage.

I will meet you at the time and place you suggested.

If nothing else, I will be able to thank you in person for becoming a true friend and advocate for Mary.

Until then,
M.W.

Nan had worked out the puzzle! Or enough to need to meet Mary face to face and exchange information.

Angie stared into the box.

Somewhere in here were the answers. Or had the meeting happened and Nan handed over something different? A report of everything she'd learned?

The letter was posted a week before Nan's heart attack. Depending on where it came from it might have taken anywhere from a couple of days to more than a week to arrive. There was no mention of where or when the meeting was scheduled.

'Wait on... your diaries.'

Nan always kept work diaries to keep track of publisher deadlines, word counts, notes about research trips, appointments which concerned her work. The current one was usually within reach of the desk.

A search of the office came up empty. Angie even peeped in

the desk drawers. Had Gramps accidentally packed it with his boxes from the study or bedroom? Darn, that was a possibility and asking him if he knew the whereabouts would likely get her told off again. She wasn't about to ruin the current good feelings between them.

Hopefully the diary might be in the bookcase in the house or else she would wait until he'd unpacked the boxes at the cottage.

For now she was going to read another chapter in the book. She had to find out what happened to Mary next.

She liked inspecting the pools of water left by the sea on the rocks. Mama never came down here but Father loved to fish and would tell her about the birds and sea life. Even at seven she knew it wasn't safe to be where the sea and land met although Father could go. He would remove his shoes and roll up his pants in case a wave splashed up. On this day the wind was strong and the ribbon tying her braid flew off. She tried to catch it, chasing it across the slippery surface until Father yelled at her to stop. She'd got too close to the ocean and quickly retreated but he was running at her along the very edge. His face was angry. She'd disobeyed the rule. Instinctively her hands went to protect her bottom from the smacks she knew would come but as Father jumped over a big gap in the rocks he cried out and vanished from view. A terrible scream. He was gone. He never came back.

TWENTY

6 February 1963

Mama never said a thing to me about what happened with the priest last year. Since then, she's gone out of her way to avoid him other than to sit at the back of the church each Sunday. I'm still proud of how she stood up to him and I think my father would have been proud as well. But what I remember most from that day was when she brought Dolly into my room.

I couldn't believe my eyes. At first I hugged the doll to me. It was the same toy I remembered but so much smaller. Then I realised it was me who'd changed. I was a teenager, not a little girl.

It occurred to me that teenagers didn't need dolls so I put Dolly at the end of my bed and there she stayed for a few days. Then one night I had a terrible dream and woke up crying for Mattie. Mama hadn't heard me and I was in the dark with tears on my face. Then I saw Dolly and remembered.

I'd been outside somewhere. There were trees and grass and I still recalled the scent of eucalyptus and sound of kookaburras laughing. Dolly had fallen onto the ground and was covered in dirt and Mattie grabbed her and dunked her head into a stream.

Even in the dark bedroom I could see him. Older than me. Curly golden hair. Blue eyes and the biggest smile ever.

Mattie was my brother.

I held Dolly against my chest. My heart pounded so hard it hurt. And I kept whispering, over and over, 'Mattie is my brother. Mattie is my big brother.'

There was no more sleep for me that night. I turned on the flashlight I have under my bed for emergencies and found a piece of spare paper from my school studies. Then I drew Mattie. Lots of drawings filling the page, getting a bit better with each one. I could see him more clearly as I thought about him.

Not that the memories came readily. Snippets here and there but always his generous smile was the same.

When dawn arrived I hid the drawings inside one of my drawers, under the paper which Mama likes in the bottom to keep it clean and fresh. I wanted to think things through rather than blurting out what I remembered. Mama has sometimes become upset when I ask about him and she has enough to worry about.

The months went by and no new memories came. I was so busy with schoolwork and Mama allowed me to take a part-time job helping one of the church families who run a shop in town. I wasn't allowed to serve customers but I unpacked stock and took care of inventory and kept the shelves looking nice. It was only for a few hours each week but I was making a little bit of money for myself. Just before Christmas my employment ended because the oldest daughter left school and went to work there during the long summer break.

I miss the money and the work. It gave me a sense of satisfaction to do my job well. But I had all of January to myself and just helping Mama as normal.

Now it's the first week in February and school started and I've had a week of much harder lessons. Mama says it will get even tougher until I finish and then teacher college will be harder again. I'm not worried because I love to learn. Another two years of study and I can take the exam even though I'm young. As long as I've completed the necessary levels there's nothing stopping me.

Today I've finished my chores and have been for a walk to Driftwood Cove to buy myself an ice cream. It feels so grown up to have a little bit of money to spend just on me. Mama would call it a waste but she's busy sewing again because her animal toys are still selling thanks to Mr Kane. She has always been right about working hard – even if it isn't the job of your dreams. If you make enough money to pay the bills and eat then there's no reason to ever resort to asking for charity. Or stealing! At church last Sunday there was a sermon about sins and the priest told us the latest local theft was of a herd of cows.

I take my ice cream and wander along the beach holding my shoes in one hand so that the water can wash over my bare feet. There are some teenagers playing in the deeper water, mostly boys. They whoop and splash and push each other under the surface but all are laughing and I can't help smiling at them. How is it a sin to be friends with people of other beliefs? Or even no beliefs? I would love to join in the fun for a bit.

But I keep walking.

The priest talks a lot about sin in his sermons. The sin of greed. Of lust... although I don't really understand what it means. Some of the sins I've read in the Bible but there are some which I've never seen. The priest says women must not own property or a business. They must never disobey their husbands nor argue, no matter the directive given. Mixing with those outside the church is to be avoided other than for work and school. It is sinful to befriend an outsider. And so on. I asked Mama about women not owning property because of our home and she laughed and said the priest gets carried away sometimes and that she doesn't own our house anyway. Father found the property one day and nobody wanted it so we moved in. Same with our car. It was already in the garage and Father had spent weeks working on it so it was driveable.

The kids in the water are shrieking with laughter and I can't help looking back. One of the boys has curly hair which looks blond despite being wet. What if he is Mattie?

I stand for ages watching and hoping there's something to tell me he is.

But why would Mattie be here in Driftwood Cove?

Why doesn't he live with Mama and me?

The way she's been upset when I've said his name gave me the feeling something bad happened to him but if he'd died, wouldn't we visit his grave? I never once thought to look for one but suddenly it is the most important thing I can do.

Our church only has about thirty members. Mama told me once that it used to have many more worshippers but people moved or died or even left the religion. Those who left would definitely go to Hell. That is the priest's biggest sin ever.

The graveyard is at the back, behind the church and the hall. I've been here for funerals but not of anyone I really know. I guess I don't know many people. We don't mingle a lot and I can't remember us having anyone to visit for dinner since all those years ago with Mr and Mrs Godfrey. I go to each headstone and read the name and the other information. Most of these are really old. More than fifty years ago. Only a few people have been buried here in my lifetime.

No Mattie.

And no Father. Not here.

Guilt fills my heart. If I'd stayed away from the edge of the rocks then he wouldn't have fallen into the sea. Mama explained much later that he couldn't swim yet somewhere deep down I am certain I remember him swimming in the sea. The memory isn't easy to summon. All I know for sure is sitting on the sand at a beach while Father went swimming. He made me promise never to tell Mama in case it frightened her, him being out in the waves. I was very young.

So why couldn't he save himself when he fell?

There is so much blurring together. Me screaming and being terrified to go to the spot where he fell. I ran all the way home, calling for Mama to come and she raced down the rocks, not stopping to take off her shoes as she jumped from rock to rock until reaching the edge. I begged her to come away but she was calling my father's name over and over. I think other people helped look. A boat went out. He was never found, only his fishing gear where he'd left it.

I let out a moan. So much of this had been buried as deep in my mind as these poor souls were buried in their coffins. My hands are trembling and I have goosebumps on my arms. It was my fault that he fell into the sea. I'd tried to explain to Mama what happened and she told me I must never repeat it. I could be taken away from her to a prison for bad children and then she'd have lost me twice.

What did she mean though? Maybe I misheard and she said she would lose us both, Father and then me.

There was an investigation into what happened but I wasn't allowed to say a word. Mama told the people that my father was alone on the rocks. She prayed a lot for forgiveness for the lie. The finding was that he had been either swept out to sea as an accident or had taken his own life. The priest decided that it was the latter and his funeral could not be held by the church. So there's a tiny headstone in the public cemetery with just his name.

'What are you doing out here, Mary. Come inside and we will talk.'

It is the priest and I shake my head and run out of the graveyard and don't stop until I am at the public cemetery. There, I find my father's headstone and sit beside it for a while. But he isn't here. I can't feel his presence and get to my feet and go look for any other graves with our surname. There's nothing. If I've always lived with my parents in the house on the hill yet remember having an older brother called Mattie, then where is he? I'm not going to ever give up until I find him.

Despite my new resolve, I have to be careful not to upset Mama. If something bad did happen to Mattie then it might deeply hurt her to talk about him. The only way I can work this out is by putting together everything I know… which isn't much. I thought about buying an extra lined exercise book like my ones for schoolwork but when I was at the newsagent my eyes kept going to the diaries.

Last year I'd asked Mama for one and that just led to me having to clean the hen house from top to bottom.

Today I paid for my very own diary with money I earned and saved.

I carry it home pressed against my chest as if already sharing the secrets in my heart. It comes with a little pen and a ribbon as a bookmark and is plain blue. I love it so much.

Mama is in the kitchen so I hurry into my bedroom and slide it beneath the mattress of my bed for later. Then I go and help her prepare our dinner.

'I should have done of all this today. You look so tired,' I say. I take the peeler from her hand and continue on the potatoes. 'Would you like me to finish it all?'

'Just the vegetables. I've put mutton in to cook for a few hours on a low heat. There'll be enough for a few meals so do all the vegetables and we can use what we don't eat tonight another day.'

She fills a glass with water and sips, leaning against the counter as I peel into the sink. Her face is drawn and a bit pale and I worry she is working too hard. Not only is she sewing toys, often all evening, but still has her other sewing customers.

'When I'm a teacher I'm going to buy us both a house and have enough money so that you don't need to work so hard.'

Mama makes a strange sound and I look at her. Why does she look ready to cry? Then she sips some more and puts her arm around my shoulder for a moment. 'You are a dear, wonderful person. A thoughtful and loving young woman. God blessed me with you, as unexpected as you were. As you both were.' She releases me and walks away. 'I might finish one more toy.'

I watch her go, longing to ask questions. Who is 'both'? Mattie and me? Or someone else? She's made little comments before. Speaking about Mary as if Mary was not me.

That night, after Mama has turned in to sleep, I write in my new diary. There are some pages at the very end which are for notes and that's a good place. Here I can share my thoughts for me. Just me.

Before long I've filled two whole pages with my words and lots of questions. Mattie is my older brother. So where is he? Did something bad happen to him? What is my real age? Some people have thought I'm younger than Mama says. She even told the priest I am young for my age. And she has said odd things about Mary, as if Mary is someone different to me.

When there's nothing left to write I go to today's date in the diary.

I've visited my father's grave even though I know he isn't there. I looked for Mattie's grave too, because I know he is my brother but can't find anything about him. And I bought my very own diary. Mama seems so tired and I want to look after her, the way she's always cared for me.

I put the diary back in its place and when I close my eyes, I smile. I will always treasure Mama's lovely words tonight.

'What have you done?'

Mama holds my diary in the air then throws it onto the kitchen table. It slides and turns and finally stops near the edge.

I don't know what to say. Why is she so angry?

'Do you never learn, Mary? Do you not listen to me?'

'Yes, of course I—'

'Silence!'

Her face is red and furious. We're on opposite sides of the table just after lunch. My schoolwork is on one side of the table ready for the afternoon session.

'I told you diaries are wasteful. A path for Satan. Yet you've disobeyed. I knew letting you have a job was a mistake and you have taken advantage of my kindness. What nonsense is in your head, Mary? Do you not understand the devil himself has taken your common sense and good upbringing and filled your mind with lies?'

'Where is my brother?'

Mama reels back, her hand on her heart.

'You have no brother.'

'Mattie is my brother. I remember him.'

'No. That is the work of Satan.'

How could I be so wrong? Mattie is real. I am certain.

'This diary is going into the fireplace.'

'Oh no, Mama please. I just want to be able to write my thoughts down.'

She gives me such a terrible look but then she stalks away. I stand near the diary, wanting to pick it up and hide it again. Somewhere she won't find. But then she's back and holding Dolly.

'You decide, Mary. Which one goes into the fireplace? The diary or Dolly?'

TWENTY-ONE

Now

Angie and Gramps drove to Daphne and John's house just after ten. It had taken Angie a few attempts to create a cohesive list which sounded less angry than she felt about Xavier, and more calmly rational.

Perhaps the last chapter she'd read about Mary had fired her up because since waking, Angie had been powered by quiet outrage rather than her default of minimising the impact on her of other people's actions… such as the man's behaviour. It was just as well that he wasn't going to be there or she would have delivered some choice words.

'Calm down.' Gramps put a hand on her arm as they walked up the driveway. 'These people are our friends.'

'Do I look upset?' She drew in a long, slow breath. 'I don't mean to be. They aren't the problem.'

What if she was making a fuss over nothing?

Which goes in the fireplace? The diary or Dolly?

That might well become her motivation for all future

uncomfortable moments. What an awful thing to do to your own child. To the child you'd stolen.

Angie stopped dead. If Mary was a replacement, then what had happened to the first child?

'Hello, Emmett and Angie! Please come in.' John had the front door wide open.

Filing the thought away for later, Angie caught up with Gramps and in a minute they were all in the living room.

'I'll just help Daphne with the refreshments so please sit wherever you like.'

After they sat Angie took out the notebook with the list. She turned to the back page and quickly wrote a reminder to herself to find what happened to the original Mary, careful to keep the words from Gramps's line of sight.

'Here we are!' Daphne breezed in carrying a plate while John followed with a tray. 'I made a lovely pot of tea but if either of you prefer coffee then that will only take a moment.'

'Tea is great, thanks.' Gramps spoke for them both.

While tea was poured they all chatted about the weather which was always a safe subject. Daphne looked tense although she kept a smile on her face the whole time.

'Now, help yourself to cookies. During one of our adventures away I had the opportunity to learn some new baking techniques and I think these are quite nice.'

John nodded. 'They are delicious.'

Everyone sipped and nibbled and silence fell. This couldn't be pleasant, hearing a complaint about your employee.

'I am so sorry—' Angie started.

'We feel awful—' Daphne spoke at the same time.

Both stopped and laughed.

John leaned forward. 'There's no need to apologise, Angie. We must. Daph and I took a drive up to the cottage after your phone call. It certainly isn't up to renting standard and we would never take on a listing which needed so much work.'

'We love our clients, no matter whether they buy and sell, rent, lease, or are landlords. After all the years John and I have served Rivers End, our reputation is for friendly, professional service and quality homes and investment properties. Sadly, the cottage in question will have to undergo some further improvements to be listed by us.'

'We've not spoken to Xavier yet to ask what his thinking was.' John didn't look at all happy.

'It matters to us though that you didn't have a positive experience with him,' Daphne said. 'Please, tell us everything.'

Referring to her notes, Angie spoke briefly about her encounters with Xavier. His dismissive attitude, his assumptions about her budget, and insistence he drive her to the cottage.

'That is odd, because we encourage people to follow us or meet us at a viewing. The previous complaint we had was about him being dismissive toward another young woman.'

'The thing is, John, and Daphne, that him being like that wasn't the big issue. It annoyed me and if he does it to others then potentially he's putting people off the business. But he frightened me during the drive and the inspection. And then there's the conversation I overheard.'

By the time Angie finished talking, Daphne had a hand over her mouth and John's face was red with anger. Even Gramps was cross now that he'd heard more of her feelings of being trapped and in danger.

'I don't know what to say, Angie. We are both so terribly sorry.'

'But this isn't your doing, Daphne. Xavier was determined to put me off the cottage one way or another. So what is he up to?'

John sighed deeply. 'Thank you for bringing this to us. Daphne and I intended to stay in Rivers End for a month but it might be for a bit longer while we sort out the future. I can assure you Xavier will not be a part of it.'

'Such a pity you have to change your plans,' Gramps said.

Daphne beamed, all the distress gone. 'We don't mind so much because we recently fulfilled one of our big wishes by locating someone dear to us after many years. There's really nothing so wonderful as hugging a loved one you thought you might never see again.'

Gramps didn't say another word in the few more minutes they were there. His eyes were almost blank and Angie's heart went out to him. He was so sensitive to any talk of loss and must harbour many wishes that he could hug his wife or son just one more time.

Gramps had an eye check-up in town so Angie decided to do a bit of shopping while she waited. He was expecting a couple of tests done with eye drops which meant no driving for a while and she preferred he didn't walk all the way back either.

She'd parked closer to the optometrist's which was just on the other side of the intersection from the main shopping area. Shopping done, she crossed on the same side of the real estate agency and hurried past when she heard raised voices from inside. One of them belonged to Xavier and she hoped he wouldn't make it any harder for the Joneses than he already had.

Once she packed the shopping in the car, she still had some time to burn so wandered around the outside of the jewellery shop belonging to George Campbell. This was one of her favourite places to window-shop in Rivers End and as a teenager with stars in her eyes, she had gazed at the array of glittering rings in one window, each prettier than the last, wondering if she'd ever have one on her finger after a perfect proposal by the sea.

In reality, Shane's proposal was a simple 'Let's get married, Angela.' Said while they were at a nightclub in Melbourne. She'd had to ask him to repeat what he said over the music. His engagement ring was huge. Lots of diamonds. He'd later sold it to pay off some debts.

'A simple solitaire. Or one with three diamonds.'

She started. How had Jack snuck up without her noticing?

'Are you planning on wearing one?' That was about the best she could come up with because for some stupid reason her heart had skipped a beat – a few beats – and his smile was making her brain foggy.

He held out his hands. 'My fingers won't fit any of those.' Then he pointed to the men's wedding rings. 'Some of those are nice.'

'Do you like the plain ones?'

'Nah. I think one with a diamond. Just a subtle one. And George offers the man-made ones now which I definitely prefer. Much better for the world.'

'I used to stare in the windows of this shop as a kid. Just reliving those memories. I doubt I can afford anything George makes but they are all so beautiful.'

'Except with an engagement ring like this one' – Jack pointed to an exquisite ring with one large and two small diamonds – '*you* wouldn't be paying for it. The man who adored you would. He'd select carefully to find the one ring which reflected his love for the woman he'd propose to.'

Oh, this is too much to take in.

She kind of laughed. 'If that's how you think then someone in your life is going to be happy. Unless someone already is?'

His smile disappeared as he gazed at Angie, his head slightly tilted and those eyes even darker than usual.

'Nobody has ever said yes to my proposal.'

'How many people have you asked?'

Jack moved closer so there were only inches between them.

She hadn't been so close to a man in so long... and never to a man like this one. He was an enigma. A genuine and funny and handsome enigma who smelled so fine.

'I've never proposed marriage, Angie. Not yet.'

Was it possible for a voice to caress? His was low and sent a delicious shiver down Angie's spine. She leaned forward, just a little, drawn to him.

'Please do come inside if you are shopping for rings. I keep some very special items in here.'

She blinked at the interruption from George Campbell, who'd emerged from the shop.

Jack's smile was subtle. Almost a promise to come back to this moment. Then as though nothing was out of the ordinary Jack turned to George.

'Nice to see you. I'm hoping you might look at my watch band which I seem to have broken.'

'Certainly.'

George returned inside and Jack followed, pausing at the door to look back. 'Walk on the beach later?'

'Sure. Yes. Maybe.'

Before she could say anything else which made even less sense, Angie waved and crossed the road, after looking both ways. Not that it would have made a difference as she could still only see Jack's eyes.

The bookstore was going to become a time waster for Angie. From the moment she stepped inside she was lost in admiration.

Every detail was there for a reason, from the inviting areas for both children and adults with soft rugs, comfy chairs, and side tables, through to bookstands which were low enough to be accessible to wheelchair users. The aisles were wide as well and beautifully stocked and presented.

Half a dozen customers browsed, one being assisted by a

woman in perhaps her late forties with a lovely, warm smile. There was no sign of the nice young woman from the window. Olive. She'd mentioned her mother as being Harriet. Angie couldn't remember them living here and the bookstore was previously the second real estate agency which had moved down the road. Being on the corner was perfect, with so many windows for book displays.

Angie selected a new release she knew Gramps would love. Although her budget was tight, with the housing crisis solved she would soon be back to earning an income and building her money up. There were so many she longed to buy. A couple were newer titles but also many from the past few years which she'd not been able to.

Not been permitted to.

Shane thought books a waste of space.

He didn't read anything which wasn't useful for his work... which Angie had believed was as an investment broker. Sure. He invested other people's money into his accounts.

'I'm so sorry to not say hello when you came in. May I help in any way?'

'Hello. Is it Harriet?'

'It is.'

'I had a brief conversation with Olive the other day while I was window-shopping.'

Harriet grinned. 'Let me guess. She ran outside to try and drag you in.'

'Pretty much. I'm Angie.'

'Nice to meet you. What if I pop this excellent choice of yours on the counter?' Harriet prised the book from Angie. 'Would you like a hand looking for anything else?'

'I could spend a day in here and not see everything. It's such a gorgeous shop.'

'Oh what a lovely comment! Thank you. Olive and I did

almost everything ourselves and we love this space. And the people of Rivers End and surrounds are just the best.'

'They really are.'

There was a small bookcase with a glass front and a lock.

'Those are collectors' items?'

Harriet wandered over with her. 'A mix of first editions, limited editions and very old books. When we first moved here, Olive and I purchased a lot of books from residents in the area in order to offer something other than the new ones. We did a whole lot of travelling, going to Driftwood Cove and even right up in the mountains.'

'Driftwood Cove? Do you have any of the books you purchased there?'

What if there's something leading to Mary?

'Good question, I think so.' Harriet took keys from a pocket and unlocked the glass. 'There wasn't a lot we were offered. Half a dozen books which fitted our criteria.' She began to go through the books after sliding the glass to one side. 'Well, that is odd. I was certain we had several of the same book. It was unique. Only small but from an obscure publisher and written by an anonymous author.'

All the hairs went up on Angie's arms.

'Was it called *The Loneliest Girl by the Sea*?'

'That rings a bell. And they are all gone. Let me check the system. It may be Olive has them in the safe for a book club or similar.'

Angie followed Harriet to the counter, almost holding her breath as the other woman tapped a keyboard and checked a screen.

'Well this is interesting. We had four copies of a book which indeed was titled *The Loneliest Girl by the Sea*. Quite evocative really.' She touched the screen. 'And all were purchased by one customer. Ah. Okay.'

Harriet moved from the computer.

'Is that a bit unusual? One person buying all the stock of one book?'

'It is. And I am surprised I didn't remember but it was only a few weeks after our opening and Olive did the sale. How odd I never noticed.'

'Do you know the customer? I mean, maybe they regularly buy four at a time of other books. For friends perhaps.' How on earth was Angie going to find out who bought them? This surely had to be the same person who'd been in touch with Nan.

'No. Usually just one at a time. Anyway, is there anything else you'd like today? And would you like this gift-wrapped?'

TWENTY-TWO

Angie stood outside the bookstore for a while. To a casual observer it would seem she was browsing the window displays but Angie's thoughts were racing and she only saw the reflection of herself in the glass rather than what was behind it.

Why would one person buy all the copies of a book? An old book, which was of little value to anyone other than the author.

It had to be Mary.

Or someone close to her. Wasn't a husband mentioned in one of the letters to Nan? One who knew some but not all of her past. What if he'd found out and was helping her?

She glanced at the door to the bookstore. If she explained her interest to Harriet, would there be any chance of finding out the purchaser? Clearly she knew and from the response of 'Ah. Okay' and then no reply to the question of knowing the customer had to suggest she really did know them. And wasn't sharing. It might be as simple as client confidentiality.

There had to be a way to gain Harriet's trust.

Angie went back inside.

The shop was empty now apart from Harriet who was pushing a small trolley filled with books down an aisle.

'Did you forget something, Angie?' Harriet smiled and headed her way.

'I was thinking about your collectors' books and thought it worth asking if you still buy any?'

'Absolutely. I warn you I am quite picky but I am happy to take a look if you have some for sale.'

'I'm uncertain about selling but I don't want them to go to waste. My grandmother was an author who is now out of print. She wrote historical novels drawing on the local region both in her setting and her inspiration about characters and stories.'

Harriet's eyes widened. 'Are you Opal Fairlie's grandchild? And Emmett's?'

'I sure am. I can't believe you know her.'

'Know her? I've read every book she wrote and if you have any copies you're selling I would love to see them. Oh, but I am so sorry... you lost her a few years ago?'

'Fifteen. Thank you, I miss her terribly. At the moment I'm going through her office and there are several pristine copies of each book which is why I suddenly thought your bookstore might be a perfect place for at least some of them.'

'I'll give you my card and add my private number.' Harriet hurried to the counter. 'I'm happy to come to you if you'd rather not transport them for me to assess.'

About to say it was no trouble, Angie stopped herself. If Harriet came to visit and there was the chance to show her a little of Nan's research then perhaps she could be the conduit between Mary – or whoever had purchased the books – and Angie. A chance to finish what Nan began. What Nan might have completed herself had she not passed away so suddenly.

Am I being manipulative?

Angie hesitated. And then came the image of a teenager being told to choose between the two things which meant the world to her.

'That would be lovely if you would. And I can show you Nan's workspace.'

'Really? Oh my goodness, that would be such an honour.' Harriet held out a card. 'Call me when you want and we can set up a time which suits you. Either in or out of work hours.'

'And you know my grandfather?'

'Oh, he is so lovely. He comes to browse and sometimes buy, so if the book you selected is for him, I know he will love it.'

How interesting the owner of the bookstore was so familiar with Nan's work. She hadn't been a huge bestseller. But she'd touched many a reader and her sales over the years were testament to that.

I must see if there's a contract anywhere about her books. Perhaps they can be re-released.

'Are you sure it isn't an imposition for you to visit me?'

'Not in the least. Olive and I love acquiring old books. Let me know when it suits and we'll be there.'

Making some tea for Gramps later, Angie was still second-guessing her decision making. She couldn't just use a stranger to help her find Mary. It was bordering on unethical. Unfair to both parties.

Except her intentions were good.

Helping the anonymous author find closure was surely the best outcome? In her letter to Nan she'd mentioned there were nine copies of the book unaccounted for, so if four had come to the bookstore via a seller in Driftwood Cove, it would leave only five. And if she happened to have tracked down and acquired those as well then only Nan's copy was left.

I could give it back to her.

Gramps was in the living room on the sofa, his glasses off and eyes closed. Angie hesitated in the doorway with the tray, unwilling to disturb him, but he knew she was there.

'Just resting my eyes. Drops made my vision blurry.'

'But the visit went well?' Angie set the tray down and poured them both tea.

He blinked a few times and straightened. 'No sign of any problems other than normal deterioration expected at my age. There's a new pair of glasses ordered and some prescription sunglasses.'

'That's a good idea.' She handed him a cup. 'And good there's no issues.'

'Thanks, lass. I meant to ask if you know what happened at the real estate office earlier?'

'I heard some raised voices when I took the shopping to the car but then I went window-shopping at the jewellery shop.'

And saw Jack.

In an attempt to stop the heat rising in her face, Angie quickly sipped from her cup.

'Well, I shall bring you up to date. I'd had the drops put in and had to wait a few minutes for them to work so went outside for some fresh air. I was under the tree out the front and as you know, the carpark behind the real estate agency and a few other shops is accessed by a driveway between them and the optometrist.'

'So did something happen?'

'A man burst out of the back door of the agency, slamming it behind him. Made me jump. Then John followed carrying a box. The kind you put files in. John called out to him – it was Xavier – then put the box on the bonnet of a car and told him that was all of his stuff and that his final pay would be deposited this afternoon.'

'So they did fire him.'

'Seems like it. Xavier began yelling and John calmly walked back into the building. Xavier picked up the box, and for a minute I thought he was going to throw it at the door because he looked so furious but he got in his car and went hurtling off.'

Angie let out a small sigh. 'I feel sorry for them. Daph and John. Instead of continuing their new lifestyle, it's now back to work as usual.'

'Better than having a dishonest or even dangerous employee.'

'True.' She put her cup down. 'Do you want to take the rest of the day off? We could drive into Green Bay to do some shopping?'

Gramps grunted. 'Not up to shopping. Might sound a bit strange but I'm considering spending a night at my new abode. Every time I'm there now that there's some furniture and more of my belongings I feel a bit more comfortable. A bit more ready to live there. Does that make sense?'

'Of course it does. You've done so much research into your new world and I admire you embracing this change.'

'It is huge, Angie. I love Seahaven. My dad grew up here and when I was little we'd come to visit our grandparents. Then much later it was my home – mine and Opal's. And we loved it. Raised our own beautiful family here...' He trailed off as his head dropped. 'Despite all the sad memories, all the lost ones, there is still so much love within these walls.'

'I'm a really good listener. If you ever want to talk about the past.'

He lifted his head to look at her. 'Talking won't bring people back, lass.'

'There's so many missing parts of my history. I know only a little about your parents and less about Nan's. And I always thought you were raised here. One day when you feel ready... would it be okay if I asked some questions? It feels important to keep memories alive, generation by generation.'

The sad smile on his face hurt Angie's heart and his voice was heavy. 'You deserve to know. But one day, Angie. Not today.'

That is enough for now. A start.

She got up to collect his cup and kissed his cheek.

'So are you staying in the cottage tonight? You'll need to take some of our sheets and a blanket.'

'I think I will as long as you don't mind being here alone. Unless you'd like to invite Jack over?' A sudden grin lit his face. 'Plenty of food in the pantry and fridge since you went shopping. Some nice wine as well.'

'Gramps!'

He pushed himself to his feet.

'Well, why not? He's a decent man and he likes you a lot.'

'I'm newly divorced.'

'It's been a year.'

'Plus... and this is important. I actually don't know much about him other than you two are friends and hang out. And that he was a police officer, has a part share in his godfather's restaurant and has a lovely family. '

'Yes, it isn't a lot to go on, except you have spent time with him. He's a good person. And while I can only imagine how cautious you must be about another relationship, you deserve happiness. You are a young woman with her whole future ahead and whether you choose to live it alone or with someone special is completely in your hands. It's just that you always wanted your own family. Children.'

'But how do I trust again?'

From nowhere, a sob followed her words and then tears were streaming down Angie's face. Gramps pulled her into his arms and held her tight as she grappled to control the emotions.

'You trust when you are ready. By watching how a person is. How they speak to others and whether they keep their promises. Do you feel safe with Jack?'

She nodded, stepping back and finding a tissue.

'Then that is a good start. I doubt that young man plans to move too far from Rivers End. Although Jack still has some dark moments when he misses his former life, for the most part he's happy here and is making a life.' Gramps collected another tissue and dabbed her cheeks, just as he had when she was a kid. 'I'm not saying you need to get married again. Or even love again. Your nan and I had a rare gift with our marriage and I'll never forget the years of happiness we enjoyed. But, Angie? It is more than time for Shane to stop living in your head rent-free. Hmm?'

Gramps was right. As badly burned as she'd been, Angie wasn't going to let her past marriage shape her future. Her life was already turning a corner now she had a secure place to live. In a couple of weeks she'd be teaching which was her absolute passion in life. Next week she had a meet and greet with the school principal and be able to have a proper look at the school again. No doubt there'd been many changes since her time there as a pupil.

Angie sent a text message to Jack.

> If you are free, would you like to come over for dinner tonight?

While she waited for a response, she browsed the shelves in the fridge and pantry. It wouldn't take long to whip up a quiche and salad. Or some pasta. Except Jack part-owned an Italian restaurant so was used to authentic pasta, not the store-bought kind she had, even if it was fresh, not dried. Perhaps sushi. She loved Japanese food and wasn't bad at making sushi rolls and poke bowls.

She glanced at the time. Almost five-thirty. It wasn't leaving her long to do justice to the latter so she took another look. There were fresh sweet potatoes which were perfect to toss in the oven for half an hour then break open and stuff with a yummy filling. And a Greek salad on the side.

After turning on the oven, Angie collected the ingredients,

softly singing to herself. When the phone beeped, she'd worked out that dinner could be ready by six-thirty.

> I'm so sorry, Angie. Already attending an early dinner. Please accept my apology to you and Emmett. Another time?

'Oh...' Angie's heart dropped and she flopped onto a stool. 'Why would I think he was free? Why would I think he doesn't have a date?' Saying it aloud just made it feel worse.

> Of course. Another time. Gramps is staying in his new cottage tonight so it is just me here and I don't usually eat until much later. Have a nice dinner.

She sent it and immediately regretted mentioning she was alone. It sounded desperate.

'Well, you did suggest a walk on the beach later,' she muttered.

There was no point cooking for one. Angie wasn't lonely. She had plenty to do without worrying about making nice meals for other people. Picking up the sweet potatoes, she tossed them back with the other vegetables.

TWENTY-THREE

Half an hour of brutally scrubbing the bathroom into submission cleared her head. She wasn't up to eating but there was little point in taking her feelings out on inanimate objects or vegetables.

Angie opened the door to Nan's office.

It felt different knowing she didn't have to pack anything up. No giving away or selling or disposing of even one piece of paper unless she chose to do so. She placed her palm on the cool glass in front of the shelf which held Nan's own books. There were six of each. If Harriet did want a set or two then Angie would negotiate with her. And any money which was made would be donated to a regional literacy program – they were always underfunded but so important for disadvantaged children. Angie had a dream of creating a scholarship or fund in Nan's name and maybe as her future changed for the better it would become a reality.

This was what life was about. Helping others was second nature and she'd missed it so much during her marriage. Being isolated from Gramps and Rivers End and her beloved work had taken a toll on most aspects of her life.

She collected the box from the desk and settled on her favourite chair. Her laptop was on the counter in the little kitchen area but not open yet. First she'd reread the letters and be sure of her facts and for that purpose she'd brought a notepad with her. As she read, she scribbled keywords and dates and some phrases which needed further scrutiny. It still touched her on many levels reading the poignant words of M.W.

That done, Angie gazed at the box for inspiration. It was close to seven and her stomach was conspiring against her, wanting food now. She should have cooked some pasta. Garlic and basil and tomato stirred through some gnocchi wouldn't have taken long. Her sudden need to eat was amplified by the very smells she thought about.

'Hi.'

Now she was hearing things.

But when Angie stood and looked in the direction of the delectable smells... there was Jack, holding a bag.

'Hi.'

'I knocked. At the house.'

'Okay.'

He lifted the bag. 'I was at Franco's for a quick dinner meeting about expanding into home delivery. We were so busy talking we barely ate. Fancy some gnocchi and garlic bread?'

I fancy a whole lot more than that. Good start though.

Deciding to ignore the first part of the thought, Angie gestured. 'Please come in.'

'I wasn't sure if you'd have eaten. I have forks.'

Angie's grin grew wider.

Jack headed for the counter and after putting the bag down, began taking out containers, each smelling divine.

'The garlic bread is in foil. Franco actually gave me a fresh one. The gnocchi hasn't been touched so you can eat it knowing nobody's lips came into contact.' He was smiling as he unpacked.

But if your lips had come into contact...

Angie pulled herself up. This wasn't the place or time. If ever.

'Would you prefer to sit outside? Or here?'

'Actually... can we sit under my tree?'

His eyes turned to hers. 'Your tree?'

'My tree.'

'Ah, the one not far from my tree.'

'Correct. What shall I carry?'

'Good choice, Angie. I am curious.' Jack unwrapped the garlic bread, careful not to break off any small pieces of foil. 'Would this be as good under my tree?'

'Are we back to that?' Angie couldn't help smiling. Her stomach was getting full from delicious gnocchi and the company wasn't bad. Not even close to bad. 'One way to find out.'

'A tree-off. Same meal. Same time of day. Same company. Good idea.'

Did I just invite myself to his house?

'Have some of this. I warn you there is a fair hit of garlic and it comes straight from Franco's garden.'

He held out the bread with the foil scrunched around the sides and Angie helped herself to a piece. It was flavoursome and strong enough that one would need to use mouthwash if you were going out in public later. She took a second piece.

It was almost scary how good this all felt. Her heart was doing its own thing. There was a spark of light and warmth – only a spark – but it wouldn't take much to fan it into a brilliant flame. Still, she was cautious. This was happening too fast to be real. Having some attention from someone who wasn't trying to use her was going to her head.

'What was for dinner?'

Angie tilted her head at the question.

'If I'd been free for dinner when you messaged earlier?'

She changed position to sit cross-legged and was facing Jack over the remains of their meal. 'A seven course degustation menu.'

His eyebrows lifted. 'Do tell.'

'Vegan. Mico-greens picked with tweezers beneath the full moon covering a slice of crispy polenta. Tofu cream piped into tiny tart cases. Miso eggplant skewers. And so on.'

'I love vegan meals.'

'And a choice of two desserts.'

'All of that to prepare and cook alone?'

'Every bit.' Staying serious was challenging her self-control. 'Actually, that's for another day. In order to better understand Mary, I'm keen to replicate the meals she's mentioned so far.'

Jack made a strange sound which might have been suppressed laughter or else horror. Either way, Angie was on a roll.

'So there's been sandwiches, mutton, lots of vegetables, eggs, mashed potatoes with green beans, chicken, and gravy. Plum pie with cream. What was the other thing? I remember. Cabbage stuffed with mince. Yum.'

'Let me know when you intend to serve that so I can be unavailable.'

'But there was some kind of sauce as well.'

'Ugh.'

'Scaredy-cat.'

'Yup.' He started collecting the containers. 'Want the last piece of garlic bread?'

'Go ahead. I'm pretty full and thank you for bringing dinner. I'd been thinking about making gnocchi but Franco's is much more delicious than mine would have been.'

'Once he has the home delivery part up and running you'll be able to order it from the comfort of your own kitchen.

Speaking of Mary though... have you read more of the book? I keep thinking about her.'

'One more chapter and it's powerful. A bit upsetting actually. Would you like to read it?'

Angie collected some iced tea from the house while Jack headed to Nan's office to read the chapter he'd missed. She handed him a glass after he closed the book.

'Gertrude wouldn't get my nomination for mother of the year.' His voice was flat. 'That poor kid.'

'I had such a happy childhood. Even though we moved all the time with Dad's work, my parents were loving and I had Gramps and Nan to visit. To treat a child that way seems so wrong.'

'A lot isn't sitting right with me, Angie.'

You are such a good human. I can see your compassion.

'I've been thinking about Mary version one,' she said.

'Version one?'

'The narrator recounts several strange comments by her mother over time. Referring to Mary as though she isn't there, saying that "Mary happened" instead of "you happened". The mention of a little lost girl. The times other people reference Mary's looks or age not being what they expect. And Gertrude's over-protectiveness.'

He nodded, his face thoughtful.

'And with her memories getting clearer about a big brother who Gertrude denies exists, it leaves me feeling something terribly wrong happened. Something sinister. But if Mary is Laura, then where is the original Mary?'

'What makes this so intriguing and so difficult is the length of time ago these events took place,' Jack said. 'We don't know yet if this is a factual account and—'

'I meant to tell you! Oh. Oh, I am sorry to cut you off.'

Angie's voice dropped to a whisper. Shane hated her doing that. He'd rebuke her in front of other people if she made the mistake of being too enthusiastic and interrupting.

But Jack didn't seem to have noticed and if anything, looked interested. 'Tell me what?'

Forcing herself to push the reaction into the background, Angie reached into the box, taking a moment to calm her rattled nerves. She pulled out the envelope with the letters and handed it to Jack.

'Last night I read the third letter. Third and final. Please feel free to look yourself but the gist is that the author of the book was going to meet Nan.'

His mouth dropped open a bit in surprise.

'Yes, but it never happened. Well, maybe it did but I don't think so.' Her words rushed out. 'Nan seems to have solved at least some of the puzzle and persuaded Mary to have a meeting. Mary didn't want to but then changed her mind and agreed to come. If Nan had worked out who Mary really was, if she was the little girl Laura perhaps, then there was a chance that between them they might have found Mattie as well.'

'What makes you think they didn't meet?'

'The date on Mary's letter. It was only a week before Nan died. I guess it is possible it reached Nan but we don't know when the meeting was scheduled for and her diary for that year isn't in here.' Angie gestured at the bookshelves. 'She kept meticulous handwritten records and all her other diaries are in here.' The ever-present grief was rising faster than she could manage. 'What if I can't find it? It might be in Gramps's boxes. Already at his new home. *Oh no*. What if we accidentally threw it out?'

Warm hands enclosed hers and pulled her gently toward their owner until she was on her feet. He tugged a bit more and somehow manipulated her until she was sitting on his lap, leaning on his chest.

'Breathe.'

He released her hands and encircled her with his arms. Not tightly. Just enough to give a sense of security.

'This has to be bringing a lot back from that time. So much loss in your life. Let me be your safe place to fall, Angie.'

With a sigh from her heart she relaxed against his body, resting her head on his shoulder. Her eyes closed and she did what he said. Breathed. At first it was all she focused on. And then, as her heart rate came down and her grief settled back into the box where she usually kept it, Angie noticed Jack. His body fitted hers perfectly. Powerful arms which were protecting her from the world. Muscular legs beneath her. His breath against her hair. And the scent of the man. It enveloped her and filled her senses.

Time passed. A minute. An hour. Angie was sleepy. But Jack shifted a bit.

'I promised you a walk on the beach.'

He had. He'd also told her he'd never proposed. And that nobody who proposed to her would expect her to buy her own ring.

'Feel up to it?'

'A walk?'

'Or can we read another chapter?'

Or we could stay like this.

'Another chapter.'

Getting to her feet was a bit awkward but Jack supported one of her arms until she was up and then reached for the book as though nothing out of the ordinary had occurred.

They got some more iced tea first which gave Angie a chance to compose herself. Ending up in tears yet again wasn't good for her. First Gramps was comforting her and now Jack and there was a sense of the emotion bubbling just beneath the surface, ready to burst through again when she least expected.

'Circling back to earlier,' Jack said, 'what is your theory about Mary version one?'

'Not really a theory yet. I just wonder why someone would take a child and raise her as their own rather than return her to her family. The psychology of making such a decision interests me at the same time as alarming me.'

Jack watched her closely. 'Go on.'

'So far, each chapter has a little intro which is written from an observer's view, although I think this was the author's way of dealing with a mix of scattered memories and speculation. They are a story in themselves and I'm keen to read them in one session once we finish the book. Perhaps they'll provide more clues.'

'I think they have already. She knew she was lost and a man picked her up. He said he'd find her family and mentioned a brother.'

'Oh, I'd forgotten that. Bet he never told his wife he had. Wait... so he was watching her when she was with them? Was it premeditated?' The idea of a stranger spying on an innocent family then waiting for the chance to kidnap their smallest child made Angie angry.

'Or had he seen her before so knew her family and stumbled across her that day? Except they were holidaying in Rivers End, not residents.'

Angie's mind was racing to connect the dots. 'An opportunity presented itself and he took it. Remember how the child woke up somewhere new, heard arguing and then met the woman who became her mother? Presumably Gertrude had no idea she was about to be given a child!'

After emptying his glass, Jack stood and stretched. 'Sorry, back tightens up sometimes.'

I have so many questions about your life.

Asking him outright felt intrusive. His sister and Gramps had both hinted at a serious injury in the line of his work as a detective but neither had elaborated. If Jack wanted her to know, he'd tell her.

'People can't just suddenly have a small child where none existed. But Laura might have been close enough physically to pass her off as their own. Except...'

'Except – what happened to the first child?'

'She must have died,' Angie said. 'Gertrude and Vernon hid her death. Isn't that illegal?'

'Yup. Even back then they had a legal obligation to tell authorities.' Jack rotated his torso again and then took his seat. 'Shall we read?'

The first months after her father fell into the sea were the worst. At first people visited from the church, some with food and others with sympathy. Her mother wanted neither. She'd be polite until they left then lock the door and go into her bedroom again, leaving the child to put any offerings away and barely eating for days on end. There were no more tears. Hours would pass when she would stare out of the window to the sea. Then she turned to her Bible and began to change. Not back into the warm and kind woman who vanished as surely as her husband did, but into a stern and demanding person. Rules were made, far more than the one not to be near the edge of the rocks or not to leave the property but about clothes and manners and silence. So much silence.

TWENTY-FOUR

8 March 1964

Someone has stolen all of the chickens. Even the rooster. The coop door was wide open when I went to get eggs yet it was closed last night. Even Mama knows it was closed because she was the last person to touch it. My hands were full carrying the newly empty buckets – one for water and one for food – and she'd shut and latched the door.

At first I thought it somehow blew open and they'd gone wandering. We let them out during the day to keep them healthy and reduce the pests in the vegetable beds so that's where I look.

No familiar cackling and chatter from them. For that matter, the rooster didn't wake me with his normal crowing this morning.

I am frantic. I run around the perimeter of the land looking and calling for them. These are almost pets for me. Mama refuses to have a dog or cat or a fish even. She doesn't know I've named every hen and they answer to their names. By the time I sprint back to the house to tell Mama, I'm out of breath and want to sob.

'What on earth is wrong?' Mama is in her dressing gown in the kitchen, about to crack some eggs.

That's enough to bring the tears.

Once I calm down enough to speak, she comes with me to the coop.

'I did close the door,' she says.

'Yes, I saw you. But how would they get out? It wasn't a fox because there's no sign of feathers or anything.'

Mama goes inside as if she'll find them hiding in the boxes and rummages around. 'Well. That's that.' She takes the gate from my hands and closes and latches it.

'But they won't be able to get back in if this is shut.'

'You said you'd looked all over for them, Mary. There's no sign of a fox so the logical conclusion is someone deliberately took them. Even the priest has spoken of how many families are suffering from poverty, so if they are so desperately in need that they'd steal then we have to accept it was God's will.'

'To let someone steal our hens?' Tears are running down my cheeks. 'But they gave us food. And we loved them.'

'Love? A chicken?'

She is already hiking back to the house and I follow.

'How will we manage though without the eggs, Mama?'

'We trust God.' She glances at the sky as though expecting hens to suddenly fly down from heaven. 'He has a plan for us. Have another quick look but then come and have breakfast.'

I retrace my earlier path, even sprinting to the rocks where I once found a lost hen having a lovely time trying to catch a tiny fish trapped in a rockpool. How I wish they were there. That Mama is wrong. I resolve to prop the door of the coop open after breakfast. Just in case.

My plate is on the bench when I go inside and Mama is washing up hers. I hadn't meant to take so long.

'You can eat it cold. We have three dozen eggs in the cupboard and need to make them last so can't afford to waste any.'

'But we'll get some more hens?' I never waste food. Mama made it abundantly clear when I was younger not to ever fuss about food or I would go without for a whole day. Even when she cooked the stuffed cabbage all that time ago I didn't dare reject it. But it was nice enough anyway.

'There's no money for chickens and what is the point? They might just be stolen again. It's God's plan that we don't have hens right now, in penance for our sins.'

My heart hurts. Are the hens alright? Will whoever took them feed them well and let them scavenge in a garden?

'Finish your plate then get properly dressed. We must go to the church.'

With my mouth already full I can't respond and by the time it's empty she's gone into her bedroom. I finish my meal. Every last bit of toast with eggs from my lost friends.

All the way walking to church I try to work out what I almost remembered at the chicken coop but it keeps slipping away like mercury. We're going to help decorate the hall for Easter Sunday. It is a joyous celebration of the rising of Jesus Christ and each year the women in the congregation prepare food and drinks for everyone to enjoy following the sermon. We've bought a basket of bread rolls and some flowers from a special garden bed of hydrangeas and carnations and others Mama tends to for Easter and Christmas.

My arms are tired from carrying so much and Mama looks just as weary. I'm not sure why we can't use the car more often. I've been working part-time again and Mama is selling a lot of her toys so I don't understand why she refuses to have it checked and fixed and I *really* don't understand why we can't buy a few hens because the eggs they produce pays for their upkeep.

At almost sixteen, I'm no longer willing to just accept everything I'm told.

Not now.

There are too many memories about Mattie and too many inconsistencies in my life. I just have to be careful not to ask the wrong questions or make Mama aware I am searching for answers about my past.

'What is going on?'

Mama suddenly stops. The church is in front of us and the front doors are closed, which on its own is weird as nobody is allowed in the hall unless the priest is here and when he is, the doors are kept open. But they aren't just closed.

'Is that a bar across the doors?' I ask.

People have gathered at the bottom of the steps, mostly women who are members of the congregation, all staring at the same thing. There's a sign nailed into the timber bar which is itself nailed across both doors. Nobody attempts to read it. For a few minutes, there's just a bunch of people standing in silence. I look from face to face. Everyone here apart from me is an adult and I know them all. Why does nobody read the sign?

These people are like a bunch of sheep who were herded into a small pen. Standing around. Waiting for someone to tell them what to do.

What their purpose is.

All of my life – at least the last eleven or twelve years – has revolved around two things. My parents and the church. Their church. I have never been permitted to ask serious and sincere questions about the values, the beliefs, or the teachings. No, I'm only a child, even now. I have to listen and obey. Everyone else is wiser and understands.

The reason I don't understand is because I have been like a sheep.

Putting down the basket, I go up the half-dozen steps, aware of the murmurs behind me.

'Shall I read it aloud?'

A quick glance at Mama's face almost destroys my sudden courage. Her eyes are wide with horror.

Too late.

I start reading using a loud voice.

'At the top it says the notice is by order of the shire council. For the attention of parishioners. Until further notice this church and its ancillary buildings are not to be entered or interfered with in any way. A warrant has been issued for the arrest of James Thurston, the person who has acted as the priest of this church, for a range of charges. These include theft from the church and its congregation, false identity, and unpaid fines. Until such time as these charges are addressed, the church and its property are being held under...'

I glance up. 'There's heaps of words I don't know. Maybe someone with legal knowledge will understand?'

There is complete silence. Some people are staring at their shoes. Others have tears on their cheeks. And more have blank faces. Mama's face is white but the horror is replaced by anger and I don't think at me. She meets my eyes and nods and I come down the steps and go back to her side. Her hand squeezes mine for an instant.

Then to my surprise, she clears her throat and speaks. 'Did anyone know this was going on?'

Everyone turns and her face goes from white to bright red but her chin is high. 'Well?'

There's shaking of heads and mumbling between people and then they are talking over each other and some go up to the door to read the sign for themselves.

'What will happen, Mama?'

'I expect the church will remain closed. There are few enough priests as it is since we broke away from the main church. Who would want to live all the way out here with so few faithful to tend to?' She turns for home and I grab the basket and catch up.

The months slip away and so do our routines. Without church services we leave home even less and Mama gives me the regular task of shopping at the grocery store in Driftwood Cove. About once a month she takes the car with boxes filled with toys to Rivers End, where she hands them to Mr Kane. Whenever she drops them off, he pays her for the previous ones. She saves the cash notes in a locked metal box in the storeroom, hidden behind dusty old bottles and only opens it for necessities.

Today she's dropping off toys and I have to go shopping because we don't even have enough for dinner tonight. She left before I could ask her for some money. I don't think Mama will mind if I take the amount we budget for because she opens it in front of me all the time. The problem is getting the key because it is in her bedroom. She's been gone for ages so I should just wait.

My schoolwork is done for the day plus I did an extra class. I'm ahead in my studies and taking more senior subjects which means I should be in a good position for final exams before applying for teaching college. Almost everything I make from my part-time job is saved for when I leave home but unlike Mama, my savings are kept in the safest place I can imagine. Inside a Bible. We have a few different ones and this is one Mama never picks up so I cut some pages to make a little hole. If it is a sin then I'll pay for it eventually I guess but at least nobody should look inside for money.

I'd rather go shopping now before it gets too late. Winter is just around the corner and although today is pleasant, I don't like hiking home when it's almost dark. I open Mama's bedroom door and go in.

It feels bad being in here. Mama is very private and I glance around for where the key might be but the room, like mine, has little other than her bed, a wardrobe and chest of drawers. Inside the wardrobe there's a shoebox at the very bottom and it looks old. I open the lid and almost drop the box.

There's a photograph of Mama and Father and me as a baby. I've never seen any photographs of us all together, I look only a few months old. Beneath is another. I'm a couple of years old and Father is holding me. I have my head on his shoulder.

The shoebox has a lot of stuff. Letters in envelopes. Ribbons. A velvet box. And a folded piece of paper which I open. It is a birth certificate. Mine. And more photos of me except... it can't be. The child smiling at the camera looks about four or even five years old and has short, straight hair. But mine has always been long and wavy. When Father died it was because my ribbon flew off and my hair was halfway down my back then, so how could it have grown so much in a couple of years?

From outside comes the sound of the car and my heart jumps. I can't be caught snooping. I put everything back in, close the lid, and stow the shoebox. By the time Mama has put the car away I am back in the kitchen pretending to add items to my shopping list. I want so badly to ask about the photos. And for my birth certificate because I will need it once I leave home. As I summon the courage she comes in and her eyes are red and puffy.

'Oh, Mama?'

'Don't fuss, Mary.' She pulls out a chair and sits. 'Mr Kane didn't pay for last month. He promised to pay double next time but we're going to need to be extra careful again.'

'He took the new toys though?'

'Yes. Apparently he had loaned a lot of money to the priest just before he absconded with so many people's donations.'

'How awful. Could we sell some toys at the markets instead?'

She shakes her head. 'I wish we could, but last month I agreed to only sell to Mr Kane so for now we'll tighten our belts. No more luxuries.'

I'm walking home with my arms full of shopping. Mama might want us to tighten our belts but we still need to eat. We decided I should shop as usual today and then tomorrow we will draw up a proper budget with all the money we have and our costs and plan ahead. I've been studying home economics which includes this kind of thing.

With all the fuss about Mr Kane I left home late and now it is getting dark. I didn't bring a flashlight and am hurrying but the bags are heavy. It would have been smarter to do half today and then come back tomorrow for the less urgent shopping.

Driftwood Cove is such a lovely area but apart from the beach and village, most of it is hills and of course, our house is not only at the top of one, but there are several in between. I follow the narrow road which heads toward our house but then diverts inland. Once that is gone there is a track which is bumpy and has holes and sometimes fallen branches. The car goes along it but at night it means I have to slow down.

I stop for a minute, putting all the bags down and rubbing my shoulders.

It is so quiet here other than the birds settling in the trees for the night. But no cars or people or— *whatever is that?*

A little way off the track someone is talking. A male voice, but not an adult. I can't hear the words but they sound upset. Mama would never approve of me helping. It isn't that we don't believe in charitable works and stuff but she's warned me so often to avoid being alone with boys.

It is just light enough to see the outline of someone through the trees.

'Are you okay?' I call.

'Hello? Would you help me?'

With what? I should ask. Actually I should pick up the shopping and keep going.

I leave the track and in a minute I'm confronted with a strange sight. There's a young man squatting near an upturned bicycle with his arms around one of the wheels. He looks up at me and grins.

'Thank you very much. The tyre came right off and I don't want to try and half-carry it all the way home or leave it overnight. I just don't have enough hands to do this.'

For some reason this is funny. Not his predicament but the idea of needing more hands than God gave us when situations arise which require more.

'I don't know anything about bicycles.'

'That's fine. Would you be able to hold the wheel steady while I prise it back on the rim? Just here is good. Use both hands now, and expect a bit of tugging.'

I figure sitting on the ground is best and take hold where he shows me. It only takes a minute or two and then he tells me I can let go. He checks the rim and then smiles at me. Even in the almost-dark, his face is friendly and I have a strange feeling inside which is nice and a bit like flutters in my stomach all at once.

'You have no idea how much trouble you just saved me. Thank you.'

We both get to our feet and he turns the bicycle right way up.

'I have to go.' I head back to the track and it is only when I lift the bags that I notice he's followed.

'Do you live far away?'

'Half a mile or so.'

'Let me return the favour.'

Before I can say a word, he takes two of the bags.

'Okay, thanks. But just to my gate.'

Mama would have a turn if she sees him. An outsider. A male outsider.

He talks a lot. He tells me his name. And that he lives two streets back from the cliff on the far side of the town. He's a little bit older than me. Has a lot of friends and his family are really great. But there's also a little bit of sadness and I wonder why. It was when he talked of his friends. Maybe I am reading too much into a casual conversation.

At the gate he hands me the bags and we say goodbye. I watch him leave. There's a terrible emptiness in my heart all of a sudden. How I long for friends. For family. For Mattie.

Late that night, long after Mama has gone to bed, I cut some flowers from the garden bed and carefully go down to the rocks. My brain is buzzing from meeting that boy and from the strange photos I found in Mama's room. I don't know who I am anymore. I'm sure I'm not Mary. And I don't know where the real Mary is.

Beneath a cold moon I drop carnations into the sea.

One for my father. Yellow.

One for Mary. Red.

The rest for Mattie. White.

TWENTY-FIVE

Now

Angie and Jack wandered along Rivers End beach, feet bare, the warm sea washing over their toes. Nobody else was here and the full moon lit their way.

Coming here after reading the chapter was a way to reset frazzled emotions. Jack had read it twice and Angie had added some information to her spreadsheet. Then he'd closed the book, put it into the box, and stood, his hand outstretched with a simple, 'Walk?'

How strange life was. She'd returned to Rivers End filled with fear and suspicion of the world, longing to shake off her past but expecting it to take a long time and result in a life alone. The brief upsetting experience with Xavier would have reinforced her doubts about other people had Jack not followed and shown her not everyone was untrustworthy or manipulative.

She glanced at him. He was between her and the sea, hands in his shorts' pockets, face serious. This book and mystery of Nan's was affecting him as well.

His eyes turned to her and he smiled, transforming his expression. 'I love it here.'

'The beach? Or the town?'

'Both. But I credit the beach most for helping me recover.'

'By swimming?'

'Some. Mostly by the magic of the sea washing away my anger and despair then replacing it with acceptance and hope.' He gestured to the lagoon. 'Shall we sit there?'

Angie nodded. She didn't want to interrupt him if he was in the mood to talk.

They perched on the edge of the lagoon with their legs in water so clear beneath the bright moon that Angie could see her toes. She wiggled them and a cloud of sand rose.

'I wonder how many people do exactly this?' Jack trailed his hand across the surface. 'Sit and talk in this spot?'

'Plenty. Even Gramps and I have more than once.'

'There's a certain peace in watching the river pool into this large lagoon and eventually trickle to the ocean. A once mighty river originating up in the mountains which slows as it navigates the twists and turns to lower ground and rests a while before becoming part of an even greater body.' His voice was wistful and he reached for Angie's hand for the first time since they'd left Nan's office. 'You must think I'm strange.'

'Hardly. I wonder though... metaphorically you are the river?'

A smile touched his lips.

'Where are you on the journey?'

'I'm here for now. The lagoon. It took a while to get here and now I'm struggling to find my next path.'

'I've not wanted to pry...'

'Ask me anything.'

'Do I get three questions? Like wishes?'

The little lines around Jack's eyes crinkled up. 'We can start with three.'

You'd better not disappear back into a lamp.

'Both Gramps and Ruth mentioned you were injured at work and you told me about being a detective. I guess my question is, if you feel like answering of course, what happened?'

'Neither of them filled you in?'

'No, other than to say you were badly hurt in the line of duty.'

He was playing with her fingers, his eyes on their hands. The night fell silent other than the waves. A minute or two passed. Then Jack sighed and released her hand.

'All I ever wanted was to be a detective. Specifically Homicide. I worked so hard to get there with a degree in criminology and a whole lot of extra training to ensure I was fit enough both physically and mentally. In hindsight, nothing could have prepared me for the darkness which comes with being exposed to tragedies so often. It changes a person... some cops become jaded while others care too much. I thought I was immune because I loved the job. Loved the investigation and research and the occasional action. Bringing some of the worst kinds of people to justice made all the hard work worthwhile. Until...'

'Until?'

Jack drew in a long breath. 'One night an arrest went horribly wrong. It should have been straightforward. Two detectives. One suspect. Except there was another person in the house with firearms.'

Angie's heart raced. The hair on her arms stood up.

'My partner was shot and down. I managed to get to her and drag her out of the line of fire but that meant my back was exposed. Just for a second.' In a sudden movement Jack stood up in the lagoon then strode a few feet away. The water was up to his hips and his hands rested on top of the water as he turned to stare at Angie. 'I felt nothing other than a bit of a kick against my back. Couldn't work out why my legs stopped working. Turns out a bullet hit my spine.'

'Oh my lord.'

'Another bullet grazed my head and I was out. Lost the original perp who disappeared for good. My partner was able to shoot the gunman. And she recovered fully from her wound.'

Angie pushed herself into the lagoon and waded to him. The water reached around her waist. She took his hands in hers. 'You survived. You saved her and you survived.'

'But the cost... oh, Angie. For a while the prognosis was grim. I was told I might never walk again. And that was when all the darkness of the job crashed down and for a while, I couldn't see a way forward. Couldn't get rid of my pesky sister though. Did she tell you she's a physical therapist?'

'She didn't.'

'Thanks to her I had no choice but to harness my natural stubbornness and begin the long path to healing. Months in hospital with multiple surgeries followed by a lot of physio. I'm as good as I'm going to get but while I look fit enough, I'll always have some issues.' He lifted her hands to hold them against his chest and his eyes were dark. 'Most of the time I can do normal stuff. Run, swim, lift things and move freely. There's days I struggle with pain. Down the track I may need another operation. My mobility is not assured.'

'I'm in awe of your determination, Jack. Whatever happens in the future you will deal with at the time. And those around you, those who care about you, will be there to support you however you need.'

His hands gripped hers so tightly she almost asked him to let go but she could see the anguish in his face and needed him to know she was right here for him.

'Remember when I said I'd never proposed?'

She nodded.

'When I was shot there was someone in my life. I had a ring... but she walked away.' He let out a small bitter laugh. 'I wasn't the man she loved anymore.'

Angie lifted her chin. 'Then she didn't know you. Love doesn't work that way, Jack.'

His hands released hers and moved to cup her face and he lowered his so they were only inches apart. 'I'm learning that.'

'You are?' Her voice sounded tiny in her ears. Despite standing in water her body was on fire. She'd never wanted to kiss anyone this much before. Nobody.

'I want to keep learning.'

His lips touched hers. A butterfly kiss which ended before Angie could react. Then his hands dropped and his face was further away but his expression held a question. One she had no way of answering. Not yet.

Without him touching her the fire ebbed away, replaced by a strange need to defuse the moment and make him laugh. Her hands went into the water like scoops and with a sudden grin, she raised them in his direction and splashed his T-shirt. After a split-second of shock, he returned the favour and then the game was really on.

Jack walked Angie all the way to her front door, their fingers entwined. Both were soaked to the skin after first one and then the other managed to fall over while evading splashes. It was only when an approaching flashlight alerted them to other people in the area that they stopped acting like kids.

Now it felt more like she was on her first date. Other than dripping hair and soggy clothes.

'We didn't talk much about the case.' She gave him a wink as she felt in her pocket for house keys, thankful of a button which had kept them inside during the water sports.

'Oh, you did hear me call it that. I'm not sure how Mary or whoever she really is fell through so many cracks. I have a few thoughts, such as looking for an obituary of her father or newspaper reports of his disappearance. Being lost at sea would have caused a local stir.'

'Why didn't I think of that? One of the newspaper clippings is an obituary page, but for much later so it should have got me thinking.'

'There's a lot of moving pieces.'

'I really want to find out about Mary version one.'

'Agree. But for now I think we are both overdue for hot showers and dry clothes and sleep.'

Angie unlocked the door and turned on the hallway lights before stepping back. Her mind was playing tricks on her. Old bad memories of Shane pushing her out of his way if she went into their apartment first, never enough to hurt her but with such disdain.

'Hey... you're shivering. Go in and get warm. I'm sorry I didn't realise earlier.'

He isn't Shane.

But her stomach was tight and she went inside and turned. 'Thanks for tonight. Sleuthing and talking and... stuff.'

Jack leaned against the doorframe. His hair fell across his forehead and it was all Angie could do not to reach up and brush it to one side where he usually wore it. The very ends around his neck had the cutest curl to them being wet.

Their eyes met and both smiled.

'I have to go to Melbourne in the morning for a meeting,' he said. 'There's a chance of ongoing consulting work on an upcoming mini-series.'

'Similar to the film you just did?'

'Along those lines. I'll probably stay overnight rather than do the drive twice in a day. Is it okay if I text tomorrow?' He leaned a fraction toward her.

'Yes. So, goodnight.'

He straightened. 'Goodnight, Angie. Sleep well.'

Then he disappeared into the night and she closed the door behind him.

Had she alienated him? Had her change in demeanour sent the wrong message? For a moment Angie considered calling out to him. Running down the driveway to get another kiss, another touch. In the last few hours she'd discovered so much about Jack but would she never be able to move beyond the damage from her marriage?

A long warm shower, fresh clothes, and a glass of wine put things into perspective. She and Jack were learning about each other. The attraction was mutual... this she knew in her heart. And he liked her.

I like him.

Friendship was the perfect base. It would be enough if one or the other decided not to pursue anything else.

Liar.

Rather than attempt to sleep or sit in the house contemplating her future, Angie walked to Nan's office even though it was late.

Turning on a lamp, Angie opened the box and took out the newspaper clippings. There had to be clues in the last few which she'd overlooked from her brief perusal the other day. The one from 1964 made sense now. A priest who was a thief. He'd stolen from his congregation and vanished, resulting in the closure of the church. How interesting that according to Mary, her mother had stoically accepted the loss of the house of worship which until then had ruled her life. Despite Gertrude's clear flaws as a human and especially as a mother, there was something compelling about the woman.

She backtracked to the photocopy of a page with classified adverts from 1963.

This made for interesting reading with such items for sale as a wheelbarrow of potatoes for a few shillings or an antique clock for a pound. There were a handful of jobs advertised – all in Warrnambool where the newspaper was based. And quite a few people looking for work, mostly men after manual labour. Right at the bottom was a small display ad for a local craft market with offerings such as homemade baked goods, clothes, and soft toys.

'Soft toys?' Angie grabbed her phone and used the zoom on its camera to read the fine print. It was hard to make out and she snapped some photos and sent them to her laptop. Perhaps she could clean one up enough to read the address where the market was held.

She was certain there'd been a conversation between Mary and her mother about selling in the local markets. Opening the book, Angie scanned the last chapter they'd read. Yes, there was mention of Gertrude making a recent agreement with Mr Kane about exclusivity, so presumably until then she'd sold the toys herself as well.

After locating her notebook, Angie scribbled 'Mr Kane and family – find them', 'Who ran the markets or is there a vendor list?' and 'What else was in the shoebox in the wardrobe?'

Mary had written about a locked metal box with cash savings and Mama kept the keys hidden.

Angie opened the second envelope and emptied the contents into the lid of the box. She'd forgotten about the hymn book and picked it up first. It was far older than she'd first thought and written in German. There was some writing in the front, also in German, and Angie understood one word. Gertrude. And the year of 1922. Gramps knew some of the language. There was nothing else to identify the hymn book so perhaps he'd take a look, even if only to translate the dedication.

And then there were the keys. One looked like a house key, another similar to a letterbox key, and there was a smaller one which she still thought might be for a padlock. Almost the kind from an old bicycle chain. All appeared to be of a similar vintage and any identifying markings were long gone.

'How on earth did you find your way to Nan?'

Of course the keys didn't answer so Angie took a sip of wine while she stared at them. There were missing parts of this puzzle. Keys from who-knew-where and when. A book by an anonymous author. Personal letters from the same writer… was it possible she'd mailed them to Nan and if so, why? Or had Nan come across them as part of her research?

Maybe Jack had contacts in the police force who would dust them for prints.

Although that might be going too far, she nevertheless added the thought to her notes.

She put the keys with the hymn book in the lid and moved back to the newspaper clippings. This one was dated 1966.

The newspaper was the same one as all the others. Based in Warrnambool which was the largest town in the region, the paper no longer existed. Angie had done a search in the hope she might be able to visit the offices and try to get hold of more information.

The page was titled Births, Deaths, and Marriages. As with the last, this one was hard to make out the details with some of the notifications but Angie tried to focus on one column at the time. None of the entries were for anyone called Mary or Gertrude or even Vernon. Whatever Nan kept this for was a mystery for now. The final one was a short article warning people to lock up their livestock, tools, and firewood after numerous reports of thefts.

Angie yawned and checked the time. Long after midnight. Hopefully Gramps was fast asleep and happy with his test-run. She packed everything away other than the hymn book. That, she slid into a pocket to show Gramps tomorrow. But what she really needed was more help brainstorming the puzzle.

Jack would find this new information fascinating and it was

all Angie could do not to send him a text message but she opened her phone. And there was a message from him.

> I can see your light on from my house. Tonight mattered a lot to me. Sleep well.

He'd sent it almost an hour ago and she'd not noticed when she'd taken the photos. Angie stepped outside, looking over the fence, but his house was in darkness. Her fingers touched her lips. Butterfly kisses would do for now.

'Sleep well, Jack.'

TWENTY-SIX

Gramps arrived home just after Angie finished breakfast and when she heard his car, she put the kettle back on. He carried his overnight bag straight to his bedroom then joined her with a smile as she pushed a cup of coffee across.

'Shall I make you some food?'

'Thanks for this. I've just had breakfast in the dining room and it was delicious.'

'Tell me.' She poured another for herself and sat again.

'Choice of a buffet or from a small menu. The latter is good for those not as mobile although there's staff to help.'

'So what did you have?'

'I'm a bit worried, Angie. If I eat so much every day I'll need to be rolled into the dining room.' His eyes crinkled. 'Toast and eggs and a hash brown and tomatoes. And pancakes.'

'*And* pancakes? Anything else?'

'Yes. A nice conversation with Annette and Bess and George.'

'George? Not Campbell?'

'Indeed. You wouldn't know this but a few years ago he had some heart issues and although he recovered very well, the toll caught up and, like me, he decided to move before he had to move. He's sold his house and moved in a few days ago. I asked about the jewellery shop and he said he'll keep going for as long as he can.'

Angie frowned. 'Is it a family business?'

'He is the last of the master jewellers to own the shop. Learned from his father and grandfather but sadly, George never married and there are no heirs.' Gramps's mood shifted and he sighed. 'Thing is, even had there been children, times have changed. Fewer younger people follow their parents into business. Particularly family businesses. I'd hoped your dad would join me building houses and he did work as a general labourer as a teenager for a bit of experience and savings but never took to it. Dreamed of a Fairlie & Son Builders sign on my cars, but not to be.'

'You know that Dad admired you? He used to say that if you want something done and done well, talk to you. And that in all the world there was no better person to have on your side because you were so trustworthy.'

'Me? I'm the last person to trust.' Gramps pushed himself to his feet and his cup spilled.

He stared at it and when Angie went to get paper towel to sop it up, took them from her hands and did it himself.

'I'll make a fresh one.'

'Leave it, Angie.'

His tone was sharp and her first instinct was to shut down but the pain on his face was raw. This wasn't about her. She'd accidentally hit a nerve.

So, she sat again and picked up her own cup, not drinking but holding it between her hands.

He made sure there was no wet patches left and then made himself a fresh coffee, taking his time, not saying anything. His shoulders were rigid and his earlier happiness gone. When he returned to his seat, he took a moment and then looked directly at Angie.

'Sorry about that, lass.'

'I trust you.'

'You shouldn't.'

'Why?'

Gramps shook his head and the set of the mouth was familiar. He didn't want to continue the conversation. There was a tap on the front door and he almost looked relieved at the interruption. 'Expecting anyone so early? Jack?'

'Absolutely not.'

I wish.

It was Daphne Jones, holding a huge bouquet of gorgeous flowers.

'Angie, just the person I wanted to see. I'm sorry to drop in so early but I have to open the office in a little bit and didn't want these sitting there until later.'

'Please come in. Would you like a coffee? We're just having one.'

'Goodness, I shouldn't. But nobody comes to the office this early so maybe I will. Thank you, love.'

Daphne followed Angie to the kitchen where Gramps was making coffee. No doubt he'd heard the conversation and his smile looked welcoming rather than forced.

'Now these are for you. Both of you really, but especially Angie, for being so forthright in talking to us about Xavier.' Daphne pushed the flowers into Angie's hands. 'We might not have found out about his dreadful dealings otherwise.'

The flowers were quite wet at the bottom so Angie put them stalks down into the sink at an angle. 'I'll find a big vase shortly but these are beautiful. And no thanks needed.'

'Oh, I disagree and so does John.' Daphne sat. 'And I want to thank you for mentioning this all to young Jack.'

'Jack?'

'Indeed. He dropped in and had a chat about Xavier. Horrid person scaring you like that and acting against our own code of conduct.'

What on earth had Jack told them? Angie was proud of herself for stepping up but knowing Jack had her back meant... well, a lot. She wasn't used to that.

'Anyway,' Daphne continued, 'John and I had already begun taking a good long look at the rental side of the business and there are a few anomalies. Worrying ones which indicate a few homes were being rented for the purpose of using them as short stay properties. They'd be making the original tenant a lot of money without the owner seeing a cent let alone approving it.'

'Like Airbnbs?' Gramps asked.

'Sort of. We have an awful lot of investigating to do and Jack suggested we contact someone he knows in the police force. Something to do with fraud. For now we're working very hard to put things right with the affected landlords but I do worry this might be our fault. John has been a good realtor for decades and the thought of losing his licence is distressing.'

'But isn't Xavier also licenced?'

'Yes, Angie, but we need to speak to our legal advisors to find out about liability and all of that. We'll do the right thing by our clients.'

Angie released a slow sigh of relief. Her instincts were right about Xavier. She could trust herself more than she had in the last few years... believe them like Jack had said she should.

Gramps and Daphne chatted for a few minutes about his impending move to the assisted living community. He repeated his enjoyment of the feast from breakfast and how he'd stayed last night as a test run.

'And what about Seahaven? If you're still looking for a rental property, Angie, then will it be sold?'

'No, I'm not looking now.' Angie jumped in before Gramps

could say anything about being tired of people trying to make him sell. 'I'll be living here.'

'Seahaven has to stay in the family, Daphne,' Gramps said. 'A Fairlie has to live here at all times.'

Angie and Daphne both asked 'Why?' at the same time.

The lines in his face deepened. 'Because. Just in case.' On that curious note, he got to his feet and disappeared into his bedroom.

'I think we need to go shopping.' Gramps gazed at the living room in the cottage. 'Not looking quite like a home yet.'

He'd spent an hour in his bedroom after Daphne left and when he'd emerged his spirit had lightened and he invited Angie to visit the cottage. They packed the most recent lot of boxes into her car and drove down. He didn't mention anything about the earlier strange comments and Angie wasn't about to remind him. It was clear he had more worries about leaving the house for good than she'd realised. Could it simply be he was afraid to lose his connection with the one constant in his life – Seahaven? By having Angie here, he knew it was still part of the Fairlie family.

After bringing the half-dozen boxes inside they'd stopped in the living room.

'What would make it more like your own home?'

'Not sure. Having most of my treasured possessions here now helps but there's nothing to tie the past and present together.'

Angie had some ideas. She was hardly a decorator but she knew her grandfather. Taking out her phone, she quickly took photos from a few angles then moved through the little house doing the same. This would help while they shopped, with colours and different touches to bring some homeliness.

When she finished Gramps had vanished but his voice led

her outside, where he was talking with Bess and Annette. They smiled at Angie and kept chatting. As before, Marge stood apart from the others and Angie slipped through the gate.

The little dog bounced in delight as she approached and then squatted to scratch his head. 'Hello there, James Regal.' She looked up with a smile. 'And hello, Marge.'

'Angie, isn't it?'

'Yes, it is. Such a lovely day to be out for a walk.'

'We are supposed to be going to the shops.' Marge almost glared in the direction of her friends.

'From what I heard just then, Gramps is still raving about the breakfast he had this morning.'

'The meals are excellent. Thank goodness for James Regal because he likes to walk a lot which keeps me fit.' Marge was lean and her bare arms were sinewy. She looked like she was active and wasn't about to gain weight from eating well.

'Gramps showed me around the other day. The swimming pool looks good, and the games room.'

'And there's a hairdresser. Everything here is special.' Marge still gazed at the other women and now her expression softened as a small smile touched her lips. 'I would never have moved in but the three of us lived in Bess's house for a couple of years and it was a natural progression.' She looked back at Angie. 'Not that I mind being alone.'

Angie straightened and the dog flopped against her feet. 'I like my own company most of the time.'

'Good. Relying on other people brings disappointment.'

Like Shane.

'Not all people though.'

Marge's eyebrows rose. 'All of those in my life. Family. Husband. Even someone who I'd come to trust but...' She trailed off and again, her eyes rested on her friends. 'Only those two women have stood by me no matter what.'

Bess noticed them watching and waved and the small smile

broadened, transforming Marge's face. Gramps turned to see who Bess was waving at.

'Come on, James Regal. Walkies.'

The smile was gone. And then so was Marge, almost marching in the opposite direction.

Angie puzzled over the encounter on the drive to Warrnambool. Gramps was napping, making her wonder if he'd been dancing again last night or just hadn't slept well in a new place. If he headed off early for bed tonight then she'd go up to Nan's office and return to the box which so intrigued her. Perhaps Jack would be free... she had to stop thinking about him. But her lips hadn't forgotten. Circling back to the conversation with Marge was a better use of her time while driving.

After Marge left, Bess and Annette had returned to their cottage which was only a few doors down and over the road after mentioning they needed shopping bags. They seemed unconcerned that Marge had already gone but it was the way the woman reacted to Gramps which had Angie curious.

What was it he'd said a while ago? He didn't know if she was standoffish or shy.

Marge didn't give Angie the impression of shyness but she was definitely on the reserved side and that might be from her history of being disappointed by people she cared for. Who was the person she'd come to trust who let her down? And why did it matter? Angie had enough mysteries to solve without delving into the private affairs of a woman who seemed perfectly content with her life.

Yet it was odd that Gramps was an issue of some sort for Marge.

You are overthinking this.

She'd seen it twice. The deliberate physical distance Marge set between herself and Gramps. Close enough to support the interest of both her friends but not have to be part of any conversation. According to him, he'd barely come across Marge over the years yet he knew Bess and Annette from various committees and through other connections.

Gramps muttered in his sleep and Angie glanced at him. He did look tired.

Was that why he'd been so snappy earlier before Daphne arrived? And even while she was there. The odd comment about a Fairlie needing to live at Seahaven at all times.

Because. Just in case.

Those were the vaguest words Angie recalled her normally articulate grandfather using. And the only thing which made sense was he was still uncertain about his new cottage and might want to return to his family home.

What else could it be?

She slowed as they reached the outskirts of Warrnambool. This town was much bigger than Rivers End yet retained a true country vibe. As a teen she'd sometimes caught the bus here to spend the day which usually included a long walk along the breakwater. As with everywhere along the coast, the town was growing and it took longer than expected to find parking close to the shops she wanted to visit.

Gramps woke with a start.

'We're here. What about some lunch before we take on the shops?'

He undid his seat belt. 'Best idea I've heard all day. Lead the way.'

TWENTY-SEVEN

The afternoon flew by between shopping and then helping Gramps decorate the cottage with their purchases. Cushions and a throw rug for the sofa; lamps, some lovely vases, new sheets, pillows, and a comforter set. There were more lamps for his study and bedroom and one for the hallway, and tea towels and placemats for the kitchen.

'When you put up your art and photos it will add even more comfort, Gramps.' Angie was pleased with the result and from his face, so was he. 'Once you move in we can go to that big garden centre in Green Bay and get to work on the garden.'

He put his arm around Angie's shoulder as they looked at the living room made bright and welcoming by the new additions. 'Thank you. Everything suits the cottage and me yet isn't old-fashioned. Your nan would've loved this.'

She rested her head against his shoulder. 'It's been fun.'

Gramps made a snorting sound. 'Shopping isn't fun. Do we have much left at the house to finish?'

Angie straightened. 'Not really.'

'My thinking is to stay at Seahaven tonight then move the

rest of my clothes down tomorrow. Although there will still be a few smaller trips, I'll effectively move in.'

So soon?

Her face must have given away her surprise.

'Whenever I leave it'll be hard, lass. But I can't drag things out, not when I now have an inviting home right here.'

'You do. And people who are looking forward to you living in it.'

Gramps went in search of his keys and wallet, calling over his shoulder. 'By that I hope you mean the existing residents rather than my grandchild longing for some peace and quiet.'

Angie waited for him to return. 'You *are* incredibly noisy to live with. Loud music at every hour of the night. And that drum kit...'

'Remind me where the drum kit is? I might like to entertain my new neighbours.'

The banter continued all the way home and they were both laughing as they climbed out of the car. Once in the house Angie located the clipboard with their lists and she and Gramps wandered around the house checking against their notes. Almost everything was completed. There was a little bit more sorting from some of the boxes neither was certain about but that wasn't an urgent task.

'So as far as I can see, you only need us to move a few larger items down,' Angie said. 'We might need to hire a trailer and ask for some help either end.'

'Jack will help.'

'Only light stuff.'

Stopping what he was doing, Gramps looked at Angie over the top of his glasses. 'Only light stuff?'

'We could hire someone for half a day.'

'He told you about his injury.'

She nodded.

'Don't you think he should decide what he can and can't

do?' Gramps continued. 'I'll allow that us men aren't the best at saying when they are out of their depth but in Jack's case, I doubt it applies. That young man is determined to be as fit as possible and live a long healthy life. He wants a family and knows he needs to care for his body more than ever in order to stay mobile. I assume he's filled you in on his worries about losing it in time?'

'Yes. He told me everything about the night he was shot and afterwards. Even about his girlfriend.'

'Well he's better off knowing the heart of a person, isn't he?' Gramps rested his hands on her arms, staring at her face. 'Took him ten months of knowing me, spending a couple of nights a week eating and talking, before he told me about her. And what... under two weeks with you?' He suddenly smiled. 'If you want my advice and actually, even if you don't, let the man be when it comes to his wellbeing. He's always said if he's not up to doing something. Trust him.'

'You're right. And I do trust him.'

'Do you have any idea how happy that makes me? After all you've been through these past years... when you arrived home you were so wary. Didn't want to upset anyone. Still see it a bit but I also see my best girl coming out of her shell again.'

'Aw... you haven't called me that for years.'

'Best girl? Well, you are. I'm going to check the letterbox.'

Angie smiled to herself at the use of the childhood endearment as he left. He was right on so many counts, not just about Jack. Something was changing in her. There was hope in her heart again and despite the upheaval of Gramps's moving, she felt more settled than since she'd left to get married. Was it the town? The reconnection with her grandfather? Her finger touched her lips. Yes, the nice neighbour with good manners did have some bearing on her increasing confidence. And Mary. Immersing herself in Nan's research was exactly what she'd needed.

It was easy to connect with a child and then teen who'd been deeply lonely. One who'd lost her father. And if she wasn't the first Mary, then she'd lost her real mother as well. Same as Angie.

'At least I have Gramps,' Angie whispered.

Mary only had the memories of a brother to hold on to. How different her life might have been if she'd grown up with her real family.

***

Night was falling when Angie let herself into Nan's office. She'd helped Gramps pack two more boxes to take which was about all the small items left, unless they found something later. Over dinner he'd begun yawning and as expected, excused himself for an early night.

She opened her laptop on the small table and added to the columns and rows in the spreadsheet. Nan had discovered so much more and Angie knew there had to be further notes or evidence she'd gathered because how else did she know enough to want to meet with the writer of the little book and suggest she might help find the original family? So far the diary from the year Nan died was missing. Gramps had a number of boxes to unpack at the cottage, so hopefully it was in one of them because it certainly wasn't in plain sight in the house.

A message beeped on her phone. Jack. And that made her heart speed up, which was ridiculous.

> Heading out for a quick meal with one of the producers but if you're up later, shall I call?

> Hope today went well. Enjoy dinner. I have no plans for an early night. ☺

Jack sent back a smiley face of his own and Angie put the phone down. If he called, then she could tell him what she found last night. The clues around the craft market and the keys and hymn book. What else would she find tonight?

Opening a web browser, Angie searched for Driftwood Cove. First in general, and then adding dates in the hope some old article might be floating around. She checked the dates in the spreadsheet and began in the early 1950s. Although the first chapter in the book was set in 1960, the little comments which preceded it were much earlier. Memories or embellishing what was real with an imagined past in order to create the novel… there was still so much to unravel.

Driftwood Cove was smaller than Rivers End and a few kilometres away in the direction of Warrnambool. Angie remembered the town as having a handful of shops which mostly faced the beach across a road. While the shopping area was flat, almost all the rest of the town was built on hills and cliffs. It married up with the descriptions from Mary's book.

Angie opened a map and changed it to a terrain view.

She narrowed it to a several kilometre radius. Mary had mentioned living two miles from the shops so she allowed a bit more distance – the equivalent to four kilometres – in case Mary had been guessing rather than knowing for certain. The description of the house on the hill overlooking a small area with rockpools rather than a beach might help.

But there were so many little coves and inlets and from the map it was hard to judge what had rocks rather than sand. She needed to visit the town and drive around. Better yet, walk along the coast until she found the right place. That reminded her of the other newspaper article which reported on abandoned houses. There'd been a photo taken from a distance showing the outline of the house, a wide gate, big shed, and possibly a chicken coop.

Angie slowly moved around the map, occasionally zooming in when she found something of interest and after a while thought she might have the right place. It was a bit more than two miles and there didn't appear to be an actual road leading to it, just a series of tracks worn over time. There was a small house and some other buildings and it was perched at the top of a hill. She tried for a street view but that offered nothing. Who'd even go anywhere so desolate to add to digital data?

After getting up to stretch, Angie picked up the book. *The Loneliest Girl by the Sea* was the perfect title.

The house Mary grew up in was about as lonely as Angie could imagine and she'd lived in some remote places. Dad's job sometimes had the family living a long way from cities and bigger towns but always around other people. The red dirt of the outback was familiar, as was life close to huge quarries.

It was the intense personal loneliness of the author which haunted Angie.

As a child it wouldn't have been so noticeable. She had her mother and school and church. But once a teenager, everything changed. Home schooling meant no daily interaction with people her own age. Her mother was an emotionally distant woman who refused to let Mary ask normal questions and stopped her making friends. She'd befriended the chickens, for goodness' sake.

Angie checked the time and her phone. If Jack was having dinner with people from the meeting then it could be longer than he expected. She had plenty of time to read another chapter. Discovering what happened to this beautiful soul was eating at her.

Winters were relentless. The house was never warm, not unless the child crouched near the one working fireplace or stood close to the woodstove. Neither gave off enough heat to take more than a little of the chill away. She learned not to complain. Not to question. Never to criticise even if it was only a mention of her freezing fingers. Put on more clothes. Wear socks to bed. And as many of her clothes she could add on top.

Outside was worse... or better, depending on the day. While the temperature inside rarely changed, there were days when the sun came out and the wind dropped and it was better to be busy in the garden or with the chickens.

Mama didn't seem to notice. For two full years after Father died she wore the same three outfits. Two were the same but rotated between washing – thick material formed into long dresses with an additional knitted jumper for winter. The other was for church and the necessary trips to the town for shopping. This one was a black dress of slightly lighter material reaching halfway to Mama's feet. Beneath were black stockings and then black shoes. Sensible black shoes kept only for those occasions.

The child had additional clothes for school but at home it was simply dresses made by Mama. And two cardigans. A coat for church. In the heat of summer little changed other than to open more windows and leave off any extra clothes.

Then one day, one important but terrible day, the child sat on the hill overlooking the sea and began to wonder what was happening in her life. And by wondering, she started to remember another time... before she lived here.

TWENTY-EIGHT

6 June 1966

I'm standing on the rocks where Father disappeared all those years ago. The tide is similar to that awful day – not high or splashing over the edge. Back then it was windy and that is the biggest difference but even so would a grown man be swept into the ocean under those conditions? For the first time ever I climb off the rocks into the sea. There's firm sand surrounding the whole area, a bit like an underwater beach. The water is only up to my waist and although my heart is racing and my breath comes so quick it almost hurts, I step away from the rocks with my arms outstretched for balance. The sand is the same depth for a few yards and then the colour of the water becomes much darker and I can see how deep it is ahead.

Although I've never learned to swim, I understand the sea more than Mama knows. I've spent so much time watching the tides and the patterns that I've formed an opinion.

My father didn't die.

He wasn't swept off the rocks. The tide wasn't high enough. And now I know that he could have simply stood up had he slipped into the sea. He could swim. There's been plenty of time to think about this. To remember. And there weren't any big waves like the ones which crash over the rocks when there's a storm.

There's more. When the people came to help search they found his fishing gear on the rocks. His rod and bucket of bait and spare hooks and stuff. But not his shoes and socks or his lightweight jacket which he always had with him. And I know his feet were bare because I reminded him to roll his socks in a ball and push one into each shoe so they didn't fly away with the wind and his jacket was beneath them. So if his shoes and socks and jacket were there when I ran to get Mama, how did they disappear by the time she got to the rocks?

Father left us on purpose. He chose a moment and pretended to die but waited until I was gone to take his clothing. Mama had said often enough he was burdened with guilt so I guess that was more important than being with his family.

Yesterday I turned eighteen. I expected something to happen... for me to feel different, but I don't. I haven't felt much for a long time apart from a dull ache in my heart which is replaced when I sleep by dreams of me chasing shadows. The shadows are people in my memories from before I came here. Before I was taken. I am certain Mary is not my real name and that somewhere I have a brother and parents.

Mama is impossible to talk to. She shuts down every conversation I start unless it is about the house or the Bible or the usual day-to-day stuff.

Late last year I passed my exams and did so well that I was offered something called a Commonwealth Scholarship. It means I can apply to attend a university instead of teaching college and covers lots of the costs. I got really high marks in Mathematics and Science subjects so can use the scholarship for eligible degrees in those fields. For the shortest time a whole new world opened up in my mind. A future of studying followed by a number of career options. I was so excited and couldn't wait to show the letter to Mama after I collected it from the post office inside the general grocery store.

She'd read it in silence, her face stern, and then she handed it back. 'Girls don't do mathematics or science and nor does anyone from our religion. Science is against God.'

'Mama, not all science. Think of electricity and medicine and all the good it can do.'

'You heard me. And while you live here and are under age you follow my rules.'

I stood there holding the letter while she turned her back and began preparing dinner. It was the moment I finally understood.

I am different.

From her – who is not my real mother. And from my father who cannot be my real father. It isn't in my heart to be so hurtful about other people's dreams or so blinkered to the reality of the wonderful, clever world we live in. Instead of arguing or running away to cry, I folded the letter and took it to my room, hiding it inside the Bible with the money I'd saved. I decided to be patient and wait.

And I have.

Months of keeping my thoughts to myself. My plans hidden. My money even more carefully protected because in the past if Mama complained of us being a bit short for groceries or for her to buy more fabric then I'd immediately delve into my savings. That all stopped. I'd decided I'd rather be hungry than not have a way out when I am ready to go.

The time is almost here.

My friend gave me a present yesterday. He knows that Mama doesn't take to strangers and my birthdays have always been just for family. We've got to know each other from taking walks and talking a lot over the last few months. He even taught me to ride his bicycle which is so much fun.

He gave me a watch.

I've never had one and I almost cried which confused and concerned my friend. He put it on my wrist and I promised I would keep it forever although he said watches don't always last. While we were walking I wore it, continually holding my arm up to admire it, but when I went home I took it off. Mama could never know. Not only would she say the watch was jewellery which is vanity but then she'd be furious because a boy gave it to me.

A young man, really. He's training to be an accountant and will work for his uncle's firm once he's qualified.

Mama is in a bad mood today. The weather is especially cold and rain is beginning to fall. I hear her banging pots in the kitchen so go to help. It is only just after lunch so she can't possibly want to prepare dinner. When she sees me she scowls.

'What's wrong, Mama?'

'The saucepans won't sit properly on the shelf. And the firewood keeps falling onto the floor so I have to clean it again. I am sick of cleaning!'

I take the pot and put it away then look at her properly. Her face is paler than usual so I touch her hands. 'You are freezing. Come and sit by the fireplace and I'll get it burning better. Then I'll make some tea to warm us.'

She shakes her head. 'I have toys to sew.'

'You have a stockpile of toys and the next market isn't for three weeks. Just take a few hours to rest for once.'

Mr Kane never paid for the toys he'd taken the day that she came home crying. Nor for the previous months. Soon we heard that his family had left Rivers End, that they were involved in the mess the priest had made. Mama waited a while but when she couldn't contact him, she prayed about breaking the exclusivity agreement with him. If God answered I never knew but one day we packed the car and took lots of toys to a local craft market and they all sold. But in the middle of winter nobody wants to go to markets.

I fix the fire, prodding it until the firewood which was barely smouldering begins to fall apart and little flames start to dance around the embers. Once I add a few small pieces the fire catches properly and warmth starts to take the edge off the chill in the room.

Mama finally comes and sits on the chair closest to the fireplace and I wrap a blanket over her legs. Her colour doesn't look right and even her lips have a grey tone to them.

'I'll bring a cup of tea. Sit there please.'

'Bossy now you're all grown up?'

But her voice is soft and she even smiles.

When I bring her cup in a few minutes later she is dozing. I've never seen her sleeping in the day and try to sneak out but her eyes open and she straightens.

'Thank you, child. For everything.'

That is kind of weird. She must be exhausted.

'Give me a few minutes and I'll fetch more wood for the night.'

'Only from the usual place.'

She takes one sip and puts the cup down before closing her eyes again.

It is freezing outside and the rain is more like sleet. People say it never snows here but today might prove them all wrong. I've donned my father's old oilskin coat which is too big but covers me from the worst of the weather and wear a pair of rubber boots which need replacing.

I run to the woodshed which is more like a lean-to beside the shed where we keep the car. We get a delivery once a year which costs a lot but then gets us through each winter, but it hasn't arrived yet.

There's hardly anything left. I climb in as far as I can but there's only about an armful of wood remaining. I grab it all and take it to the house, leaving it at the back door. I want to cry. How am I going to keep Mama warm if she is really unwell? Or cook?

I remember a shed near the furthest boundary fence. It is completely out of sight of the house and I've never stepped foot inside. Father and Mama terrified me when I was little, saying that it was once a wood shed but became filled with evil spirits and must never be visited, not even the outside.

Any evil spirits will need to fight me for the firewood if there's even one piece in there. Mama is freezing.

But as I approach the area I hesitate. The trees are really tall and dense and I can't even see the building. The rain is like a heavy shroud of mist. I shake myself. There is nothing here which isn't natural. I don't really believe in religion anymore so shake off the feeling of dread.

Pulling the coat tighter, I find a path between trees and the hut comes into view. In here, where the canopy above is so thick, there's no rain and hardly any wind. Just an eerie darkness.

The timber door takes a lot of pushing to open but at last it surrenders to my persistence. There's plenty of firewood. I fill my arms but even as I do, a shiver runs down my spine.

I carry this to the house and leave it next to my other armful before collecting a flashlight. From the garage I get the old wheelbarrow. I'm too puffed and cold to keep carrying only a few pieces at a time. The wheelbarrow just fits between the trees and I leave it outside the door of the hut. If I'm quick loading it then only the top layer will get a bit wet going back to the house.

After carrying a few armfuls out I take more of a look at the hut. The flashlight reveals cobwebs all around the ceiling and walls. It is about twice the size of my bedroom in here and half the space contains firewood, packed liked my father used to do. The rest is empty other than for the last thing I'd expected to see. An old pram.

The shiver travels down my spine as I turn the light onto it.

A thick layer of dust covers everything but it is clear there is a baby blanket inside, folded into a neat square. And across the top of the pram hangs a row of elastic with wooden toys. The elastic has sagged with time making the toys slip into the middle and that detail is the one which is too much to deal with. I back away and hurry through the door, almost tripping over the wheelbarrow. It isn't full but I don't think I can go back for more.

There's something so wrong here. I walk right around the hut and there, between two trees, is a cross in the ground.

My legs are shaking and there's a lump in my throat as I go closer.

Stones cover a small rectangle area in front of the cross, laid in a pattern of sizes and shapes as though someone made an effort.

The cross is hardwood timber. A simple piece hammered into the ground and another nailed to the first. And on that piece a word is carved deeply into the wood.

Mary.

I sit on the ground beside the grave of a little girl lost. Just like me. Except I am alive, living *her* life. I don't cry. Just gently stroke the stones and keep saying sorry over and over.

After a while I realise I have nothing to be sorry for and say I will come back to talk to Mary soon. Leaving the wheelbarrow and the firewood I run to the house and inside, strip off the coat and boots.

Mama is staring at the fire and when she looks at me, her eyes widen.

'Your hair is soaked through, Mary. Come and sit by the fire.'

'I'm not Mary.'

Her hand goes over her mouth as I continue.

'I was at the hut. With all the firewood and the pram. Right near Mary's grave. The *real* Mary.'

'No, no, you don't know what you're saying.' She pushes herself to her feet, the blanket falling away. 'There's an explanation.'

'How did she die? And who are my real parents? Where is Mattie?'

Mama looks confused and she sways on her feet but I don't care. I understand the truth now. My life was stolen from me. Just like I was stolen from my real family.

'How could you? How could you and Father do such a thing?'

'What thing? We gave you a good life. A Godly life. A purpose.'

I can barely speak because the anger inside is choking me.

She reaches for me, holding my wrists with her hands. 'When Vernon came home with you I was shocked. But one look at your sad little face and him telling me how your own family didn't care that you'd wandered off... it was like God himself brought you here. You came from very far away.'

'Where, Mama? Where is my family?'

'Here. You are Mary in other ways.'

'I am not Mary!' I pull my arms away and raise my voice. 'What is my real name?'

Her face is contorted.

'Tell me or I will go and talk to a policeman.'

'No. No, you can't. They won't understand. Not outsiders.

We took care of things our way. God's way. It has to be kept secret.'

Mama drops onto the seat and her hands both go to her heart. I can't tell if this is all an act to get sympathy. 'If you tell... they'll put you in jail. For pretending to be Mary.'

'I did nothing wrong.'

She's struggling to breathe and I finally notice her lips are distinctly blue. She's having a heart attack.

'Sit back and I'll get some help.'

'Stay... Mary.'

Her eyes show her fear and despite my anger I drop to the ground beside her and let her grip my hands.

'Tell nobody. Take the... money. Birth certificate. Be Mary.'

'Mama, you'll be fine. I'm going to get a doctor.'

'I love you. Mary. Both my girls.'

With a sudden jerk she releases my hands and slumps back. A long moan leaves her mouth and her body shudders. Her eyes stare at me. But Mama is dead.

TWENTY-NINE

Now

The book was back in the box and Angie was on the floor, sobbing so hard she didn't hear the phone ringing until just before it stopped.

She lifted her head from her hands to listen and when it began ringing again, saw Jack's name and answered without being able to speak.

'Angie?'

A quick breath.

'Yes.'

'Are you okay?'

'Yes.' Angie sniffed and put the phone on speaker to free her hands for tissues.

'It doesn't sound that way.'

'Just a sec.' She muted the phone and blew her nose a few times. 'I'm back. Sorry.'

'Who has upset you?'

'Mary. Her mother. And little Mary.'

'I gather you've read some more of the book?' His voice was

soft. 'I'm back at my hotel room and I'm a good listener. Tell me about it.'

Angie moved to her chair, drying her face. 'Just hadn't expected what happened. I can't really explain.'

'Are you up to reading? To me?'

That made her smile. Until now he'd been the reader.

'How long have you got?'

'I'm planning to check out at about seven tomorrow morning...' he chuckled. 'Let me get a glass of water and then let's start.'

It took Angie longer than she wanted thanks to stopping twice to wipe away more tears and blink to stop the blurriness. Each time Jack made soothing sounds which only made her wish he was here rather than several hours' drive away. Him reading the chapter might still have made her cry but it wouldn't have slowed the process. When she finally reached the last few words, she forced them out then grabbed yet another handful of tissues.

'That poor kid.' Jack's voice was strained. 'Finding out on her own about Mary but not the whole story. And now her mother's died in front of her.'

'Not her real mother.'

'At least she knows it is true. All her memories and suspicions were right. And now we have an unexplained death on our hands.'

Angie straightened. 'Gertrude's?'

'Mary. The first Mary. I'm not up on the laws back in the late 1940s or early 1950s when the child must have died, but these days home burials have to be approved by the relevant authority and are not at all common. It is unlikely she'd have been cremated and her ashes buried.'

'Because of her parents' religious beliefs?'

'Possibly. Cremation in a small country town was probably not an option back then either.'

'You think Mary died at home and was buried without anyone knowing?' Angie could visualise the tiny grave with its stone covering. 'We need to tell authorities. Because if someone already did, if our Mary did, then wouldn't Nan have added more information about that development?'

The line was quiet for a moment and Angie took the opportunity to flick on the kettle.

'I feel that if the body of a young child was found in this situation there would have been considerable press coverage. Unless there was a criminal case involved which somehow stayed quiet but they never do. Not for long.'

'Nan would have alerted the police. Well, I think she would have.'

Unless there was a reason she didn't.

'Jack, this is just confusing me further. I need to work out the timeline of Nan's investigation because it feels like there's important facts missing. She was going to meet with the book's author so what if she didn't say anything to the police because she wanted to speak face to face first? To find out for herself if the grave was reported to authorities?'

'Now you sound upset again. Angie, this was decades ago. Lifetimes ago. It needs investigating but it isn't going to change the course of history, and possibly your nan knew that. Remember that as far as we know she didn't have the identity of the author. And she likely had no facts about where little Mary is buried. Not an address or knowledge of what happened. Just an anonymously penned book and a handful of possibly unconnected clues.'

'So what do we do?'

The kettle finished boiling but Angie no longer wanted to make tea. A deep restlessness had her on her feet, slowly walking back and forth in the small space.

'Would you like to take a drive to Driftwood Cove tomorrow?' Jack asked.

'Yes. Actually, I'd like that a lot. I've been looking at maps and have narrowed down the possible location of the house on the hill.'

The laughter on the other end of the phone was infectious and Angie's heart lightened a little.

'Of course you have. Next you'll be telling me you've narrowed down who Mary might be... the second one.'

'For that I need to find Nan's diary for that year. If I'm lucky.' She turned off the lamp and stepped outside. 'How was your meeting? I can't believe I didn't ask that first.'

'Too busy breaking your heart over something which happened last century, to people you don't know. Angie, you have no idea how much I admire your compassion.'

In the act of locking the door, Angie stopped and leaned her forehead against the timber. Shane used to laugh at what he called her sentimental breakdowns. Say she was weak and pathetic.

'The meeting went pretty well. The new show is a Melbourne-set major crimes series with a female detective as the lead. I really love the concept and the people behind it have not only an eye for detail but a desire to be a bit more realistic than some television tends to be.'

As Angie wandered back to the house they talked about his day and that was calming. Everything about him was calming... other than his kiss.

'Still there?' he asked.

'Just outside the house. I don't want to disturb Gramps because this is his last night here.'

'So soon?'

'I know. But he feels he's ready.'

'Are you?'

'Quite honestly, I don't know how I feel. I'm so proud of him for approaching this big change in his life with such dignity and calmness. The house won't be the same without him living in it.'

'New era for Seahaven.'

Angie gazed at the house. It was a new era for the family home and for her.

'What time shall we go to Driftwood Cove?'

'Can I let you know once you are home? I don't know when Gramps is leaving and he might need a hand,' Angie said.

'Text me whenever you like. So, goodnight?'

'Goodnight, Jack.'

Still restless, Angie picked a bunch of flowers from around the garden then walked to the beach. Although it was after midnight, this time she felt completely safe. It hadn't taken long for the sense of peace and security to creep back in.

She wandered along the river to the lagoon, smiling at the memory of the silly game with Jack. Splashing each other like kids.

He was unlike any man she'd ever met but after what she'd gone through with Shane the sensible thing was to safeguard herself. Her heart. And she needed to do that soon because every time they spoke, every minute they spent together, she was getting closer to Jack. It felt natural. As if they fitted. As if they were supposed to meet. The trouble was this was happening all too soon.

If not now, then when?

Angie sighed and headed for the jetty. Her life was less uncertain, thanks to Gramps, but she had a big year ahead with the new job and addressing some underlying issues around her self-confidence and fears from the past few years. The way her mind had gone back to how cruel Shane was when Jack offered a compliment proved she needed help. While she couldn't wait to be teaching again, the rest of it was daunting.

About to step onto the jetty, she realised someone was standing at the far end.

She turned back. As safe as the town was, this was the dead of night on an isolated beach. Strangers visited here all the time. And it wasn't as though Rivers End had no crime.

Instead, she walked along the beach. The tide was low and the water pleasant as it ran across her feet. As always the steady beat of waves and scent of the sea relaxed her mind and body. She could sleep now. First though, she wanted to set the flowers free. Under an almost-full moon it was clear that whoever had been on the jetty was gone, so Angie trudged back.

Tonight these flowers were for two little girls who never met but shared the same life.

One was lost far too young.

The other paid a terrible price for being in the wrong place at the wrong time.

Angie squatted on the end of the jetty and dropped the flowers in one by one. She'd never met either girl but somehow they'd always remain in her heart. Perhaps it was the connection to Nan which made it so poignant.

The flowers drifted away, then some were washed back by a low wave.

And with them, other flowers. Carnations.

But these are same ones Mary used to take to the rock pools!

Angie climbed to her feet and took another look. Same flowers. Yellow, red, and white. Lots of white ones.

In an instant she was running off the jetty, eyes scanning the exit points. No movement around the stone steps. It was impossible to see if anyone was in the tunnel beneath the cliff so she headed that way.

Her heart pounded as she sprinted across the sand.

Surely only one person would leave flowers in the water the exact same species and colour as Mary did?

She slowed along the path beside the river where the light was dim.

On the other side all was still.

No traffic. No pedestrians.

And no sign of a woman who was once the loneliest girl by the sea.

The person couldn't be that far away, not unless they'd come by car and Angie didn't recall seeing any parked when she'd arrived... unless it was in the carpark at the top of the stone steps. Even so, she'd only spent a few minutes wandering the beach before turning around. She must have missed them by only a moment or two.

After a quick check that no cars were around, Angie stepped into the middle of the road and looked both ways, trying to see as far as possible for anyone walking. That was fruitless so she crossed over. Whichever way she chose would be hit and miss but a main road made some sense. If it was Mary then she'd be in her late seventies. Gramps was a bit older than that and still sprightly and fit enough to walk fair distances so if she was the same then she might well be still on her way home.

Angie sped up to a jog, reaching the shopping area and continuing past Rivers End Inn. The majority of homes were wrapped around the town centre and she briefly stopped to check down a street. Nobody. She must have been a bit too late to find them.

Then she saw a figure ahead.

The distance didn't allow her to identify the person who was walking at a fair pace.

That galvanised Angie and she broke into a run. Once she crossed the next road she'd call out to the person... to say what?

She had the presence of mind to check behind and abruptly stop on the kerb as a taxi pulled around the corner, before taking off again when it was safe.

But where was the person? They'd been perhaps a hundred metres from this corner and now they were gone.

'Mary! Mary, you know my grandmother. Opal Fairlie.'

Her voice rang out in the night air but there was no answer.

She was outside the assisted living community.

Angie ran all the way past the sprawling property but there were no houses on the other side. The closest was too far for anyone of any age to have reached in those few seconds.

Panting, she turned to walk home.

If only she'd checked the jetty earlier.

If only she'd run a little faster.

She gazed at the wide glass doors of the assisted living community. Was it possible Mary was a resident?

Could the author of the book be living right under my nose?

THIRTY

Angie barely slept, jerking awake several times from dreams of chasing a figure down a dark alley and just when she almost caught up, she would find herself in a field of flowers. When the sun rose she showered and dressed in shorts and halter-neck top then made fresh coffee. Not ready for real life to begin or to disturb Gramps before he rose, she took her cup outside, intending to sit on the bench out the front.

Gramps was already there.

He was wrapped in his checked dressing gown with slippers on his feet and was staring into the distance. She retreated to the house and made a second coffee then approached from an angle which would give him time to notice her and collect himself. If he then preferred to be alone, he'd say so.

But his face brightened when he saw her. 'Early start for you as well?'

'Didn't sleep all that well for some reason.' Angie offered the cup. 'Thought you might like a coffee.'

He took it with a nod. 'Thank you. I thought I heard you come in late.'

'Oh, sorry. I just went for a long walk and lost track of time.'

'Are you planning on sitting down?'

'I won't disturb you?'

'Never.' He patted her usual spot. 'I've been thinking about your nan. My Opal.'

Joining him on the bench, Angie said nothing, taking a sip of coffee.

'I was thinking specifically about this bench. It belongs here. In this garden. The memories I have of her are in my heart and all I'd ask is that you let me come and visit this spot now and then.'

A lump formed in Angie's throat and tears stung the back of her eyes. She'd thought she was cried out but this was a whole new level of emotion. Personal.

'You're not about to cry, lass? Is it the idea of finding me out here some mornings like you did today and not knowing what to do with a strange old man?' His lips smiled but his voice was heavy. 'Saw you trying not to be seen.'

'Coffee. You didn't have one. And Seahaven is always your home, Gramps. All you are doing is living somewhere else. I truly don't mind you taking the bench but I understand that it being in this spot is important.' She reached for his spare hand and squeezed. 'You will think I'm imagining things but a little while ago I was certain I heard her speak to me here.'

'Sounds right. She speaks to me. Helps me puzzle stuff out. Told me it was alright to leave Seahaven. Maybe I can't risk moving the bench in case that disappears.'

'Well, you are still a talented carpenter and we've already made the decision to leave your tools here, so why not make a new bench for the cottage?'

'I like your thinking. Actually, I really like that idea and it gives me an excuse to visit to make the copy.'

'Not that you need one.'

'Maybe not right now but later... when you and Jack have tied the knot and have children for me to spoil.'

'Grandfather!'

He threw his head back and laughed but Angie didn't know where to look. It was like he'd met Jack and decided the man was perfect for his granddaughter.

'You do still want children?'

'Well yes, of course. You know I love them. Shane was never going to be a decent father and he was against the whole idea. A good thing, in hindsight.'

Being connected to him by children would have created even more problems and how hard for kids growing up with their father in prison. And once he got out, how could she have prevented him wanting access? She shivered.

'Cold?'

'No. Just thinking about, well, Shane.'

'Best to focus on the good in your life. Hard times pass. Mostly.' He gazed into his cup. 'Never worked out why terrible things happen to good people but what I do know is we humans have an amazing capacity to keep going and even live a good and happy life.'

'Gramps?'

'Reckon I'd like another coffee, lass. And I'm cooking breakfast for us.'

It was late morning when Gramps hugged Angie for the third time, climbed into his car, and slowly drove away, his arm shooting out the window to wave at the last moment. She couldn't help a few tears. It didn't matter than he was moving only a few minutes away and they'd see each other most days. But now it was real.

Life was changing again.

She closed the front door and carried the remaining boxes in the hallway into Gramps's bedroom. He'd said to use it however she pleased and her initial thoughts were to transform it into a reading room. She'd use his old study for her work and probably bring a lot of Nan's precious things down to it as well. She might buy a new bookcase – something elegant and narrow – to showcase her grandmother's remaining books.

That reminded her, she'd not spoken to Harriet about coming here.

Before she forgot again, Angie found the business card she'd been given and made a phone call. Harriet was happy to visit after work today and they arranged a firm time and address details.

No sooner had she finished the call than Jack messaged.

> I saw Emmett head off. Shall I whisk you to Driftwood Cove for lunch and exploration to take your mind off him going?

> Yes please. Ten minutes?

> Meet you at the bottom of your driveway in ten.

Angie quickly changed into her favourite shorts which had lots of pockets then threw a light blouse over her top and tied it at the waist. At the last minute she swapped her sandals for sneakers in case they ended up walking a lot, then tossed a sunhat, sunscreen, keys, phone and wallet into an oversized bag.

She got to the gate as Jack pulled up. He had the top down on the car and wore black sunglasses, black shorts, and a white shirt open a couple of buttons. Angie tried not to stare as she climbed in. He really could be an actor or model or just about anything he wanted with those smouldering good looks and sharp mind.

But he's here with me and seems to like that.

'Hi there,' he said. He smiled at Angie and didn't seem in any rush to get going.

'Hi, yourself. When did you get back?'

'Couple of hours ago but didn't wish to intrude.'

'Gramps wouldn't have minded.'

Jack pulled down the sunglasses a bit and looked over them. 'Gramps wouldn't?'

'I guess I'd have tolerated a visit.'

Angie pulled her own sunglasses from the top of her head and looked straight ahead, trying hard not to laugh.

'Maybe you should ride in the back seat.'

She glanced behind. There was barely room for a child let alone a woman.

'Or I could get my car and follow you.'

Warm fingers suddenly touched her chin... held and turned it, more accurately. Jack was closer and he'd removed his sunglasses. Angie's pulse raced and her skin was on fire where he touched it.

'You could. But then you wouldn't experience the wind in your hair and the sheer joy of my company.'

'Hmm. Let me think. Fine, I'll stay. But in the front seat.'

'You drive a hard bargain.'

'So, shouldn't you start driving? You did promise me lunch.'

His lips quivered.

The moment stretched then he released her chin, touched her cheek ever so gently, and settled back in his seat as though nothing had happened.

Thank goodness he didn't speak for a while as she had no hope of getting a coherent answer out. She wanted to touch her chin and her cheek. To ask him to pull over and kiss her. She was willing to admit to herself how deeply she was attracted to Jack. Physically, mentally, emotionally. It wasn't some passing fancy. A crush. This was serious.

Once they were outside the town limits, Jack accelerated and Angie's hands itched to rise into the air and catch the breeze. Or pull her hair out of its ponytail but all of those curls might be a bit too much being buffeted all over the place. She peeped over the side of the door, fascinated by the ground rushing past.

'Have you never been in a convertible?'

Feeling a bit silly, Angie sat back in her seat. 'Never.'

The car slowed, then pulled over on a wide shoulder.

'What's wrong?'

He grinned and climbed out. 'Have a drive.'

'Me? Drive... this? But it's expensive.'

That made him laugh and he held out a hand. 'Come on. You won't break it.'

He was serious. Angie joined him and he waited until she was buckled in before closing the door and leaning on it.

'Indicators are on the left. Adjust your seat however you want using the controls on the side. Here.' He reached to show her and moved her seat back and forward. 'Get comfortable.'

Once he was in the passenger seat, Angie checked over her shoulder and gently touched the accelerator. Not much happened.

'I can't hear a motor so it is kind of weird.'

It took a moment but once she had the car on the road everything fell into place. The car was responsive and had more on its dashboard than she'd ever seen but nothing was overly distracting. She watched her speed like a hawk, well aware how easy it would be to lose track of how fast the car was going on this open road.

They turned onto the road to Driftwood Cove and Angie glanced at Jack. He looked relaxed and unconcerned at being the passenger in his own car. Another glaring difference from Shane, who insisted on driving everywhere, unless he'd drunk too much.

'Are you enjoying driving?'

'Loving it.'

'Better driving it than being run over by it?'

'Will a time come when you don't remind me of my poor road-crossing skills?'

'Definitely. Maybe when we're in our nineties we won't remember fine details like that.'

Angie's heart did a small flip. Or was it a skip of delight? He sounded like he meant they'd be together then. Rather than spoil the thought by asking for clarification, she focused on the road, slowing as they approached the town.

It had barely changed since her last visit which was years ago, other than a lot of new houses on the hills around the bay. She found a parking spot alongside the park which separated the beach from the road and even worked out which button to press to turn off the motor.

'No key?'

'There is one but it doesn't start the car. Oh, and another for unlocking the charger at home,' he said. 'Shall we get some food and eat over there?' He gestured to a picnic table which was vacant. 'I fancy chips and a cola.'

'Gramps and I had this on the jetty the other night,' Angie said. She helped herself to one of the few remaining chips on the white paper open between them. 'He was the one who got me onto this combination and I hadn't had it in years until then.'

'Making up for it with two in a short time.'

'Simple and simply delicious in an unhealthy yet compelling way.'

Jack grinned. 'Full disclosure? I'd never done anything like this – eating chips by a beach and drinking anything during the day which wasn't water or a protein shake – before Emmett insisted I give it a try. He has a lot to answer for.'

'So you were a health junkie?'

'Never say junkie to a cop, Angie. Not even a retired one.' His eyes were amused. 'But I did take care of my body, or at least, what I thought was good for it. Turns out that sometimes it is better to eat what you crave. Better to do what you crave. Good for the soul.'

Unsure if he was still talking about food, Angie reached for the last chip.

So did Jack.

His fingers got there first and he lifted the chip triumphantly and then directed it toward Angie's lips. She opened her mouth and let him feed her. Their eyes were locked on each other and as she bit into the salty, crunchy potato, the laughter lines around his mouth deepened. This was ridiculous. She was falling in love over a chip. More likely, falling in lust with this gorgeous man.

'Angie?'

She swallowed and tilted her head a little.

'Shall we go and find this house?'

I would prefer you kiss me. Even out here where anyone might see.

'Thank you for lunch. For the... chips.'

His smile deepened.

'We should do this again. More... chips.'

Before her face could turn bright red, Angie did her best to casually get to her feet and collect the rubbish.

With Jack behind the wheel again, Angie became navigator, using her phone with several maps she'd saved. They took a road out of the town up the hill on the side furthest from Rivers End. It became quite steep with several sharp curves but at the top it evened out and they were on a more open area.

'Not many houses here,' Jack said. 'Did you see the size of some of them facing the water?'

'Massive.'

'Up here, not so much. Do you feel this is the right direction?'

'I think so. If you go another kilometre there looks like a road on the left.'

The road turned out to be barely a track and Jack parked the car on a patch of dirt near the corner. As he raised the roof, Angie gazed around. There were some larger properties along the first road, mostly acreages with livestock or horses. If this track was the one in the book, it should lead them to thicker bushland but where she stood was relatively treeless.

'Do you want your bag?'

'Oh, no that's okay. I've put my keys and wallet into my pockets. Sunhat on head. Shouldn't you have a hat?'

After reaching behind the front seat, Jack held up a daggy old fishing hat.

'Oh my goodness. Is that one of Gramps's?'

'It is.'

He locked the car then put on the hat which was more grey than its original white. It looked ridiculous and when he added his sunglasses and struck a pose Angie burst into laughter.

'You do realise I might make you walk home.' His air of offence was as fake as the pose.

Still laughing, Angie went around the car and adjusted the hat. 'A bus will come along at some point. Or I'll phone a taxi.'

'They have taxis?'

'Of course. I saw one in Rivers End last night.'

'After we talked?'

'Ah. There's some new information.'

They began following the track while Angie recounted the events at and after the beach. Jack listened without interrupting.

'I've thought about this a lot, Jack. I'm sure the person had to have gone into the assisted living community. And if it is the author...'

'It would mean she's stayed in the general area, or at least returned to it. There can't be a ton of people in the right age group who grew up in the region. How many do you know?'

'George Campbell is a bit older but always lived in Rivers End. Thomas Blake as well. He's a well-known artist. They are literally the only people I know for certain have the age and residency but neither are female. Oh, and there are the ladies who Gramps is getting to know better. Bess, Annette, and Marge.'

'So what do you know about them?'

Jack casually took her hand as they walked.

'Gramps has known Annette for a very long time because her husband was his doctor. Actually, she is definitely a long-time local, now I think about it. Bess? Not so sure about her history but again, Gramps has been on committees with her over the years. Marge I am uncertain about. We've spoken a couple of times and she said something about people disappointing her. She's divorced. Still gets on well with the ex and they share custody of the dog. Gramps has only spoken to her once or twice so it doesn't seem like she's lived in the area her whole life.'

'I imagine there are a number of residents there who might fit the bill. While Rivers End is a small town, there's heaps of people one would never really get to know. We need to find out who the family is who lost Laura so hopefully someone might remember.'

'Agree. The family being from Melbourne doesn't help even though I've tried all kinds of online searches. And they might have moved long ago or all be deceased. Although I'd have needed to stay here.'

'Needed?'

'Imagine your child vanishes from a fun family day out. She's little. Three and a half? How would you ever stop looking?' Angie's voice was broken. 'Your baby. Lost. Wouldn't you hope she'd come back? Never leave in case she did?'

Why does this resonate with me? It isn't my family.

The track led over a rise and on the other side was bushland. Lots of gum trees and undergrowth. Once under the canopy the track all but vanished and it was only by following the map that Angie noticed a path off to one side.

'Do you think this is around where Mary met the boy with the bicycle?' Jack asked.

'Possibly. If so, we're getting closer to the house.'

The trees gave way to barren ground. And then, as they rounded a long bend, they saw it.

Old fencing and a gate hanging off its hinges. And beyond, a small house.

THIRTY-ONE

Neither of them spoke. They'd reached the gate and stopped while Angie checked the map. She nodded and Jack lifted the gate so it would open enough to give them access. It hadn't been touched in years if the amount of weeds and grass growing through its wire was anything to go by.

They approached the house, stopping again when more buildings appeared.

'That has to be the shed where the car was garaged,' Jack said. 'Do you want to look inside?'

'I think we should knock on the door of the house first.'

'The place is abandoned.'

'It feels the right thing to do though.'

'Let's knock.'

If he was humouring her, his face didn't show it. The closer they got to the house, the more uneasy Angie became. This place was private.

'I'm happy to take a look around on my own if it isn't comfortable, Angie.'

'How on earth did you know?' She flashed a smile his way. 'Thanks, but I want to look as well.'

'In that case, do you want to knock or shall I?'

They were on a small porch at what must be the front door but it wasn't obvious, being solid timber with no doorbell or knocker.

Angie reached up her hand and tapped a couple of times. 'Was that too quiet?'

Jack knocked, much more loudly, and with a creak the door clicked open. 'Whoops.' He pushed it wider and peered in. 'Hello? Anyone here?'

Stale air was expelled like a heavy sigh. How long since anyone was in the house? Was Mary the last person to live here and if so, had she stayed after her mother died?

'Nobody is here, Angie. Let's have a look.'

They stepped in, leaving the door ajar, but it was hard to see, so dark that Angie turned her phone's flashlight on. Under their feet was a rough timber floor and the walls of a very narrow hallway looked damp.

'We won't stay long without protective gear. In case there's mould and the like,' Jack said.

'Oh my gosh... what if she's still here!' Angie grabbed his arm. 'Gertrude?'

A sudden image of the woman propped upright in an armchair with a blanket on her knees, somehow perfectly preserved, almost made her turn and run. Jack took her hand again.

'I'll go first but there won't be a body in here. Quite likely the person who photographed the house had a poke around already. Or do you want to wait outside?'

'Yes, yes I do but I owe this to Nan and Mary.' She gripped his fingers. 'Let's go.'

Each room was tiny. The bedrooms had only space for a single bed and small wardrobe with a little desk in what must have been Mary's. Angie refused to do more than peer into each of them so Jack had a quick look inside the drawers and hanging spaces.

'Nothing at all left behind.'

There was a room with an old wooden table and six chairs. Against a wall a sideboard of sorts held a collection of plates and linen, all thickly covered with dust. This was the dining room the family only used for special occasions.

When they went into the lounge room Angie's chest tightened and she couldn't breathe. A sudden gust of wind blew in, collecting dust in a whirlwind. The front door slammed. Angie screamed and a second later was somehow wrapped in Jack's arms.

'Just the door, my love. Take some slow breaths.'

Did you call me... my love?

The scent of his body overwhelmed Angie but in a good way, pushing aside the rankness of the house. And his arms were so comforting.

My love?

She reluctantly stepped back. 'Just startled me. Sorry. And I thought I was feeling...'

'Feeling?'

'Ridiculous saying it aloud. But my chest went really tight.'

'You're sensitive. Empathetic. You knew that Gertrude had a heart attack in here.'

'You don't think it was a ghost?'

'Do you believe in ghosts?'

'I don't know right now.' She managed a short laugh. 'Kitchen?'

The rest of the house was how Angie envisioned it. The kitchen had a wood stove from over a century ago. There was an ancient cold safe inside the back door. And the storage room still had a lot on the shelves. Ancient preserved food. A few boxes filled with toys. The ones Gertrude made. Anything which didn't fit elsewhere in the house. But no metal box with a lock.

'Did you notice any books in Mary's room?' Angie asked.

After closing the front door behind them they were walking toward the big shed and it was so good being out in the fresh air.

'There was a shelf which was empty. If you are after the Bible where she kept the money then I expect she took it with her.'

'Along with just about everything else. I wish I'd kept reading last night.'

Jack's arm came around her shoulders. 'We'll keep going later, okay?'

'Okay.' Sitting in Nan's office with Jack reading to her was becoming something special.

At the doors of the oversized shed they were confronted by a large padlock.

'I wonder if one of these fits,' Angie said. From a pocket she pulled out the set of keys from Nan's office and tried the mid-sized one. It fitted but wouldn't turn. 'Can you try?'

'So rusted.' He wiggled it then removed the key, smacked the padlock against the door a couple of times, then tried again. 'Sadly I no longer have tools for opening locks. Ah, here we go.' With a click the padlock gave up.

Inside the shed was a surprise in the form of an old and dilapidated car. It had a massive bonnet with small spotlight-style headlights and a single, squarish cab.

'I can't believe it. This looks like a Ford Coupe Utility.' Jack walked around the vehicle, stopping to peer through the windows. 'These were built in the thirties in Geelong and there's not a lot around, let alone in this condition.'

'Wait. Is it in good shape?' Angie could see rusty patches and bald tyres.

'Might not look it but if it's been in the shed since what... the early fifties that we know of, then yes. Someone who loves restoration would adore this.' He took some photos, including the registration plates.

'How on earth did a family who didn't even have electricity and all but lived off the land afford it though?'

Jack put his phone away. 'We know that Gertrude and her husband were pretty much squatters. Doesn't Mary's book say they came across this property which was abandoned after being built without proper permits? The original owner might have gone to war and not returned. I think we can track down the car's history or at least the name of whoever originally purchased it.'

Outside was a lean-to with a few pieces of firewood. The stories were adding up. And there was a chicken coop, surprisingly well built but as empty as everything else.

'You nailed it,' Jack said. 'Finding the right place first time. Where do you think the hut is?'

Angie pointed. 'This way, at least that's where I imagine it is.'

The hut sat close to the ground beneath tall, protective trees and outside it was a wheelbarrow filled with water and the remnants of firewood. Jack went inside for a minute and came back with a solemn expression.

'Pram. Firewood. I took photos.'

Together they circled the hut and found a tiny rectangle of pebbles with a crude wooden cross etched with the word 'Mary'. Tears poured down Angie's face and Jack's eyes glistened. For a while they sat on either side.

'Poor little one,' Angie said. 'Buried and forgotten by the world. Replaced with another child who grew up in a world of abuse and lies and deceit.'

Jack spent some time on his phone, messaging back and forth to someone.

'My friend Ben Rossi used to head up Missing Persons. Turns out he's moved on but he's going to reach out to the appropriate people. He's also called this in to the local police and a unit will be here in the next hour.'

'Do we need to be here?'

'Just to show them this. Which I can do if you prefer to find a spot under a tree and watch from a distance.'

'Thank you. For everything.'

He stood and held out a hand. 'Walk to the rocks while we wait?'

Angie had picked a spot to sit halfway down the hill to watch the ocean. Jack was on a phone call and wandered as he talked but he wasn't far away. She was so happy he was here. The house was incredibly hard to be inside and that little grave…

She gazed at the water. Unlike the first time Mary described this spot, the weather was pleasantly warm with a light breeze rather than icy winds and grey skies. The sea was calm and deep blue and there were a number of boats sailing one way or another and far out at sea, a huge cruise ship. This was where Mary would have chosen to sit as a kid, high enough to see the world go by but not in the line of vision from the house.

There was a sense of aloneness more than loneliness but as a child without friends or siblings it would be desolate.

Jack plonked down at her side, the action of sliding his phone into a top pocket drawing her eyes to the V at the base of his neck. The breeze ruffled his hair. His lips were slightly parted. He lowered his sunglasses to give her a 'what?' look and when she felt the heat rise in her face, she went back to watching the water. His fingers found hers and he lifted her hand and kissed it.

When her eyes shot back to him he still looked as relaxed as ever. Nothing seemed to disturb Jack's calm nature. Was this what life would be like married to him?

Angela, what the heck are you thinking?

'I just hope the police give first Mary a proper history and second Mary might even find her family.'

'I'm not giving up on you though.' Jack smiled. 'Between your grandmother's hard work and your sleuthing skills, I expect you to work it out. And after you found those flowers last night, either she is still alive living in Rivers End or someone close to her continues the tradition.'

His confidence was reassuring. And knowing there were professionals out there who would take this all seriously added a new layer of hope.

'I'd like to go down to the rocks.'

Without a word, Jack stood, still holding her fingers in his, and once she was on her feet, walked with her.

The way down was steep but there was a track of sorts which gave a bit of firmness beneath their feet. At the bottom, the grass ended against the first of the flat rocks. With the tide out, it was easy to walk right to the edge where small waves sploshed against the limestone.

They looked down, straight to a sandy bottom through clear water.

'If the tide was like this the day Mary's father disappeared, there's no way he was swept to sea.' Jack took off his shoes and climbed down into waist-high water. 'Good thing these shorts dry quickly. Now, even if it was higher or the wind was buffeting the surface about, it would need to have been a king tide or else driven by storm conditions and there's no indication in the book of that being the case.'

'Quite the opposite. Mary reinforced that her earlier memories were sound when she bravely stepped into the water such as you have.'

Jack waded a fair way out then stopped. 'Gets deeper here. It's too deep to walk.'

'In your experience, could her father have slipped and hurt himself enough to become unconscious? Although Mary looked for him only a few seconds after he disappeared and couldn't see him.'

'My gut says he deliberately dropped into the sea, probably swam along the bottom and then took advantage of little Mary running for help to climb out, collect his coat and shoes, and vanish. I'm sorry but I think he took off. Abandoned his family.'

'But why? And where did he go?'

After returning to the rocks, Jack perched on the edge and Angie slipped off her shoes and joined him. The water was cooling and little fish darted around her legs.

'Why did he leave that way? My guess is he intended to fake his own death but rather than having people coming looking for him, waited until Mary was around to see him fall. She was too young to understand and never allowed near the edge so had no concept of how shallow the ocean really is here.'

'And by the time Gertrude got there it was fair enough to think his body had drifted away, let alone once a boat arrived hours later,' Angie said.

'For all we know he might have been in debt or afraid of being caught after taking Mary from her parents. It was cruel, exposing a young child to his deception. Frightening for her. As for where he went? Long deceased. Made a new life for himself somewhere. You'd be surprised how often it happens.'

'Do you think your friend, Ben, might know how to find out?'

'I think we need to finish reading Mary's book.'

Angie agreed. There probably wasn't more than another chapter left by the feel of the book so it might offer some resolution or at least something for her to go on with.

Jack eased himself back into the water.

'If you're going swimming you might want to take that nice shirt off.'

He grinned. 'Do you think I should?'

'Swim?'

'Take my shirt off.'

He stepped in front of Angie so that her legs were touching the front of his and inched forward. She made space for him to move closer, repositioning her knees to either side of his thighs. It felt completely natural when he slipped his arms around her waist to touch her forehead against his. His warm skin against hers felt oh-so-nice.

Of their own accord her arms went around his neck and her fingers played with his hair. He sighed, a long, slow exhale, then moved enough that he could gaze into her eyes.

'I really want to kiss you, Angie.'

'Yes.'

'Yes... you know I want to kiss you?' His lips were tantalisingly close. 'Or yes, I can kiss you?'

'Yes.'

'That clears it up.'

'Hello down there! Rivers End police.'

The call came from somewhere at the top of the hill.

'Yes, please kiss me,' Angie whispered.

Jack slowly straightened. 'Not with an audience. It matters too much.' He looked as disappointed as she felt. 'Let's take care of Mary for now. We have forever.'

The police visited the hut and grave with Jack while Angie wandered around the property taking photos on her phone. She couldn't bring herself to return to the little grave nor the sad hut but it seemed important that there were images to add to the book and Nan's other information. Once there was an investigation they'd probably not be allowed back here.

At the back of the house was the door Mary had described several times. It led to the small area where she and her mother kept their boots and coats as well as the room with all the shelves inside. There was a small pile of firewood pieces, deteriorated by weather and time but clearly from some hardwood tree. This must be what Mary had collected from the lean-to and the first armful she'd carried over from the hut.

Did you leave the same day?

More likely she'd just never brought the wood inside. What had she done once she knew for certain her mother was dead?

Angie stopped walking to better think.

Gertrude had told Mary to get the birth certificate and the money and go. Even with her dying breath she'd known the young woman needed to leave. But leave what? The life she'd been given? The church? The lies and deception?

For Mary to have moved forward in life she must have kept the identity of the first Mary. Angie had assumed the anonymous author had created a whole new life, including a new name.

Is it really that simple? Can we locate her by finding who Gertrude and Vernon were? Who the first Mary was?

Angie headed to the trees surrounding the hut. Jack stood out of them in the sun, again on his phone. She waited until he hung up and gave her a questioning look.

'I think I know how to find Mary. Will you help me?'

THIRTY-TWO

Jack dropped Angie at the bottom of her driveway and went home to shower and change, promising to be back within an hour. He wanted to make further phone calls, starting with a friend who was a private investigator.

It was almost five in the afternoon and in another half hour Harriet from the bookstore would arrive. After a quick shower of her own, Angie put on a sundress and sandals and pulled her hair up with a claw clip. After the visit she'd work out what to make for dinner. If she and Jack were going to keep reading then they'd need to eat at some point.

And if he's ever going to kiss me…

She stopped in front of the mirror in the hallway and redid her hair to get the waves more under control. It needed a decent cut, something easier to manage for when school began. Soon her days would be filled with running a classroom and the sound of children and it couldn't happen fast enough. Hair finally fixed, she stared at her face. The sun had added a slight glow to her skin today and her eyes were… happy. Despite today's sometimes sad findings, there was a new joy in her heart. When she'd come home from Perth with a broken soul she'd barely looked at herself because she couldn't hide the sadness and anxiety.

The difference was profound.

I really have started again. Started to build a new life. A joyful life.

When the doorbell rang she answered, still smiling. Harriet and Olive smiled back.

'Oh, how lovely to see you both! Please, come in.'

Olive held out a cake-sized white box. 'I'm training as a pastry chef and would love your critique of some goodies I made today. There's two veggie pies, two quiches, and some bite-sized mixed sweet pastries. Of course if you hate them, just give them to the chickens if you have any or failing that, your worst enemy and we'll never speak of it again.'

'Are you kidding me? There's no way I won't enjoy these! Thank you.' Angie accepted the box. 'Would you both like something to drink?'

Harriet closed the door behind them. 'No thanks, we're so keen to see these wonderful books!'

Angie left the box on the kitchen counter and led the way through the back part of the house and then up to Nan's office. 'It might be a bit warm inside because I've not had it open all day and I need to warn you it is a mess because I'm sorting through her things.'

Olive happily followed Angie but Harriet stopped in the doorway, her eyes wide as she took in the bookshelves and desk.

'This was where she wrote her books?'

'The last couple, yes. Before then she worked in the house, sharing Gramps's study. He built this for her and when I came to live here as a younger teenager, she'd let me sit in here and read or even help her research sometimes.'

Harriet finally stepped in. 'I read somewhere she wrote her books longhand.'

'First two drafts. Then she'd type it up and work on it

further.' Angie collected one of the boxes from a bottom shelf and opened it on the desk. 'She kept impeccable notes from the research.'

'For each book?' Olive asked. 'You should write her biography.'

'That is a good idea,' Harriet said. 'I don't suppose she has any unfinished novels?'

'Anything is possible but so far I've not come across anything. However...' Angie put the lid back on the box and looked at the women. She needed every bit of help right now. *Mary* needed it. 'I found a cryptic box and I'd love your opinion.'

When Jack arrived a little later, the three were sitting in a circle on the floor with the box open between them.

'Oh, do you all know each other? Jack lives next door and has been working in this puzzle with me,' Angie said. 'I've shown Harriet and Olive everything.'

He took his usual chair after greeting everyone. 'You're familiar with the book, Harriet?'

'Yes, we had several copies at one stage. They were purchased by one person and I did look them up but it wasn't a regular customer.'

Olive had been carefully going through the newspaper clippings and glanced up. 'It was done over the phone, Mum. They paid by credit card and wanted them sent to a post office box in Melbourne.'

Angie and Jack exchanged a glance.

'Like the letters?' Harriet asked.

Although Angie hadn't taken them from their envelopes, she'd shown them to Harriet.

'You saw that? I don't suppose you kept the address, Olive?'

'Maybe. Could be in the computer at work. But I wanted to ask about these.' Olive gestured to the clippings. 'Mum and I solved our own puzzle not long after we arrived in Rivers End.

We found a diary and it had a treasure map and we followed the clues and stuff.'

Is Rivers End filled with old secrets? I never heard any until I came home.

'Are you thinking about the little girl who was lost?' Harriet asked Olive.

'Mary?' Jack leaned forward. 'Well, her real name.'

'No. This was a child with a tragic story. But I distinctly remember there'd been another child disappear a few years earlier who was never found. Not a body or any sign and now I'm wondering if this is the same child in these reports.' Olive's face was sad. 'She was mentioned in the diary but not her name.'

'It was Laura. And that is all we know.' Angie felt her hopes dash.

Harriet stared at Olive.

'What are you thinking, Mum?'

'Remember the book from Palmerston House? Elizabeth White loaned it to us to help our research.'

Olive nodded.

'Did you read it all?'

'No. Did you?'

Shaking her head, Harriet stood. 'I was more interested in the 1960s but Laura was before then. Maybe we should see if Elizabeth might let us borrow it again.'

Olive was on her feet in an instant. 'Let's go right now.'

'Wouldn't you like to see Opal's books?' Harriet laughed. 'That's why we came.'

'Fine, fine, yes. Then we'll visit Elizabeth.'

While Angie heated the veggie pies and found a bottle of wine in what was left of Gramps's collection, Jack whipped up a salad. He insisted, saying he was trying to improve his skills and doing more than opening packets or buying takeaway.

'I'm happy that Harriet will take two of each of Nan's books for her special bookcase. It still leaves me with plenty.'

'And they'll be a great addition to the bookstore. I've been going there weekly almost since I arrived and am always impressed by the place.'

Angie agreed. It wouldn't take much to spend a lot of time in there.

'How did you go with your friend? The private investigator?'

'Do you have any fruit I can toss in?' Jack went in search himself, finding some blueberries in the fridge. 'Sorry. He suggests we finish putting together the spreadsheet you've worked on and once we've exhausted other avenues, talk to him. When I mentioned the difficulty of finding out Mary's real name he said what you did – find the mother's name and go from there.'

'Yes, but how? I guess we could put in a request with Births, Deaths and Marriages for girls born between 1946 and 1948 with the first name of Mary but that seems a long shot. So far we've not found anything mentioned other than first names and not even one of the husband. I did a search for him. Did I tell you?'

'No. What did you find?'

'Not a thing. Actually, that's not true. There was a one paragraph comment in a newspaper which said the search for a man presumed washed off rocks near Driftwood Cove was called off. No names nor photographs and it was only the similar date which gave a clue it was Mary's father.' Angie checked the pies. 'These are nice and hot.'

'And this is finished. I might take a photo.'

Jack took several, angling the bowl to get the best light.

'Looks delicious. Shall we eat here?'

'Oh no.' In the process of moving the bowl in between two plates, Jack stopped, his expression aghast. 'I didn't think... no dressing.'

'There is olive oil and balsamic vinegar in the pantry. Mix equal parts in a small bowl.' Angie handed him a cup-sized glass bowl. 'Add half a teaspoon of sugar if you want but it doesn't really need it.'

Leaving him to sort that out, Angie added the pies to the plates, got cutlery, and poured two glasses of red wine.

'It doesn't stay mixed.' Jack emerged from the pantry, rapidly stirring the bowl then stopping. 'See? It separates.'

She struggled to contain a laugh as she took her seat.

'Are you mocking me?'

'Nope. What shall we toast to?'

The bowl went onto the table and a glass of wine into his hand. 'To extraordinary women.'

'Oh... well, that's nice, Jack.'

'Seeing you and Harriet and Olive working on Mary's story was... well, insightful. Half the time you didn't even say that much to each other but then there'd be a sudden focus on one thing and the suggestions would flow.'

'They are both wonderful.'

She held up her glass and Jack tapped his against it.

'So are you.'

For once she didn't look away in embarrassment or try to brush off the compliment. Instead, she touched his arm with a quiet, 'Thank you.'

They took refilled glasses up to Nan's office after dinner and a surprisingly animated conversation about music. Their tastes were similar for the most part apart from Jack's love of jazz and Angie's of country. Both promised to convert the other which led to a non-monetary wager of who would win, with the prize to be decided by the winner. It all felt very domestic-bliss.

Back in their usual seats, Jack opened the little book to the last page of the chapter Angie had read over the phone.

'This chapter led us to the house where Mary grew up. And to what appears to be the grave of another child,' he said. 'We didn't find Gertrude's body in the house and there's little left in the way of personal items.'

'Probably safe to believe Mary called for help and stayed long enough to take what she wanted from the house. If she kept the identity she'd been given then her life could continue without questions from authority figures... the kind of people she'd been raised to fear. The alternative was to go to the police with her suspicions.'

'She'd have been terrified of being in trouble even though she did nothing wrong. And remember, she believed her real family lived a long way away. How would she even begin to start looking when she had no worldly experience?' Deep lines etched Jack's forehead. 'If only she'd had some support.'

He turned the page, then another, and a third.

'No more chapters, Angie.'

'What?'

'It looks like more of her third person writing. But longer.'

'How sad to not hear her voice again, Jack.'

His hand reached for hers. 'Let's see what she has to say.'

And so the full circle had closed. The child who was brought here against her will was an adult who could leave. The false mother joined her true child in the stillness of death. And hopefully, the peacefulness of whatever afterlife existed.

After the shock and initial grief came practicalities.

A funeral to arrange. Nobody they'd known from the church

cared. It was Tim, the young man who'd become a friend, who helped. He and his parents. They were the only ones at the grave in the furthest part of the public cemetery. And it was them who offered a place to stay when she was ready, until she knew where she would go.

Before she could begin to face the future she had work to do and remained living in the lonely house by the sea while she searched each room for even the smallest clue of where she belonged. Where her parents lived. Where Mattie was. Even Mama's private belongings were no longer off limits.

The contents of the shoebox in the wardrobe were taken out and spread across the kitchen table. At first she didn't want to take the birth certificate. It wasn't hers, it belonged to the little girl in the grave near the hut. Yet Mama had told her to be Mary. She'd been Mary since her first day here. The birth certificate sat on the table for days as other pieces were collected.

A hymn book in German belonging to Mama's grandmother was put with the old cookbook and a handful of other books. The young woman didn't speak a word of the language but she searched for names or anything handwritten in case there was something other than the marriage certificate to show more about Gertrude's parents. In the end she decided it didn't matter. If Mama was so deceitful as to keep another family's child then she would hardly have told her own relatives the truth. But the hymn book had some words handwritten in the front and something made her keep it.

She didn't want the photographs or the letters which were in German. Nor the marriage certificate of those who'd stolen her. None of the Bibles – other than the one she'd kept as a safe place to hide her money for so long. When there was nothing more to find, she opened the metal box and counted the money.

There was more than she'd ever imagined. Enough to buy new clothes. Pay for teacher college or toward university if they'd still have her. For the first time since Mama died, she wept. And she finally understood. If she told anyone she wasn't really Mary then the money and the opportunities would be taken. She might even be accused of breaking the law, somehow. And she might lose her only friend. Tim.

Everything on the table she didn't want fitted into the metal box, other than the books, including the Bibles. Those she carefully wrapped in several layers of fabric left over from making the toys. Before closing it right up she added one of the toys, almost crying again as she did. She only kept the hymn book to take.

She locked the metal box and took it and the other parcel to the hut, collecting a shovel from the shed on the way. Within sight of the small grave she dug a hole. It took hours but eventually it was deep enough to place the parcel and box in and cover with the dirt. That way the things which really belonged to the lost little girl were close to her.

Once she returned the shovel, she said goodbye to the car and locked the big doors. At the chicken coop she shed more tears. By the time she was inside the house, she was calm. She'd made a decision. Knowing she would never find Mattie and her real family made the choice for her. She only had herself now. And to be her best self, she would stay being Mary.

One final time, she sat halfway down the hill to watch the sea.

THIRTY-THREE

An overwhelming and unspoken need to leave the utter sadness of the little book behind led Angie and Jack to the beach. For a while they simply stood at the end, each deep in their own thoughts, breathing the salty, healing air while the tide stirred in anticipation of turning.

Then Jack's phone rang. 'Won't be long.' He wandered a few metres away to answer.

There were two messages on Angie's phone when she checked. The first was from Harriet.

> Elizabeth and Angus are away tonight so I've left a message about the historical book we discussed. I'll be in touch once I speak to Elizabeth. Oh, and thank you so much for this afternoon. Olive is convinced we should be private sleuths!

The genuine desire to help was touching and Angie knew she had new friends in the mother and daughter team who owned the bookstore. Olive was especially a good person to know if her baking skills continued to be as yummy as their dinner.

Gramps was the sender of the second message and only a few minutes ago.

> Made my first dinner here and didn't burn the place down. Going to watch some cricket and maybe read a book.

He added a photo of sliced chicken breast on top of roasted vegetables.

> Looks delish! Enjoy the cricket. Do you still read German?

> More or less. Why?

> Found something in Nan's office which is in German and I have no idea what it says.

There was no reply. No little dots moving.

Her heart sank. She knew he didn't want to have anything to do with Nan's office yet thanks to her need to solve the puzzle of the anonymous author, she had ignored his wishes.

The phone rang.

'Gramps? I'm sorry. I shouldn't have asked.'

'No, lass. I'm the one who is sorry because you deserve to know about your family history. You've asked often enough.' His voice was thick with emotion. 'Something happened today. One of the other residents came by when I was in the front garden. Stopped and said the strangest thing and I've been thinking about it ever since.'

Jack was off the phone and heading back and Angie pointed to her phone.

'What did they say?'

'Exactly these words, Angie. Etched into my brain. They said, grief is not a reason to pretend the past doesn't exist.'

'Grief is not a reason to pretend the past doesn't exist? What a strange comment. Did you ask what they meant?'

'I was a bit taken aback, as you might imagine. By the time I took in the words sufficiently to form a question, there was no point as they'd moved on. At first I wondered if it was even directed at me. People sometimes wear earbuds while they are on the phone, for example.'

'True.'

Jack leaned back against the railing, listening.

'Anyway, the point is it made me have a proper think. You tried to ask me something about Opal's research a while back and I cut you off. I can't keep doing that. Are you around to come and talk to me tomorrow?'

'Of course. Thank you, yes.'

'About ten?'

'I'll be there.'

'Goodnight then.'

She slipped the phone into her pocket. 'Gramps wants to see me tomorrow, to talk about the past. About Nan's research.'

'That's good. Do you want me to come with you?'

'Not this time. It is a big step him being willing to talk to me but he might clam up with anyone else there.'

'We can have lunch after, if you'd like?'

'I would like.'

'What was the thing about grief you were saying to Emmett?'

'He said somebody said that to him today. I guess they were a stranger as he didn't mention a name but it feels kind of personal, don't you think? When Nan died, Gramps closed down for a long time. I remember him not answering the door for about a week and I'd do it and accept the flowers people kept sending and their cards of sympathy.'

Her heart was heavy as memories rushed back and as if he knew, Jack gently pulled her toward him and wrapped her in his arms, loosely enough that he could see her face.

'How old were you?'

'Fifteen. I was in my own world. My parents had died only two years before and it all came back, of course. Gramps and I eventually got through the worst of the grief but he shut out anything to do with Nan's work, as if it was too painful to think of her doing what she loved. I remember emptying the letterbox after the funeral and there were a dozen or so letters addressed to her. He flicked through to check none were bills or the like and put the rest in a box along with all the sympathy cards and a few gifts people sent.'

'What kind of box?'

'One of those he uses to keep files. Now I'm wondering if her diary for the year is in it as well.'

'It isn't in the house?'

She shook her head. 'Not that I've found, so I might ask him tomorrow.'

Jack kissed her forehead. 'Can we go home? I'm feeling the effects of today a bit. The back is, anyway.'

'Should I run home and get my car?'

He tightened his hold on Angie and her hands went around his waist then began rubbing up and down the muscles on either side of his spine.

'Oh my... that is nice. Bit more to the middle and a fraction higher... ooh. Are you a masseur?'

'Hardly. I'm so sorry to have dragged you all over Driftwood Cove today.'

'You didn't drag me anywhere. Remember I drove home from Melbourne this morning and too much sitting can play havoc sometimes.'

Angie dropped her arms and they started walking back, Jack taking one of her hands as he did so often.

'The phone call I had before? It was a courtesy update from the local senior constable at the police station here. We met her and the constable at the old house.'

'So is there news?'

'The trees around the hut and grave are taped off, not that anyone is likely to suddenly visit there. There'll be detectives from Warrnambool there tomorrow who will evaluate the situation and arrange forensic assistance. I mentioned that we believe there's a metal box and other items also buried in the area and she's passing that on.'

This is really happening. Mary's story will be revealed to the world.

'The author of the book never wanted this to come out. She changed her mind about the book after it was published and has gone to great lengths to find the few copies which sold. What if we're about to destroy her life?'

'What if we're about to give this lady her real life back?'

'Do you think we can?'

'All I know for certain is that the real Mary deserves more than a shallow grave in the middle of nowhere. Legally we've done the right thing and now we have to ensure that if the author of the book is affected that there is help for her.'

'Will she be in trouble for keeping Mary's identity?'

'That is something for serving officers to decide. Let's not get ahead of ourselves though.'

Have I just made the worst mistake?

Long after Jack left her at the front door with another kiss to her forehead, his face drawn with tiredness, Angie fretted over Mary. By visiting the house in Driftwood Cove she'd turned a story into a frightening and stark reality. And although she agreed that the truth of how the real Mary died needed uncovering, it was the living Mary who might pay a price for doing nothing more than believing she might be someone else. Surely no court in the land would charge her with identity theft or whatever it was called?

She sat behind Nan's desk with the box open. There was so

much new information, including her sighting last night of the person who'd left flowers in the water near the jetty. Was it even possible Mary would have stayed so close to the place she grew up when all she would have was distressing memories?

Or had she gone to university, perhaps moving to Melbourne? That was where her postal address was – even now – assuming Olive's mystery customer was the same person. Maybe she'd lived a full life as a scientist. Married and had a family of her own. And then on retirement returned to the area, settling in Rivers End... but why? Was it because of the new assisted living community? She had to be in her mid-seventies, which certainly didn't preclude her from living independently but with the person last night vanishing close to the buildings, it added to the speculation.

What was it Gramps had said? Something about there having to be a Fairlie living in Seahaven, just in case. His 'just in case' was nothing more than a desire to keep the property in the family or for him to have a back-up plan if he changed his mind about his new cottage.

But what if Mary had doubts about Gertrude's information? If she thought there was a chance she came from this region, would she feel she had to be here – just in case?

'So *are* you Laura?' Angie whispered. 'Were you drawn home because your oldest memories led you back?'

Tomorrow she would ask Gramps if he knew anything about the family whose little girl was taken. He'd have been so young himself but surely it would have been local knowledge, even if the family wanted privacy. And if he didn't, then she'd ask George Campbell or even Thomas Blake, although she'd only met him once or twice in passing.

As she closed the lid on the box, Angie knew she had go to the bench out the front. She locked the office and wandered down beneath a starry sky.

. . .

There was just a hint of a breeze. Angie checked the time and was surprised it was almost midnight. Today had been long and eventful.

She gazed over the fence to Jack's house. It was in darkness. They'd walked home slowly, at his pace. He was in some discomfort and kept apologising for needing to cut the night short. All Angie wanted was for him to know that she was there for him, no matter what, but perhaps it was still early days for that kind of discussion.

Angie closed her eyes. She let the soft air surround her and reached out to Nan. If there was ever a time she needed the wisdom of her grandmother, it was now.

How do I find Mary?

The breeze dropped to absolute silence. Minutes passed.

'You find the box, child.'

Her eyes flew open.

There was nobody here.

'Where, Nan? Where is the box?'

The air remained still and the only sound was night birds going about their business. She closed her eyes again and placed her hands palm-down on either side of her on the timber. Somewhere in her brain were the answers. Was the guidance.

When something touched her hand she didn't move or open her eyes. For all she knew it could be a leaf from a tree. Except it felt like warm skin.

'You know where, Angie. You've seen it. Finish what you started and get working to bring a family back together.'

The warmth on her hand evaporated and she let her eyes flicker open again. Nan wasn't here. Of course she wasn't – this was all her subconscious at play. But Angie felt loved and protected in the way only her grandmother ever did.

'Thanks, Nan. I love you.'

Her words vanished into the night as the breeze picked up.

Bring a family back together.

Was it even possible? And where had Angie seen the box... at least since she returned to Rivers End?

Finish what you started. You know where.

Getting to her feet, Angie initially headed for Nan's office but she was certain Gramps's box wasn't there. So she deviated to the house and turned on every light. With so little of her grandfather's belongings still here, apart from bigger items yet to move, checking each room wouldn't take long.

Starting with his bedroom she opened every drawer and door, looked under the bed and turned off the light so she'd remember she'd finished in there. Then his study, her bedroom, the spare bedrooms, all the living areas, kitchen, laundry, and bathrooms. Only the light in the long hallway remained on and she double-checked the handful of packing boxes against a wall, opening each with no result. There were two sideboards but again, no sign of the box in question.

All that was left was the linen cupboard which she'd emptied days ago.

'Oh, Angela!' she chided herself aloud and hurried to open the door.

Gramps had interrupted her before she did the very top shelf.

And sure enough, beside a couple of rolled sleeping bags was a box exactly like the ones he used for files.

With only a solo light on above the kitchen counter, Angie opened the box and began taking out the contents. This was what Mary did when she'd searched for clues of her identity.

And now I'm trying to find it.

First was the pile of cards and letters from after Nan's funeral. Beside them she placed a collection of gifts, all still wrapped. Gramps was such a meticulous man regarding social obligations. For him to have packed these and the cards away gave Angie a glimpse into the depth of his grief because ordinarily, he would have replied to the sender of each with a thank-you note. Those and the cards and letters, yet everything was unopened.

There was a photo album. All about Nan and her work. A photocopy of her first advance cheque. Letters of rejection from publishers and the one 'yes' which began it all. Copies of her book covers. Photos from awards nights and talks she gave. Angie had never seen any of these and had to wipe away more than one tear.

It hurt knowing Gramps had kept this from her and hopefully it was part of what he wanted to speak about in the morning.

Beneath was another album which looked older but Angie left it for another time. She didn't want to be crying rather than looking for the diary.

At the bottom was Nan's beloved winter scarf and Angie had to give herself a moment before gently lifting it out. She'd knitted it for her grandmother, a long thick scarf in deep purple, which was Nan's favourite colour. Neatly folded, it was only when Angie held it against her chest that she felt something tucked between the layers.

Carefully she unfolded the scarf on the counter until revealing a thin book.

It was the diary from the year Nan died.

THIRTY-FOUR

I'll only look for the day she was meant to meet with the anonymous author. Nothing more tonight. Not a thing.

Angie had made tea, unable to simply open the diary and start reading. She should go to bed. Rest. Look at this... all of the items... with a clear head.

Except she wouldn't sleep. Her mind raced with possibilities and the only way to quiet the thoughts was to answer the burning question of whether Nan met with the author. Anything else could wait, even though she'd almost begun opening all cards and letters while the kettle boiled.

After a few sips she opened the diary, almost closing it again at the sight of Nan's handwriting proclaiming this year was going to be the best of her life. Angie turned the pages until about two weeks before the day Nan died.

Today's phone conversation was both a delight and profoundly sad. How dearly I want to meet this courageous woman and help her reunite with the family still left alive. I'm almost certain I know who she once was but still I do not know who she is today. If only she will change her mind and agree to meet.

Two days later there was an appointment reminder to see the local doctor. Had Nan suspected her heart was failing? Always fit and active, the collapse was a terrible shock and one which Gramps was later told could not have been foreseen or avoided. But Nan might have felt something was off. Angie finished her cup of tea before proceeding, trying not to let emotions overtake her.

She has agreed to meet! I've agonised over whether to tell Emmett what is happening and what has been happening these past months and more. As dear as he is, there are times he is so stubborn and talking about his youth is always a sticking point. So I will go to our meeting and then decide the next steps. Oh, how I look forward to finally seeing her face. If I can reunite her with her Mattie, then my greatest work will have been accomplished.

Why the reference to Gramps's youth? And Nan's hesitation with filling him in on her plans to meet another author? Was it possible Gramps was traumatised by the abduction? That made some sense. Possibly all the children in the town were affected to some degree.

Angie turned the page.

There was only one more entry.

Rivers End Jetty. 2pm. Bring a white carnation. If the weather is inclement, meet at the cave near the bottom of the stone steps.

And there was a love heart drawn.

The date was the day Nan had the heart attack at exactly one in the afternoon.

. . .

How Angie longed to talk to Jack right now. She even checked her phone to see if his messages showed 'active' but no, he was sensibly asleep.

A peculiar calm settled on her. Nan needed her to finish the work she'd started and at last she was close to doing so. How awful to expect to go to the jetty, to meet the person she'd spent months researching, and then...

'Stop it.' Saying the words aloud helped jolt her out of the spiral into old pain.

It was the final entry in the diary. Angie closed it and placed it on the counter.

With no chance of going to bed just yet she began going through the mail. Days and days of sympathy cards and letters. The latter caught her attention.

One in particular.

The handwriting was the same as those from the anonymous author: M.W.

Taking a knife she cut the envelope open, heart thudding with the thought of what she might read. She stopped long enough to draw a deep breath before unfolding the paper. There was a twenty-dollar note and two pages, the first addressed to Gramps.

Dear Mr Fairlie,

My heartfelt condolences for the loss of your wonderful wife, Opal. I cannot begin to comprehend your grief and am so sorry to intrude at this time.

Opal and I have corresponded for some time as well as spoken on the phone concerning matters deeply important and personal to me. She had in her possession a small book which she'd promised to return to me and I respectfully ask you do so on her behalf – when you feel ready. In addition, if you would be willing to part with the contents of the box she keeps the book inside I would be forever grateful. It contains information which she believed would lead me to locate long-lost family members.

The address is above and I shall add enough money to cover the postage. The name you can use is Mary. That will be sufficient.

Enclosed is a letter I was compelled to write to your dear wife and it seemed to matter that I sent it to you.

Yours faithfully,
Mary

Gramps had never opened the envelope. Never read the letter. How heartbreaking for Mary to never hear a word back. And this was confirmation of who the author of the book was. Angie turned to the second page.

My dearest Opal,

How I wish we'd had the chance to meet and had I only found courage earlier, we would have. Your determination to help me find out my real identity touched me deeply. No other person has cared so much about my story and you had me believing I might really find Mattie, or at the least, what happened to him and my parents. I'd begun dreaming of an extended family.

I've asked your husband to return the copy of The Loneliest Girl by the Sea to me as well as the research you mentioned to me on the phone. If he does then I shall attempt to piece together what you wanted to tell me. I know you wished to ask several questions before saying any more in case your conclusions were leading to the wrong answers.

Thank you for believing in the little lost girl. Attending your funeral was incredibly hard yet also heartwarming with so many people there to say goodbye and rally around your husband and lovely grandchild.

So now I shall say my own private goodbye, Opal. You are missed.

With love,
M.W.

Angie reread the letter to make sure she hadn't been mistaken. Mary was at Nan's funeral. She might have seen her or even spoken to her and never known. The day was a blur in her memories.

That was enough for tonight. Angie put the letters and the scarf and the diary back in the box. Then the album celebrating Nan's work and all the wrapped gifts. They could wait for another time. The lid back on, she carried the box to the linen cupboard and left it on a middle shelf this time, then returned to the kitchen to wash up her cup.

She'd accidentally left the other photo album out.

Bring a family back together.

Angie opened it.

These were old photographs. Black and white and mostly small and square. The first few were of the house, of Seahaven, and Angie dropped onto a stool with a smile. The gardens had the same structure as today, just not as developed. There were lots of flowers and a swing set in the front.

Then came several images of after a wedding, the bride and groom being showered with confetti outside a church which was the one near the school. The groom looked uncannily like photos of Gramps in his twenties so this had to be his father and mother. She'd seen one photo only of his parents, when they were in their fifties, solemn and even sad rather than joyous as in the wedding ones.

A couple of larger photos followed. Three actually. Portraits first of a little boy then a little girl and then one together.

Angie caught her breath.

The little boy looked about eight and was the image of one she had of her dad around that age. But Dad was an only child and besides, this was clearly from the fifties based on the clothes and style of pose. So was it Gramps?

The girl was younger with wavy hair below her shoulders and a serious expression. Why was there a photo of a little girl in the family album? A cousin maybe? The third image was more relaxed with both children smiling at each other and the similarities in their faces and obvious love for each other made Angie gasp.

Ever so gently she extracted the photo from behind the plastic sleeve and with trembling fingers, turned it over to read the writing on the back.

September 1952. Emmett (8) and Laura (3 1/2)

The air seemed to be sucked out of the room as Angie checked the back of the other two photographs.

Laura (Lou Lou) aged 3 1/2

Emmett (Mattie) aged 8.

This was *Gramps's* history. One which Nan had worked out. She was about to reconcile him with his sister. His stolen little sister. Gramps was Mattie.

Angie dropped the photos on the counter and ran to her

bedroom, slamming the door and throwing herself onto the bed. Curled up in a ball, sobs racked her body until, exhausted, she fell into a fitful sleep.

THIRTY-FIVE

Jack shook his head in disbelief for about the twentieth time since he'd arrived just after nine. Angie had texted him to say she'd found out who Laura was and he appeared a few minutes later. His first response was to cup her face with his hands and gaze at her puffy eyes and lines of exhaustion. Then he'd held her against him for a moment before they went to the kitchen.

'I can't believe I never knew about Laura. She's my great-aunt and I should have been told. And I don't think even Nan knew… not all the details anyway. She must never have seen the photos either.'

'Am I missing something?' Jack frowned. 'Laura's family were just on holiday in Rivers End when she disappeared. But Fairhaven has been owned by your family for generations.'

'The other day… why didn't I put it together then? Gramps mentioned something about coming to Seahaven to visit his grandparents as a child. I thought he meant they lived somewhere locally but maybe not.'

I should have asked Gramps to clarify that. I should have risked him being upset.

'Emmett must have been devastated, being the last one in the family to see her. While we only know the version of events from Laura's memories, he was older and may have felt responsible.'

'And my heart is shattered for him... for the big brother whose life changed because of the evil of those who took and then kept Laura.' Her voice broke and she turned away to get her under control. 'If Mary is Laura...'

'All the circumstantial evidence points to it.'

'I'll go and see him soon.' Angie poured a glass of water. 'Listen to what he wants to tell me first and make a call on things after that.' The water helped enough for her to sit at the counter near Jack, who'd returned the photos to the album. He looked so worried and she forced a small smile. 'I'm just a bit in shock. Everything Nan was researching, all the heartbreak we felt for Mary, when all along it was far more personal than I could have imagined. If anything, I'd wondered if Gramps had known of the family.'

'Not that it *was* his family.'

She nodded. 'In between dreams I woke and realised we may still have a way of finding Laura... Mary. I need to ask Harriet and Olive if they still have the address of the person who bought the books because if so, we know it must be Mary and I can write to her. Even if not, then I can write to the one on Nan's letters.'

'Good thinking. And more than that, police may find cause to ask Australia Post for the details of the box owner. Hey, don't look alarmed. Not every search is for an arrest. Missing Persons will dig up the Fairlie cold case if I have anything to do with it and if you are willing to share your nan's research then it will naturally lead to things such as post office boxes. This is a good thing.'

Angie wasn't convinced. Sometimes bad things still

happened to good people thanks to situations outside their control.

Like me. Investigated in case I was involved in Shane's criminal activity.

'I know you said you want to visit Emmett alone, but do you mind if I hang around? Not like a stalker,' he laughed. 'In case you need me.'

How could she say she already did? Needing Jack was a constant. He'd found a way past her frightened defences by being a kind and decent human. It was telling him how much which terrified her.

'I'd like that, Jack. Thank you.'

Gramps made coffee and talked about his delicious breakfast in the dining room which was at a table with George, Marge, Bess, and Annette.

'Hopefully in time I'll stop snaffling food like its going out of fashion. Reminds me of the cruise I went on with Opal once. As soon as I saw a buffet table she had to hold me back.' He collected cups. 'This morning I filled up a plate with all the good stuff and pancakes so when I sat down I asked Marge if I could join her when she goes walking. I've seen how fast she is and that's exactly what I need to stay fit.'

Oh, that's great that you're settling in so well.

'And she agreed?'

He shook his head. 'For some reason the woman dislikes or distrusts me and I don't know why. I honestly can't remember doing or saying anything offensive and I wish I knew so I could put it right. She mumbled something about preferring her own company, then picked up her plate and left. Felt bad but Annette and Bess said Marge is a loner by nature.'

'I like her. We've spoken a couple of times and she's very intelligent. I get the feeling she carries a lot of heartache.'

Gramps finished making coffee and carried the cups to the living room. 'Don't mean to keep on about Marge but I thought I could make her feel a bit more comfortable around me after what she said the other day.'

'What other day?'

'I told you. She said grief is not a reason to pretend the past doesn't exist.'

'That was *Marge*?'

'I thought I told you. She walks past the cottage a few times a day.'

Before her imagination could run away with her, Angie put down her cup and leaned a bit forward. 'Gramps... what did you want to say to me? About the family history?'

His face dropped and he nodded. 'I never spoke of it to anyone, not really even your grandmother. Not all of it. The events of one afternoon damaged me, lass, destroyed my family in some ways. My pa and mum never recovered and both died in their fifties. I'm sure of broken hearts.'

Angie moved to sit beside him, taking one of his hands. It was shaking and she squeezed it.

'I had a sister. A bonnie child filled with mischief and curiosity. Took herself off to find a wretched toy she'd put on the ground, up in the hills after a family picnic. I'd been watching her and she disappeared. Looked everywhere.' He closed his eyes and drew a shuddering breath and when he opened them again, they were glistening. 'Never found her. Nor the toy which had some stupid name I can't remember.'

'Dolly.'

'What? Yes, that's it, but how do you know?'

'Your little sister, was her name Laura?'

Gramps pulled his hand out of Angie's and his face darkened.

Her heart dropped at the distress and anger in his eyes and Angie stood. So did he.

'Nan had come across a book written by—'

'This was Opal's doing? Prying into the darkest time of my life?'

'No. Well, yes, but by accident. And I don't think she ever knew for certain. But I don't understand why you wouldn't have shared this with her anyway?'

'Because it was my fault and my business.' He crossed his arms. 'I think it best you go home.'

'Not until you hear me out, Gramps. I know you didn't find Laura but there's a chance she's still alive and Jack and I—'

'Jack? You've dragged him into this?'

He stomped to the front door and flung it open.

'Listen to me, please, just for once!' Angie followed him to the door. 'I love you and I'd never do a thing to hurt you.'

His voice rose. 'Well you have. Please go, Angela.'

'Emmett?' Jack stood on the footpath outside the front garden.

She almost ran from the cottage and into his waiting arms.

'You okay?'

'I've upset him. He won't let me speak so let's go.'

'Do you want me to try?'

Angie stepped back and shook her head. 'Stubborn, stubborn grandfather.' She looked at the cottage where Gramps had closed the door in her wake. How on earth would she get through to him?

Sitting in the shade of a large umbrella at the café forced Angie to calm her nerves and start thinking, rather than reacting. Jack was inside ordering coffee after suggesting she give Gramps some time alone.

Upsetting him was the last thing she'd wanted to do.

'Someone will bring our coffee out in a minute,' Jack said.

He slid into the seat opposite and offered his hand. 'How are you doing?'

His skin was warm and comforting. 'Instead of blurting everything to him I should have rehearsed what I wanted to say. Given him time to absorb it. But the problem is I can't give him the important piece of this puzzle.'

'Laura.'

'Exactly. I feel I have a bunch of clues but can't make sense of them. Would you help me?'

'You know the answer to that.' But Jack's smile gave away his pleasure at being asked. 'Start with what you have about Laura.'

'Okay. Laura is Gramps's younger sister and was abducted by Vernon and kept by him and Gertrude as a surrogate for their own child, Mary.'

'Stopping you there. We know Laura is a Fairlie. How do we prove she is Mary?'

'Mary remembered Mattie. And on the back of his childhood photo he is called Mattie as well as Emmett. And Gramps told me about the toy called Dolly. I have no doubt Laura and Mary are the same person. But how do I find her?'

A young woman emerged from the café with a tray and a smile, setting down two coffees and a plate of pastries.

'Are you hungry?' Angie asked Jack.

'Thought a sugar hit might help us both.'

There was something about the pastries which played in the back of Angie's mind.

He helped himself to a treat but Angie couldn't eat. Not now. She sipped the coffee, eyes on the next table, which was empty.

'In the letters, Laura said she lived where there was no bookshop in town. That was a long time ago and Rivers End only got one quite recently. And that night I was at the beach... with flowers. The person I noticed at the end of the jetty placed carnations in the water, the same colours as Laura did in the book.'

'Coincidence?'

'I guess.'

'Keep puzzling it, Angie.'

'Perhaps it was a coincidence that the person I caught up – almost – vanished around the assisted living community. So if it is someone who lives in Rivers End, leaves carnations in the sea, and is old enough to be in the same place as Gramps... then it has to be Laura. Doesn't it?'

'Circumstantial.'

'Don't say that!'

He grinned. 'Sorry. I actually think you are reaching sound conclusions. Just a pity we have no other names to connect Laura to anyone today. Once the police have more information about first Mary and her parents, this will get easier.'

But it could take ages and what about Gramps? He deserves an answer.

Jack pushed the pastries closer to Angie and she looked at them, then at the next table again. Where the three ladies had sat and talked about Gramps all that time ago.

'Tim.'

'Tim who? Oh, that was the young man who befriended Mary.'

Angie got to her feet so fast she almost knocked the table.

'We have to go back.'

'What about the pastries?'

Gramps was in his front garden with a watering can when Angie and Jack hurried past. He put the can down and folded his arms. Angie smiled at him and kept going.

Annette and Bess stood on the footpath outside Marge's cottage, each carrying a shopping bag. Marge was locking her front door and James Regal's tail was wagging madly at the other ladies.

'Hello, dears!' Bess waved at Angie and Jack. 'I think you missed Emmett's house though.'

'Actually, I would love to take a moment of Marge's time.'

Marge was at the gate by now and gave Angie a curious look. 'We're off to do some shopping.'

I should come back. Another few hours won't matter.

Angie glanced back at Gramps, who had moved to his own gate with an unreadable expression. He must wonder what on earth was going on.

I can't lose your love. I have to fix this. I have to do it now.

'It will only take a minute or two. I just had a question. Please?'

'We can wait, Marge.' Annette took Bess's arm. 'Let's go talk to Emmett.'

'No, stay here. Angie said one question.' Marge came through her gate. 'What do you want to ask?'

Sudden nerves made Angie's throat dry and she quickly swallowed. 'I wondered... were you married to a man named Tim?'

'Is that the question? Yes, we were together for a long time.'

'And did you meet him in Driftwood Cove?'

Something flickered in Marge's eyes. Caution. 'It is pretty common knowledge that we lived there. He still does.'

'But... you met him there? Or at least, you met him a mile or two outside it. When his bicycle wheel came off.'

Marge audibly gasped and put a hand to her mouth.

'Whatever is wrong, dear?' Bess hurried to her side.

And here I go again, blurting everything out.

'There's only one way you would know that detail, young lady.' James Regal pawed at her and she lifted him into her arms. 'I would like my book returned please.'

'What book?' Annette looked from her friend to Angie. 'What is this about?'

Marge's face had lost its colour. She suddenly forced the little dog into Annette's arms. 'I need to walk.' She did exactly that, stalking away until she was almost opposite Gramps's cottage. She stopped, wavering, then crossed the road to him.

Angie hurried over with Jack at her side and the other ladies followed.

'Why did you never answer my letter, Emmett Fairlie? Why did you not fulfil the wish Opal had of returning what was mine?'

'I have no idea what you mean. What letter? What did Opal want you to have?' His voice was gruff.

'The letter I sent after the funeral. After her funeral.'

'I never got it. Maybe I did. Everything went into a box.'

'Without opening it?'

'Why does it matter?'

'Because what dear Opal collected is all I have left… of who I really am.' She snapped her mouth shut then abruptly turned on her heel and stalked away.

'Wait!' Angie chased after her again.

Annette passed the dog to Bess. 'Come on, we need to go to Marge.'

Marge didn't seem to care what anyone wanted and went through the gate of her own cottage.

'Please, please, Marge, can I talk to you?' Angie suddenly noticed the flowers peeking through the fence. 'Oh… carnations.' She squatted to touch one flower. 'White. And red and yellow.'

The hairs rose on her arms as she slowly straightened. Marge was back at the gate, one hand gripping the fence post.

'You tossed carnations into the sea at the jetty.'

Jack and Gramps were just a few metres away and the two other women had put James Regal on the ground and were catching their breaths. The dog softly whined at Marge. It was as if everyone was here who needed to be here right this minute.

'I send the flowers off to sea every week. Have done for years.'

'For Mattie.'

Gramps stiffened and his mouth dropped open.

'I knew you were like Opal. Clever and compassionate and determined.' Marge let out a long sigh.

'You were Mary.'

Tears welled in the other woman's eyes. 'I was Mary for too long. Now I'm Marge.'

'What's going on, lass?' Gramps's voice was almost a whisper and he had a hand on Jack's arm for support.

'And your real name... at least I believe so, is Laura. Laura Fairlie.'

'No. I don't know.' Marge shook her head. 'I was taken from a picnic by a man, that much I remember, but Laura isn't my name. You're mistaken. And Mattie is probably not even alive now.'

Angie had never seen Gramps struggling for words like now. He opened and shut his mouth twice, his hand on Jack visibly tightening. When Marge dropped her head and began walking to her cottage, he found his voice.

'Lou Lou. And Dolly. Do you remember Dolly?'

'What did you say?' Marge stopped in her tracks, her back rigid.

'You could never manage Emmett so you called me Mattie. And you were Lou Lou to me. Is it true? Can it be possible?'

Gramps almost tripped over his feet in his hurry to reach Marge, who slowly turned around.

'You put Dolly's head in the stream.'

He burst out laughing.

'And laughed at me all the time.'

'You were funny all the time. Even when you got cross

because you couldn't blow out the candles on your own birthday cake.'

Jack was right behind Angie and she leaned against him.

'It isn't possible though.' Marge gazed at Gramps. 'You are not the Mattie I remember.'

'And yet I am. Good grief... it is you, Lou Lou.'

Gramps and Marge both had tears pouring down their faces and as one, they threw their arms around each other.

THIRTY-SIX

Somehow six people and one excited dog squeezed into the kitchen in Marge's cottage. She and Gramps sat holding hands and smiling non-stop at each other while Jack was relegated to making coffee.

Angie briefly filled everyone in on Nan's box of secrets and where it had led her, and more recently, Jack. Not everything though. The small grave and terrible upbringing weren't hers to share so she kept to the basics.

'We knew nothing about your disappearance, dear,' Annette said. 'It was only when we had our own dreadful misadventure as teenagers that we were told another girl had gone missing some years previously.'

'Marge, why the Melbourne post office box address for your letters to Nan? That really confused me.'

'When I decided to stay anonymous with the book the last thing I wanted was correspondence from the publisher coming to my home. Tim and I were accountants working for his father and there was a Melbourne office I attended several times a year so I just checked it then. Much later, the year Opal died, I'd started having the mail redirected to the local post office but of course that slowed things down. I just was so afraid of being found out as a fraud.'

'Finding out anything other than Laura's first name was my biggest problem.' Angie glanced at Gramps. 'All of the newspaper clippings Nan had plus every search I did kept the Fairlie name out of it but I didn't know to dig deeper as the family was here on vacation.'

'And you couldn't ask me, nor would Opal have. Both of you knew I'd shut you out. I'm truly sorry, lass.'

Jack began putting coffee cups in front of everyone. 'I can't imagine how hard it was not knowing where Laura went.'

'I blamed myself. My parents said it wasn't my fault but it was.'

Marge tapped the back of his hand. 'It most certainly was not! I was too intent on finding Dolly to answer your calls and then I was walking for hours and hours. That man... I'm sure he'd been watching us and he told me he'd bring me home.' A single tear fell. 'I forgot my name. And you and our parents and home. Eventually I remembered you but the rest never came back. I even married my Tim and stayed in Driftwood Cove without a clue how close I was to home.'

Bess kept dabbing her eyes with a hanky. 'You need to tell him.'

'In time. He never knew the details of my life. I always felt terrible guilt.'

Angie reached out for Marge's spare hand. 'You did nothing wrong and I hate that you've lived with guilt for so long.'

'But you've read my book. The letters to Opal. You know about the real Mary and the woman who raised me. I stole someone's identity.'

Jack cleared his throat and they all looked at him. 'Speaking as an ex-police officer, one who dealt with genuine identity theft at times, my opinion is that the circumstances you were in was the only factor in you keeping the name you'd been raised with.

You were also only seventeen, not eighteen as you believed. The police will need to speak to you but I believe conversations will be focused on Mary and of course, your abduction.'

'We'll get you the best lawyer possible, Marge,' Bess announced. 'Besides, if they want to take you away they'll need to come through me!'

Laughter replaced all the tears. Angie could hardly believe what she was seeing. Gramps kept grinning and it was more than his mouth but his whole face alight with happiness. Marge no longer appeared stern and seemed younger. Annette and Bess still looked slightly puzzled but thrilled by the turn of events. And Jack? His eyes met hers and Angie knew she could easily get lost in them.

Dinner was finished and the washing up done. This was the first time Marge had been home to Seahaven since the day she was taken and tears were shed more than once. She'd remembered parts of the garden from childhood visits – mostly the carnations which were dotted in clumps between other plants. They'd been in her subconscious for all those years. She picked a large bunch and formally presented them to Gramps.

The four of them wandered outside to enjoy the sunset, all fitting onto the bench out the front.

'I can't believe almost a week has passed since this dear child, my grand-niece, finished solving the mystery Opal started.'

Marge was a different person. She smiled often and had arrived for dinner with her hair all curly – its natural state when there wasn't a hairdresser straightening it, and possibly to be worn like that more often.

'Seahaven belongs to you now.' Angie had thought about this a lot. 'And Gramps, if you want to return.'

'Goodness me, no,' Marge said. 'I'm happy where I am and

it would be annoying if Mattie moved away now. I've just got used to having breakfast with him again.'

'And I need my little sister close by to keep me walking if we're going to keep eating from the buffet table.' Gramps glanced from Angie to Jack and back. 'Besides, Seahaven needs to hear the laughter of younger people. Children even. It needs a family.'

Once the sun set, Gramps and Marge went in search of an after-dinner drink.

Jack and Angie wandered around the boundary of the garden, finding themselves at Nan's office. Angie hadn't been back inside other than to collect the box and take it to Marge the other day.

'Did I tell you Marge has a theory about how Nan came to find the keys and hymn book and so on?'

'You did not.'

'She kept those hidden inside a shoebox at the bottom of a wardrobe.'

'Like Gertrude had.'

'Yes. It was when she was living with Tim and his parents and years later, long after they'd married and gone to their own house, his mum and dad did a clear-out of their house before retiring. Nan loved digging around old sales and thrift shops so possibly found those and only much later connected them to the story of Mary.'

Angie had put one of the chairs out the front of the office and Jack sat then pulled her onto his lap.

'I *can* get another chair,' she said.

'This is better.'

Laughter carried from the house. If Marge and Gramps could get through all of their trials and grief and find peace and a future, then so could Angie.

'Jack?'

'Hmm?' He played with her hair.

'I like you.'

A slow smile lit his face. 'I like you, too.'

That wasn't so scary.

'So... would you please kiss me?'

His arms tightened until their hearts were against each other and his mouth was close to hers.

'This time nobody will stop me, my love.'

EPILOGUE

February next year

The birthday cake was huge, three-tiered, chocolate, and on the top was white chocolate icing in a message – *Happy Birthday to the best sister ever.*

'Do you have any other sisters, Emmett?' Jack handed Gramps a cupcake-sized version with four candles. 'I'll take the big one.'

'Wait, we need to light these candles,' Angie said. She quickly did so. 'Onward.'

The trio went outside, Angie leading the way to a marquee erected in the front garden. Beneath it was a long table seating at least thirty people, all here to celebrate Marge's first real birthday since 1952. Gramps had overseen every detail, including the guest list, catering, and music. Next to the marquee a dance floor had been created and a local DJ was ready to help the guests dance the evening away. As a number of the guests were from the assisted living community, he'd arranged for their minibus to do drop-offs and pick-ups.

Angie waved both hands in the air until the chatter quieted, then nodded to Annette and Bess, who sat to the left of the birthday girl.

'Close your eyes, dear,' Annette said.

Like almost everyone else, Marge wore a birthday hat over curls which were almost touching her shoulders these days. She squeezed her eyes tightly shut and Angie gestured for Gramps to quickly place the mini cake in front of her.

'When you're ready, open your eyes and blow out the candles,' Bess instructed.

She and Annette knew all about the little cake but the other guests looked confused.

'Alright, I'm opening my... oh my goodness! Emmett, explain yourself.'

'Thought it might be best if you had another shot at blowing four out rather than close to a hundred.'

Marge shot him a fierce look. 'A hundred? How old does that make you then?'

'Old enough that I can still outrun you.'

'Dear? The candles are dripping.' Annette mentioned. She and Bess had huge grins on their faces, as did most of the table.

'Come closer, Emmett. Last time I couldn't manage this on my own so you'd better help.'

Gramps leaned down and together they blew out the little flames.

'Make a wish, Lou Lou,' he whispered.

Her hand lifted to cup his cheek. 'Got everything I need, Mattie.'

'Have you even eaten yet, Angie?' Olive was in the kitchen cleaning up. She'd been part of the catering team headed by Harriet's partner. 'All you've done all day is make sure everyone else is happy and has a full plate. Which we appreciate because there was a lot of food!'

'And all of it was delicious.'

'How do you know if you haven't eaten?' Olive put her hands on her hips. 'Let me put a plate together.'

'Oh, you don't need to! I will have a glass of wine though. Somehow the glass of champagne to toast Marge ended up lost before I had more than a sip.'

'In that case you will find it.'

'I don't understand.' Angie found an open bottle of white wine and poured a glass.

Olive's hands left her hips to gesture widely if rather vaguely. 'Um, hello? You single-handedly solved a cold case which dozens of police and reporters failed to do.'

'Not on my own, but thanks. It's made a difference in so many lives.' From here Angie could see the dance floor through the living room window. Gramps and Marge were dancing together. 'I can't believe it sometimes.'

'Well you didn't need me or Mum which is just as well. That book of Walter Bell's from Palmerston House appears to have overlooked a lot of the history of the town. Just has the bits he wanted. Now, eat.'

Angie turned around to find a plate of delicious food on the edge of the counter. She hadn't noticed a gnawing hunger until now and she put down the glass and went to Olive to hug her.

'You and Harriet are such good friends. Thank you.'

'Go on. Take your plate and find that man of yours.' Olive grinned. 'I have work to do or your lovely kitchen will be left in a dreadful mess.'

With a smile, Angie collected the plate and her glass and returned to the marquee.

She found a vacant seat and began eating. Almost everyone was dancing or wandering around the front garden. The music was an eclectic mix across the decades and her feet tapped the ground.

The music changed to a waltz. Marge began dancing with

her ex-husband, Tim Walsh. He'd been around for family dinners a couple of times during the year and adored Marge, as she did him. But she was happier living alone and her tolerance for people was sometimes tested, other than with Bess, Annette, and now Emmett.

Gramps was dancing with Bess and they were deep in conversation as they slowly crossed the dance floor. There was a growing connection between the two and Gramps had told Angie only recently that he would never forget Opal, but was ready to love again.

Nan would approve.

Angie still talked to Nan late at night at the bench. She'd told her about reuniting Gramps with his sister and thanked her for leaving such good research. And then when Marge was told by the police they had no intention of considering historical charges for a seventeen-year-old doing as she'd been instructed by her parent. She'd been happy to update that John and Daphne were free of legal worries after months of investigation found Xavier completely liable for the rental scandal. Most recently it was to share she'd been to a funeral for Mary... the first Mary. There was no definitive proof of how she'd died but it was suspected to have been from natural causes. She'd finally been given a proper burial.

Warm hands rested on Angie's shoulders and she pulled herself out of her memories and looked up with a smile. 'Hello, stranger.'

Jack leaned down to kiss her forehead then pulled out the next chair. 'I'm not the one who hasn't sat down all day – until now. Good to see you eat.'

'Nothing more to do, other than give a hand with the cleaning up.'

'Such an amazing party.'

'Thank you for doing so much. Your help made such a difference.'

For a few minutes they danced, their eyes on each other. The music stopped but still they slowly moved together, bathed in moonlight.

'I've won everything I could ever need,' Angie said. 'Gramps's love and respect, Marge as a new auntie, a whole town of friends. And teaching... oh how happy that makes me.'

'You believe in yourself again.'

'It's easy when people I love believe in me.'

He seemed to catch his breath. They weren't dancing now, just holding each other.

'Emmett is right.'

'Sorry?'

'Life is too short. I'd given up on love when I moved to Rivers End. And I've seen how your marriage harmed you. But Angie, we can't see into the future. I don't want to wait to be with you for the rest of my life.'

Her heart was racing as he took her hands in his.

'I've loved you from the second I met you. Being allowed to share your search for Marge only reinforced it as well as growing my respect and admiration. I love you, Angie.'

'And I love you so much. You've trusted me with your fears about the future and I think you know I'll always be at your side, for as long you want me to be.'

'Forever, my love. Might I become your prize? Will you marry me, Angela Fairlie?'

A cocoon of warm air settled around them. Angie was certain she heard Nan tell her to say yes. She didn't need any encouragement and lifted herself onto her toes to touch Jack's lips in a butterfly kiss.

'You are my prize. And yes, Jack. Yes, I will marry you.'

A LETTER FROM THE AUTHOR

Thank so much for reading *The Lost Girl of Seahaven*. I hope that Angie and Mary's lives took you on a journey of the heart. I love keeping in touch so if you want to join other readers in hearing all about my new releases and bonus content, please sign up for my newsletter.

www.stormpublishing.co/phillipa-nefri-clark

If you enjoyed this book and could spare a few moments to leave a review, that would be hugely appreciated. Even a short review can make all the difference in encouraging a reader to discover my books for the first time. Thank you so much.

Thanks again for being part of this amazing journey with me and I hope you'll stay in touch – I have so many more stories and ideas to entertain you with! From my heart to yours.

Phillipa

www.phillipaclark.com

facebook.com/PhillipaNefriClark
instagram.com/phillipanefriclark
tiktok.com/@PhillipaNefriClark